All the Water in the World

**Center Point
Large Print**

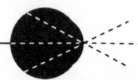

All the Water in the World

a novel

KAREN RANEY

CENTER POINT LARGE PRINT
THORNDIKE, MAINE

This Center Point Large Print edition
is published in the year 2019 by arrangement with
Scribner, a division of Simon & Schuster, Inc.

Copyright © 2019 by Karen Raney.

The text of this Large Print edition is unabridged.
In other aspects, this book may vary
from the original edition.
Printed in the United States of America
on permanent paper.
Set in 16-point Times New Roman type.

ISBN: 978-1-64358-386-0

The Library of Congress has cataloged this record
under Library of Congress Control Number: 2019946721

This book is dedicated to
Summer Dale (1996–2012) and Kelly Morter

PART I

Eve

1

A lake is a black hole for sound. The wind, the crack of a hammer, the cries of birds and children weave a rim of noise around the water, making its silence more profound. When a turtle or a fish breaks the surface, the sound appears to come from within. Maddy, who is a natural philosopher, would want to know whether it really is sound, or just the possibility of sound, that issues from such breaches. I mention Maddy because to have a child is to have a twofold mind. No thought or action belongs to me alone. This holds true more than ever now.

Every morning that summer I made my way to the dock, moving my cup of coffee up and down to prevent a spill. Some days when I arrived, the mist was a thick white lid. Some days it was lifting to expose the pan of still water. Some days I could see circles of rain popping out on the lake before the drops reached my skin. Robin never came with me. He was busy building the new room in the attic, a blank place that smelled of raw wood and glue and had a completely different light from the rest of the house. Being up in the thick part of the pines, it should feel like a tree house if it's ever finished.

When I reached the shore, the day I met our

neighbor, the mist had already cleared. The colors were intense, almost unbearably so: sap green, white gold, blue of every kind. The dock wobbled underfoot as I stepped down, making me aware of both the mass and the instability of water. I set my cup on the low table at the end and brushed the dew off the two Adirondack chairs, whose green surface was bubbled and flaking. Those chairs needed repainting, but I knew if I mentioned it to Robin he would say in his hearty voice, "Hey, Eve, that's a good job for you!" and I have more than enough to do while I'm here.

Standing to face the lake, I indulged in a moment of play, as though I were on a stage with the curtain closed behind me. I swung my arms. I did fifty jumping jacks. I mimed a person singing or shouting, until I felt myself to be rising, clothed in feathers and scales, a creature that forgets everything and lives by its wits.

I sat and sipped my coffee. Before me, the pine trees pointed up and their reflections pointed down, just as convincing as the real ones, and I allowed myself a few moments to believe in this second world.

At the far shore, something puckered the glassy surface. A kayak, paddling purposefully in my direction. There was plenty of time to retreat, but I stayed put. Must be the newcomers who were rebuilding the house across the way. They'd painted the house yellow. It is so exposed that we think they have violated the bylaws of the lake association charter. We think some shoreline trees must have been cut down to give them a better view. This also gives us an unwelcome view of a bright yellow house. It has even found its way into the reflection. Maddy would agree the color yellow is garish for a house. *Garish* may not be her word, but it is perfectly apt. Tawasentha, the highest natural lake east of the Rockies, has always been, and will always remain, a no-motorboats, cabin-in-the-woods kind of place, no matter how big the cabins have become. Forty years ago, when my father bought the lot, people built their own houses. Dwellings are still supposed to be some shade of brown or gray. The world needs all the trees it can get.

The kayak advanced toward me, dragging the shattered reflection along behind it. The occupant was a woman of about my age. She coasted alongside the dock, smiling openly. Her hair was pulled back into what resembled a reddish ball of yarn, and her arms and face were covered with freckles, which the sun had blurred but not managed to melt into a tan. The paddle across her knees was dripping from both ends. She certainly wasn't the person I imagined would come from that house. I sat above her on the dock and waited.

"Is everything okay? You were waving. I thought maybe you needed help."

"I was doing yoga," I said, touched but annoyed to hear the word *help* spoken so casually.

The stranger's intense blue eyes passed over me. I don't think she believed me for a minute. "I'm Norma. Your new neighbor." She gestured with her paddle, scattering drops. "We're doing things to the place before moving in. I hope it hasn't been too much of a nuisance. The noise, I mean."

I shook my head. When I said nothing, she raised her paddle as if to lever the kayak backward. That was when I surprised myself by inviting her to join me on the dock. By the time she had tied up her boat, wiped her hands on her shorts, and sat down, I was already regretting my invitation. Our chairs were awkwardly close, but I could hardly adjust their position now. Nor could I finish drinking my coffee in front of her, or give in to the solitary pleasure of holding the mug between my hands and inhaling the steam. There was nothing to do but gaze together lakeward. Chitchat was in order. Better to get it over with.

"You have a family?"

"Three kids. Luke's eight, Ben's six." Norma grinned. "Tanner's forty-two."

"I've got one of those. He's in his playroom at the moment." I nodded in sisterly fashion toward the house, although in spite of the messy marriage he'd left behind and occasional bouts of glumness, Robin was as grown up as they come. I leaned forward to study a dragonfly shimmering on the arm of my chair. I've always been fascinated by the way they alight and lift off without warning.

Looking up, I said: "I guess your house needs a lot of work."

"Gutting, boiling, starting over from the ground up? According to Tanner. He's an architect. I kind of liked it the way it was."

"I don't think the Gibsons had touched that place since the seventies. They kept the wood shingles. They left the shoreline trees alone . . ."

"Rustic charm, I think it's called," said Norma.

"You've picked an unusual color."

She waved at her kayak, moored below. "First thing we did. I have a thing about yellow. My mother's favorite color."

I did not mention the bylaws. Instead I steered the conversation toward the goings-on of the association. Any pause I filled with a question. Was she native to Pennsylvania or a transplant? How had they come to buy the lot? Did her husband's practice give him much time with the boys? I learned about Tanner's loopy business partner and Ben's tantrums. I studied Norma's face as she recounted her children's foibles in tones of high bemusement, as if motherhood were a hilarious accident that had happened to her while she'd been looking the other way.

She stopped talking and frowned into the sun. Under the freckles her skin shone as if lit from within. I felt a longing for the easy company of women. I know my smile is an unnerving thing these days. Still, I smiled at her when she turned, and she reached out and put her hand under mine, making me jump.

"Classy," she said, meaning I did not look like the kind of person who would paint my nails. Purple this week, with diagonal white stripes. I snatched my hand back. What on earth was she doing here? How much did she know?

"I do it for Maddy," I said.

Norma held my gaze. "Who is Maddy?"

Maddy

2

Just say. For the sake of argument, just say it was true. How would it work? One hundred and seven billion individuals right back to the cavemen—a hundred and eight on some websites—each one still remembering who they are? I lie on my side, stroking Cloud. I do my best thinking this way. I can think whatever I want. I can even tiptoe into places that are totally, strictly off-limits for someone with a mother like mine. Under the fur I could feel my kitten's skull and the buttons of her spine. So tiny. Breakable. She stretched and opened her toy mouth and closed it again, and into her ear I whispered, "Even the cavemen?" until I felt her tongue scraping my face. Soft on the outside, grainy on the inside. Well, maybe it's not like here at all. Maybe you can dissolve in and out. Be yourself when you want to be, or just disappear into the soup.

I got up feeling not supergood but okay. I put on my dream-catcher earrings with the little hanging feathers. Holding my door open at least a foot, I told Mom it would be a pajama day. She was fine with that. She had an article to write. But she still stood there, needing something.

My mother's hair has grown back. She shaved it off in solidarity after my first round of chemo.

There's no point in both of us being bald forever. It's in a pixie cut now, which I think really suits her, even with the little shoots of gray coming in. She thinks it's completely unfair that Grandma has almost no gray whatsoever, and neither does Uncle Chris. The way genes go together and create a person is totally random. I think about that a lot.

She put the back of her hand on my forehead and then my cheek. I let her step inside and hug me, and smell my orange-flower body spray, a present from Fiona. My mother has always liked sniffing me. She says it starts with smelling your baby's head and then you just keep on doing it.

"Is your kitten with you?" She wants me to have company because she can't stay with me every minute of every day, though she tried to at first.

"Right here, Mom. Where she always is." She got Cloud for me during my last treatment. Ragdolls are the most adorable cats in the universe. Blue eyes, white fur, pug-type nose, and the best personalities ever. Cloud will stay next to me the whole day, even when I'm throwing up or lying on the floor for a change of surface. She sleeps on the fleece blanket I got for her because it's the color of the sky. When I pick her up, she droops as if someone's removed her bones; that's the Ragdoll in her coming out.

When my mother left, I put Cloud on my

stomach and went back to reading *To Kill a Mockingbird*. They're having me work my way through the tenth-grade syllabus, but I only want to reread books I already love. If I had a father I would want one like Atticus. He always does the right thing even if he has to pay for it, which he almost does with the lives of his children. Whenever I read anything nowadays, I skip to the end to see how it comes out. This story, of course, I know how it ends. Scout and Jem get out alive, though Jem has his elbow broken, which he doesn't care about as long as he can pass and punt. After the arm was put in a cast, Atticus sat by his bed, and he would be there when Jem woke up in the morning. I know it might not be fair, but I always wanted to ask my mother: Do you like having a father? Didn't you think I might want one?

After I had my little cry about Atticus it was hard to go back to the courtroom scene. There are some words that make me feel physically sick. I could not get the line "Ruttin' on my Mayella" out of my mind, like it was the title of some awful country song. The accused man, Tom, is so polite and soft-spoken I know he would not be capable of anything as cold as that.

Going to see Jack Bell tomorrow, I texted Fiona. *For Science.* Checked my watch. Fourth period just started. She might look at her phone in forty-five minutes. Fiona and Vicky come after school every other day; they feed me chicken nuggets if I'm eating, and all the gossip. Though I have to say, after five months, high school is starting to seem like some extraterrestrial place that I know about in perfect detail but could never actually visit.

I folded over the page at the part where Scout stops them taking Tom from the jailhouse. Because she was a small child and reminded the ringleader he was a father, Mr. Cunningham took the lynchers away and they did no harm. Atticus must have been smiling to himself at the courage of his daughter. Though if you ask me, courage doesn't come into it, because Scout didn't understand what danger she was in. I wish I could be that innocent.

How can any live creature be so silky? Why is it sad the way kittens squint up at you when you pet them? Like they're thanking you for giving them everything they ever wanted.

I let Cloud go to sleep on my stomach and lie back, hands under my head. I once sneaked a tube of croissant dough to my room, not realizing—duh!—that you had to bake them first. To split open the tube, I whacked it on my dresser so hard that the dough circles flew up and made a grease mark on the ceiling. Mom just laughed. The stain stayed there all these years because interior decoration is not our thing. And Mom gets busy, especially since Robin moved in. It's a joke between Fiona and Vicky and me, because the stain is *exactly* the shape of a you-know-what, though I did not notice that at the time. I was only eight, but how naïve can you be! We laugh about it almost every time they visit. Vicky, who I'm sure has seen lots of them by now, laughs the loudest, in this croaky guffaw that I love to hear.

One thing I wonder is: Can you make new friends there? Or are you stuck with the people you already know? I have to say that would severely limit my friendship group. Does anyone even talk? It's possible talking is irrelevant in a way that is only obvious once you get there. If I made friends with a cavegirl, for example, I could stroke her fur and she could brush my hair like Suzy does when I babysit.

Used to. Suzy *used to* brush my hair.

I frowned, noticing that I assumed I'd have my hair back. But forget hair! What if you can't even figure out where to draw the line between humans and everyone else? Do you draw the line at monkeys? Rabbits? Where? The more I thought about it, the more unbelievable the whole scenario became, even allowing for what we might not know or understand until it happens. Okay, Mom: you win. It's all a story. No world without end. That's when I got this choking feeling of being sealed up in a place where nothing could get in or out.

I stood up so suddenly I banged my shin on the

bed frame. Cloud jumped to the floor, astonished and possibly insulted, but she did her Ragdoll thing when I lifted her back on the bed and I was forgiven. At the window I watched Robin get into his VW and grin like a chimpanzee in the rearview mirror to check his teeth before driving off. He is more vain than Mom, who is one of the least vain people I know. I'm always catching him in the hallway mirror, pulling faces. If he sees me he laughs and shouts, "Hey! Can't a person have any privacy around here?" Maybe it's because, no offense, he is quite ordinary-looking and not very tall. It's obvious to anyone that he is not my real dad. Don't get me wrong: I like Robin. He is a Good Thing in Mom's life, especially now.

I went to my dresser and picked things up. The charm bracelet Grandma gave me when I was ten. I love the little scissors. They even cut. The picture of me and Mom at Cape Cod. She's in a black one-piece, holding both the hands of this bald munchkin who is turning around and screaming because the waves are on her feet. How weird is that? I know it's me, but I don't really believe it, as in *really* know it to be true in the way that I know I am standing at my dresser holding this frame, which has silver flecks on it, and I know my fingernails are painted half red and half pink. I did them last night before bed. I am absolutely, one hundred percent certain that I am in my bedroom looking down at my nails and they are half pink, half red, with black spots on the pink side. Whereas in the frame, that could be any cute kid.

Who would have guessed that heads are so glossy underneath? And that I would ever be seeing mine?

Wink at the reflection. Tuck chin. Do that pistol-fingers thing. Give him the come-on smile. Click fingers of both hands twice, high in the air. *Olé*, suckers! Flamenco *señoritas* are the queens; those ruffled men stomping around them are necessary but, let's face it, somewhat ridiculous. Anyway, this is my parentage coming through, and you can't get away from that.

My hand is always going up to touch my head. It's a shock every time, like reaching for my kitten and finding a reptile there instead. People say how stunning I look, that I have the perfect bone structure for it. Not everyone has the right bone structure. My mother, for instance, discovered after she shaved her hair off that unfortunately she doesn't have the right bone structure. She looked like one of those aliens in the Roswell Incident. Onion head, enormous eyes. I think they were actually crash-test dummies. I'm only saying this because Mom admitted it herself and kept telling me how beautiful I looked compared to her.

I guess mothers don't mind if their daughters

are prettier than they are. Maybe they have some special hormone that makes them *want* this to be the case. Come to think of it, maybe that's why my mother wears those clunky shoes and leaves her shirts untucked. One of the reasons, anyway. The other reason is that she is a truly unique individual who does not care what people think. Biology is amazing. You can be an individual, or even a feminist, while at the same time this mothering hormone gives you a kick out of not upstaging your daughter.

Knock on the door.

"Come in." She has read the books and knows you don't enter a teenager's bedroom without asking.

"Come in!" What does she think I'm doing in here?

My mother stood in the doorway, looking shy. "Just taking a break. Just wanted to check in."

I've been hearing that voice forever. Musical, slightly nasal, very warm. By the way, Mom, explanations are not necessary. I know why you're knocking on my door! I read somewhere that babies, before they're born, can recognize their mother's voice, and even their father's, if he's around. If the family has a dog, the kid is born wanting to be near that particular breed of dog. Which means I have a built-in love of golden retrievers.

My mother handed me a spiral sketchbook

and a box of pencils. "If you get bored," she said. "Just an idea." When she speaks in that overly casual way, you can be sure she has been planning the thing in question for days. "Drawing can be relaxing, you know."

"Thanks, Mom, but I'm extremely relaxed. You're the one who needs relaxing." I grinned when I said this so she wouldn't take it the wrong way, and accepted her offering. Like everyone else, I drew pictures when I was little. Unlike everyone else, I kept it up till the end of middle school. Kids used to put in orders for me to make them drawings, from a photograph, say of their dog or their sister, or a scene from *The Simpsons*. By high school I mainly did what I had to do to stay in favor with the art teacher, Mr. Yam. "What would I draw, anyway?"

"It doesn't matter," said my mother. "You could draw what you see out the window. Your clothes hanging in the closet. Or in your case, thrown on the floor."

"Ha! Look who's talking."

"More interesting to draw if they're thrown on the floor." She kept standing there. "Are you okay, Maddy? Do you need anything? Just say."

"I'm fine, Mom." I put down the sketchbook and held out my hands. "Do you like my nails?"

"Love the colors!" she said a little too quickly. "Love the spots!"

I could see she was having a not-so-great day.

"Can I do your nails, Mama?" From the corner of my eye I saw my mouth talking in the mirror, as if it had started leading a life of its own. "Puleeese . . . ?" I said this in my Tweetie-Pie voice, knowing that although my mother is a sucker for my Tweetie-Pie voice, she was still going to say no. She always says no. She won't even wear subtle shades of lipstick.

"No offense, Mom, but the way you look at the moment? Believe me, nail polish would help!" She laughed, so I thought it was safe to follow this up with: "You should listen to the younger generation. Let us show you the way."

Since I've been sick, my mother gets this look as though someone is forcing her to stare into a light that's way too bright. I should have known better. Teasing strikes her as cute, and cute means sad, and sad brings on the look, which I was in no mood for today.

"I know it's me doing this to you, Mom! Do you think I want to do this to you?" There. I'd said it out loud, though not necessarily in the right tone.

We stared at each other.

I could also say: I'm the kid around here!

I could also say: Well, you're the one who made me! But that would be mean, because what's happened is no more her fault than it is mine. Grandpa's always telling me that.

My mother was smiling and frowning at the

same time, like someone had just told her a terrible joke. "Of course you don't!" she said. "No one *wants* this. We didn't ask for this. But we do have to bear it. All of us together."

Well, thumbs-up, Mom! Earnest-motherly I can take. When I go to pieces she gets strong, and vice versa. She always comes through. *Eres una estrella.* In fact, that was so stellar, there might be a two-way eye-watering thing going on here soon if we're not careful. But I feel we can conclude with dignity.

"Thanks," I murmured. "Mama mia." She likes it when I call her that. Our favorite slushy movie. I gave her one of the back-patting hugs I learned from her. Bony spine, sharp shoulder blades. We both need fattening up.

"And yes, please," she said, pulling away. "I want you to do my nails. Makeup too. The works."

Good thing she can't read my mind. The afterlife! I'm the kid around here! You're the one who made me! If they turn on you like that, I never want to have children. But I guess if I did, I'd get the hormone, and then I would be exactly like my mother.

3

Jack Bell had recently had his braces off, and his teeth looked blank and unused, like he was trying them out for the first time. I am five nine and a half, one of the tallest girls in the tenth grade, but he had passed me by a good two inches. What pimples he had were confined to his chin. His broad cheekbones narrowed his eyes in a friendly way. We stood there like we had both been hypnotized. I hadn't had much to do with Jack since sixth grade. We weren't mean to him—Fiona, Vicky, and me—but he was so quiet we tended to forget he was there. Now I felt sick to my stomach, standing on his porch in my beret, staring at his teeth. If only I had hair!

There is a thing I do at moments like this, that I've done since I was little. I imagine wrapping myself in some big thick material until everything is muffled and distant. Then I imagine I am being observed by someone I can't exactly picture, who knows everything I'm thinking and loves me anyway. It makes me feel I can do all kinds of difficult things.

I considered Jack from inside my invisible cloak. "I've come about the campaign."

"I know."

"Miss Sedge's idea."

"I know."

He went up the stairs in front of me, dragging his sneakers on each step, his big wrists swinging. At the top he turned. "Want a Coke? Water? Cranberry juice?" I hesitated. "Vodka and tonic?" Jack asked, grinning with his new teeth.

"Water, please." I pretended to look around. "Nice house." Though I don't like split-levels. They remind me of a doll's house where everything is in view.

"It's my dad's place. He's at work."

"Lucky you." I had met Jack's father when we were young and they lived in their other house, predivorce. Tall, talkative, nice is all I remember.

Jack went to the fridge and I took a seat at the breakfast bar. On the counter a laptop was open to a website, *Tar Sands Action 2011*, next to a stack of books and a DVD. Did that mean I was to be dealt with quickly and ushered out?

This kitchen didn't even have a door on it. Anyone could see us from the landing or through the windows that started half a floor below. My eyes kept flitting down to the front door, expecting a lordly version of Jack to charge in at any moment to see what his son was getting up to.

He was taking his time by the fridge, his back to me, head tipped down. Enough thick brown hair for both of us. Judging by the bony, stretched-out look of him, Jack had grown tall a little too fast.

In fourth grade he used to come over to my house and we'd cut out constellations from *National Geographic* and prick the pages to make light-box planetariums. Back then he was a pigeon-toed kid with a buzz cut. We went on our bikes to the new subdivision at Sligo Creek. The creek had been drained to build the houses, but water came up anyway in all the ditches. We brought pollywogs home in pails. Some of them grew tiny back legs. Some even grew front legs, but we never got as far as a real toad. Jack said the pollywogs couldn't grow up because they had been taken out of their natural environment. I said I didn't think a stinking hole on a construction site was very natural. Jack said it was more natural than a pail.

Hiss of a bottle cap.

Don't turn around yet . . .

Second hiss.

I whipped off my beret. When Jack faced me again, a glass in each hand, I was there with my naked head out in plain sight.

It is a blink reaction people cannot help. I was prepared for his surprised look. I had planned to get some satisfaction from it. What I was not prepared for was the expression that immediately took its place: This is curious. But: It is what it is. And: No huge deal. Maybe it is the look of someone with a scientific turn of mind. Miss Sedge has a very similar expression. If you believe everything is part of the world, then everything is equally astonishing, so nothing by itself can be too astonishing.

"Beer?" He held one out, looking proud to have prepared me a stronger option.

"Sure," I said. We sat in worldly silence, sipping our drinks. I hate beer.

It was up to me to say the next thing. "Miss Sedge tutors me at home. Even between treatments there is no point in me going to school." He nodded. "Dr. O says I could, but Mom thinks I'm too tired and I could catch something." He nodded again. "I probably shouldn't even be here." Further nod. "I'm about to go through another round." I was taxing Jack's nodding faculties.

"Do you like to talk about it?" he asked. "Or not? Fine if you don't."

"Sometimes yes," I said. "Sometimes no."

"How will I know?"

"I'll post it on Facebook: 'I now wish to speak about my cancer. Please make an appointment.' "

I liked the way his eyes almost shut when he laughed and I liked him asking "How will I know?" as if it were up to me but in theory I could talk about it if I wanted to. As if there would be lots of times to talk about it. I guess the campaign meant he'd be seeing me again.

"Miss Sedge is pretty cool."

"I know." After a minute: "We weren't very nice to her."

"You weren't?"

"Way back in ninth grade," I rushed to say. "Vicky drew a cartoon of her on the board. One time she caught us outside the library, making fun of her voice." She told us to get to class or we would be in big trouble, but the look on her face before she covered it up is something I don't like to think about, even now. Especially now.

I picked up a book and read the title out loud. "*Life as We Know It: Varieties of Global Catastrophe*. Well, catastrophe's better than warming! What I hate is these words. *Warming* sounds so cozy. Who wouldn't want to be warm? Keystone Pipeline. How could something called a 'keystone' be dangerous?" In Jack's presence, with the air flowing freely around the bare bulb of my head, I didn't know what would come out of my mouth before I heard myself say it.

"It's impression management," said Jack. "The extractive industries are good at that."

"Where do you get this stuff from? Impression management. Extractive industries." I felt subdued by his earnestness, by what he knew that I didn't.

"My dad, mostly," he admitted.

"What I don't understand is, aren't the people making the pipeline worried about the planet? They live here too."

"It's the biggest mystery of my life," said Jack, so stiff and serious that I couldn't help smiling.

He spoke rapidly. "I mean the fact that people aren't more interested in what's happening to the earth. Maybe they can't take too much reality. No. It's money, basically. The companies will rake in billions if the pipeline is built. But it's *our* future—" He was in the middle of a you-and-me loop with his hand when he stopped. I could see him backtracking for a second, then deciding to go on. "For you and me, if we want a future, we have to leave fossil fuels in the ground. It's that simple."

He said some more things about the Anthropocene, the Faustian bargain, the two degrees Celsius. I could see he loved the science of it and the details and the words. Facts were facts, and I could read them and even try to let them become, as Miss Sedge said, part of my worldview. But Jack was wrong. It was not simple. Nothing was the least bit simple.

I could think about supereruptions and methane burps with calm curiosity during the day. But at night the images conjured up by the facts would wash over me until I was lying rigid in the dark, my whole body thumping with fear. What I couldn't explain was the thrill it gave me to imagine it. Especially the tsunamis. As the ocean floor got shallower, the waves grew bigger and stronger until the shelf ran out and the waves were set loose. Then the buildings and the scattering people, dignified on their own scale, were just crumbs. Over and over the images ran through me in the dark. I felt each wave slowly gathering power into itself, like a creature thinking cruel and merciless thoughts, and on the other hand like a creature just doing what it couldn't help doing, and what it would not stop doing until it was finished.

"So . . ." I could hardly admit any of this to Jack. "What are we going to do?"

"Have a look at this."

He angled the laptop toward me and together we leaned in to the screen. I could have stayed there for a long time near the heat of his shoulder, scrolling through the site as he told me about the march students were planning from Georgetown to the White House. The point was to demand that the president follow through on his promise to reconsider the pipeline.

"It says here, 'Participants must be at least eighteen years old.' "

"That's just for the civil disobedience." Jack tilted away from me, gripping the edge of the table with one hand and balancing on the back legs of his stool. "That's the best part! But we can raise money. We can publicize it. We can go on the march. We've got a permit to be on the sidewalk in front of the White House for the whole afternoon."

"Do you know what they call it?" I read off the screen. "The picture-postcard zone."

"As long as you keep moving, you don't break any regulations. But if you sit down there and refuse to move, you could get arrested. That's why minors can't take part."

"I wouldn't mind getting arrested," I said.

"Well . . ." He was still balancing on his stool, trying to impress me with his acrobatic skills.

"I might have minded before."

"I'd love to get arrested," said Jack. "But it could damage the campaign." With his free hand, he took a slug of beer. I watched his Adam's apple moving up and down under the smooth skin of his throat, and smiled like I knew some joke he didn't. The beer had trickled down onto my legs and made them warm and pliable.

"I'm thinking," I said dreamily, "what will the picture-postcard zone look like when the White House is underwater?"

His stool hit the floor with a thump. He slapped the counter and sprang to his feet.

"What's wrong?"

Jack turned around once, waving both arms in the air. I saw the muscular back of his neck, the loose seat of his jeans, and for a second the complicated front of them before he sat down again, grinning.

"What a great idea! We can make postcards of the White House underwater and sell them to raise money!"

He was looking at me in this easy way, and

it seemed as if the fourth-grade, crew-cut, planetarium Jack was saying, "Remember me?" At that exact moment I made a decision. I would find a way to do it. Not right now, but soon. To know what it's like. And just as that thought entered my head, Jack Bell in his enthusiasm about the postcards laid his hand on my arm, near the wrist. He removed it instantly, and went to the sink on some pretext or other, but my arm was fizzing and sparkling so much where he'd touched me that it didn't even feel like an arm anymore. I knew then that it wasn't just a matter of curiosity. The thing was this: I wanted to be with someone who, unlike my family, didn't *have* to love me but just decided to. Even if it was only for one day.

Fiona collapsed on my beanbag chair, more than an hour late. With her fierce blue eyes and white blond hair, she looked like some third-string angel down on her luck.

"Sedge caught me at my locker between fourth and fifth. No pass."

"Where's Vicky?"

"Home with a temperature. Hundred and two point six. She had such an unbelievably sore throat in French, she was almost hysterical—"

"She should try chemo," I said, reclining on my cushions.

"I know," said Fiona in her motherly voice. "It's

a good thing we didn't come see you yesterday. She might have already been contagious."

"Dr. O says I have more to fear from my own germs than other people's." I'd had enough science forced on me in the past six months to last a lifetime.

"So I took her to the infirmary," Fiona went on. "Guess who tagged along just to get out of French? Guess who inveigled the nurse into letting her stay, so was *not* in the hall when the bell went?"

"Natalie Flynn?"

"Sniveling sycophant." Fiona was famous for her vocabulary, which never seemed to match her flyaway appearance. She jabbed herself in the collarbone. "*Who* took Vicky to the infirmary in the first place? *Who* knew all the symptoms of spinal meningitis? Hel-*lo?* I thought I'd make it to study hall in time. I only stopped for a second to check my cell, and *I* got the detention."

"Bad luck," I said, though I know how Fiona thrives on close calls. As I see it, the occasional detention is more like a close-call tax than a major miscarriage of justice.

"She's vile." Her nail-bitten fingers sliced the air. "She's de*test*able."

"Annoying, maybe," I said, stroking Cloud. "Not detestable."

At first I'd said no way when I heard Miss Sedge would be one of my tutors. I'd thought it

39

was someone's idea of a joke. But my mother refused to get me out of it. She has this idea about the glorious benefits of facing things. Personally, I'd rather look the other way. But in this case she was right. Miss Sedge is not at all like she is at school, where she has no sense of humor whatsoever. At our kitchen table she acts as if I'm not a pupil or even necessarily a kid, let alone a sick one, but just another interesting person to talk to.

"Did you get my text?" I asked, to move us off the subject.

One great thing about Fiona is she doesn't stay mad. "I was reading it when she caught me. I'm lucky she didn't confiscate my cell phone." She scrambled upright on the beanbag, working her eyebrows cartoonishly. "Jack *Bell* . . . ?"

I did not want to let her down, and I do not believe in lying to your best friend. However, a certain coolness had taken hold of me. "I went to see him," I said. "I didn't know his parents had split."

"And . . . ?"

"We talked about the Keystone Pipeline."

"What's that?"

"They pump oil down from Canada and ship it to the Gulf Coast. There's a campaign to stop it. Miss Sedge wants Jack and me to get involved." I tried to look demure. "He's nice. He's cute."

Eyebrows hitched up and down.

"Don't get too excited. Nothing happened."

"Nothing?"

"But it might."

"How do you know?"

"He touched my arm." Pathetic! Just when you're wanting to lie, you find yourself telling the truth.

She sank back in the beanbag, unimpressed. Fiona was almost fifteen when she got her period, and she still had the high-waisted, spindly look of a middle school girl. Her wrists were so small she had to punch extra holes in her watchband. "But Jack Bell? Isn't he kind of basic?"

"He's different now. He gave me a beer. He wanted to talk." Each sentence I said about Jack made me feel as though he and I were in actual communication. "He's going to be a scientist."

Fiona brightened. "Can I tell Vicky?"

"No!" Vicky was thirteen and a half when she got her first boyfriend, a sophomore linebacker. There was another one after that, and now Wade, who worked at the Coffee Bar downtown. If Vicky found out, she would never let it go.

Fiona was staring at me.

"What?" I laughed. I forced out a solemn look. "What?"

"Are you sure nothing happened?"

"I'd rather mention it to Vicky myself, that's all."

"Okay," she said. "That's fine."

I stared. "What do you mean, 'That's fine'?" In days gone by, she would not have stopped there. "What if I told you he kissed me?"

"Get *out!* Where?"

I took a second: architecture or anatomy? "On his dad's window seat." It was easy, the move from partial truth to outright lie.

That look again, like a safety bar coming down. "But, Maddy?"

"What."

"Oh, I don't know." Fiona crossed one leg over the other, chewed her thumbnail, and pumped her foot up and down. "Are you sure he's a nice guy?"

It was my turn to stare. "You think no nice guy in his right mind would want me?"

"Oh, don't be ridiculous!" She flashed me a smile. Not a real one. "You more than any of us, you idiot!"

"You think a boring nice guy is all I could get?"

"Just saying . . ." She put on her wheedling voice. "I am your *fwend,* you know."

The elation that came from speaking Jack's name and making up things about him was gone. So was the coolness I'd felt a moment before. It was the tone of her voice that did it. Her tone told me that no matter how far ahead of Fiona I'd always been when it came to periods and overall polish and style, no matter what we'd been through together as best friends forever, no matter if she came to visit me three times a week, minimum, I was in another category now. This made me feel so hollow and alone I couldn't at that moment imagine anything good happening to me ever again.

"No, forget it. I'm talking crap," she declared. "I'm just jealous. Go for it. Promise you'll go for it."

I stood up so fast that dark spots flashed around the room. Fiona leapt to her feet and steadied me while I groped for the bed and sat down again, bowing my head to keep away the stars. From the corner of my eye I could see Cloud sitting upright on the quilt, ousted from my lap and awaiting instructions. Fiona pretended she had come over just to pet my kitten.

"Poor girl . . ." She pressed the fur back with her thumbs until she was crooning to the face of a little wide-awake gnome. "Poor baby! Have you lost your place?"

4

Another sip?" asked Grandma, steering the straw to my lips, her voice a wavier version of my mother's. I sucked in without opening my eyes. Ginger ale. Essence of chemotherapy. It's supposed to help the nausea, but now the taste itself makes me feel sick. I sipped it anyway, because it also tastes of comfort. My whole life is like that. Nothing is just one thing or the other.

I opened my eyes. My grandmother's face was frowning down at me, her hair puffed around it in light brown scallops. My grandparents live downtown, only half an hour away, but they come and stay with us when I'm going through chemo. They were here when we got back from the hospital. I knew my grandmother had gotten a cut and perm for her visit, and this fact alone made me want to cry.

Funny when people are looking at you at close range. Our heads were practically touching, but what was inside hers and what was inside mine were a million miles apart. Or maybe not. We would never know. I shut my eyes. Light doesn't help. But my grandmother's presence does. I think it's because when she sees me heaving into the bowl and falling back on the bed, moaning from my sore mouth, or bawling into my pillow, she is putting me into a larger picture she has in her mind. I like to think there is a larger picture. Even if it's her scientifically dubious one of suffering people being rocked in the hands of God.

"Grandma?"

Cool hand on my forehead. "Yes, Punkin?"

She's called me that forever. I kept my eyes tightly shut. I had to keep them shut in order to squeeze out such a question. "Have you always believed in God?"

It must be sad for my grandmother, living with heathens. She removed her hand and did not answer right away.

"No, not always," she said at last. "Not genuinely."

"So when did you start?"

"When your mother was born."

"Why then?"

"Shall I tell you?"

"Well, *yeah* . . . ? I asked you, didn't I?"

Grandma gave me one of her looks. She thinks sarcasm is the lowest form of humor.

"Yes please," I said meekly.

"Your grandfather and I were so happy when we found out I was expecting. The pregnancy went fine, the usual morning sickness and so on. But as soon as I went into labor, we knew something was wrong. The contractions would start and then stop. This went on for more than a day. The baby was in distress. They couldn't find the heartbeat at one point. It was very scary. Then I started bleeding. Turns out your mother had the cord, the umbilical cord—"

"I know what cord, Grandma!"

"Of course you do." I heard the smile in her voice. "The cord was wrapped around her neck. She very nearly died. Actually, so did I, from the hemorrhage—that means losing a lot of blood all at once—"

"I *know!*"

"They rushed me to the operating room. I was out of it by then. And while I was out, I had this amazing experience . . ." She stopped.

"What kind of experience?"

She seemed hesitant to go on. "I'm not sure I can explain it to you." My grandmother put her lips together. "It was like I was not inside myself anymore. I was looking down on the heads of the doctors and nurses, and while I watched them trying to save me and save the baby, there was this . . . *presence* isn't quite the right word. Being? No. That sounds like it was all in one place. Anyway, there was *some*thing with me that was completely good and generous."

"Must have been a dream."

She smiled. "Maybe. When I woke up, I couldn't see any baby and I got scared, so I started talking to God. We came to an agreement that if I lived and my baby lived, I would devote my life to Him."

"But how did you know someone was there to talk to in the first place?"

"He spoke first."

I opened my eyes. Grandma was sitting on my bed in her yellow cardigan, the ginger ale glass forgotten in her hands.

"Not the usual way of speaking," she said. "It's mental."

"Sounds mental."

"Spiritual, then. But that's not a word your generation uses."

"*Mental,*" I said, "means it's in the mind. The mind comes from the brain."

"Mmm," said Grandma.

"So if the brain stops, there's no more mind."

"That's why we say *spiritual.*"

"Spiritual's not in the brain? Then where is it, exactly?"

Long silence. "Do you wonder about these things, Maddy?"

"Sometimes."

"Of course," said Grandma, as if it were the most natural thing in the world. "Maddy," she went on, "do you suppose that everything around us . . ." Her knobby hand took in my lavender walls, my Snarky Puppy posters, my dresser with its jewelry stand in the shape of a ball gown and its rows of Muji candles, down to my blue fleece blanket, on which Cloud was curled up acting out her name: all the fixtures of my life that I didn't under any circumstances want to leave. "Not to mention where we come from, where we're going, what makes you *you,* is all figured out already? Already known?"

"Someone must know."

"How would they?"

"Have you ever heard of science?"

Grandma wrinkled her forehead but decided to overlook it. If you have cancer you can get away with lots of the lowest form of humor.

I turned over with difficulty. Either my muscles were going soft from disuse or the chemo was attacking them too. Grandma helped settle me on my other side and put her hand on my cheek. Where she touched me was the only part of me that didn't hurt.

"Science is certainly a powerful way of understanding the world. Never underestimate science. But it's not all there is."

"How do *you* know?"

After a long pause, she said: "I don't."

"Oh, great." I turned my head away.

"Do you want to come to church with us sometime, Maddy? Your grandpa and I would love it. Remember you used to go to Sunday school when you were little? To our other church?"

Of course I remembered. Graham crackers and orange Kool-Aid in the basement room. Wooden fire engines. Maps in impossible colors. Sitting on the carpet in a circle around a lit candle, while the lady spoke in an unnaturally gentle voice. I kept my eyes on the candle flame, the only interesting thing in the room. At the end she said: "Now it's time to change the light," and lowered her candle snuffer over the flame, trying to fool us into thinking she was only "changing" the light, not putting it out.

"Thanks, Grandma," I said. "But I'm not going to start believing in God because I'm desperate."

"You mean like I did when your mother was born?"

"That's not what I meant!" I shot back. That's exactly what I meant.

After a pause, Grandma asked, as casually as if she wanted to know whether I was hungry: "Do you feel desperate sometimes, Maddy?"

I shut my eyes. "Not really." The nausea had come back. Both feet were half-numb and prickling painfully, like when the blood rushes in after they've gone to sleep. "Does Mom know what happened when she was born?"

"She knows about her birth, yes. I've told her the whole story. Not that she necessarily . . . sees it the way I do."

"Mom isn't into that stuff. She would never change her mind, even if *her* baby is sick."

Grandma laughed. "Your mother has always had her own ideas, ever since she was small. Like you."

"I don't agree with everything Mom says, you know."

"Of course you don't." Lightly she added: "You have a first-rate mind, Maddy. Don't dismiss things just because they're out of the ordinary. That's all I would say. There's more of everything than we think."

Are all old people so cryptic? More of everything than we think? I liked the sound of it, but I knew liking the sound of something was not enough, and I knew the conversation had to end. It was not just that my feet were hurting and I was ready to sleep. There was something in me that wanted to poke its nose into the world and be seen and be stroked, but if anyone tried too hard to coax it out, it burrowed back inside and hid. I feigned sleep. After a minute or two, my grandmother eased herself off the bed and tiptoed out.

"Long story short," I announced at dinner, "I'm going to church tomorrow." Third week postchemo, I was still weak but on the up and up, or at least on level ground with rising potential. As soon as I'm almost myself again, they knock me flat with another treatment.

"Oh?" My mother glanced up.

"With Grandma. Dr. O says I can go out if I want."

"Are they driving you?"

"Is that all you want to know? My method of transportation?"

She laughed. "What do you want me to ask?"

"What about 'Why are you going to church with Grandma tomorrow?'"

"Well, why are you?"

"She invited me."

"Good for her."

"And there's this cellist playing Brahms."

"Which Brahms?" asked Robin from the head of the table, where he sits to make the point that he is sitting at the head of the table. Robin is a classical music fanatic. He taught himself to play the piano when he was thirty-two, which is pretty impressive. But he never got the knack of learning to read the notes because his brain was too set in its ways. He has to memorize. Whereas I've taken lessons since I was eight and I am a great sight reader. Or at least I was when I used to play.

"I don't know." I spread my chicken potpie around the plate to make it look half-eaten. "They're picking me up at nine-fifteen."

"Aren't you hungry, Maddy?" asked my mother.

"Not very. Don't you want me to go?"

She gave me her mock-exasperated look.

"Apparently it's Palm Sunday," I said.

"Wasn't that when he rode through town on a donkey?"

51

"You're the expert. You're the one who went to Sunday school every week!"

"I was an expert until ninth grade," said my mother.

"Is that when you became a heretic?"

"That's when I started having my own ideas."

"Want to come?" I said. "We could all go."

My mother gave me her everything-under-the sun-is-acceptable smile. "Not this time."

"Why not?"

"Go and have a day out with your grandparents. They'd love that."

I fluttered my eyelids at Robin. "Come to church with me? The family that prays together stays together."

He glanced at my mother while levering the last of the salad onto his plate. "She's been reading bumper stickers again."

"I do love salad," I remarked. "Salad is the one thing I'm in the mood for . . ."

"Oh, sorry, Maddy! It's yours. Dressing? Garlic bread?" When everything had been offered except what I was really asking for, Robin said in a muted voice: "You know church is not my thing. And I have work to do. Unfortunately."

"Thanks for the support."

Again they exchanged looks. My mother drained her wineglass.

"If it's the C-major Trio," said Robin, "get ready to cry."

5

As usual, Grandpa was driving. I got in and slammed the door, calling goodbye to my mother, who was waving from the porch in a way that meant she regretted leaving me to face God on my own. Grandpa gave me the almost smile that his face settles into when he isn't trying to make it do anything special. I used to ask, "Grandpa, why are you smiling?" He always replied, "I'm not." It became a joke between us. Now I see it as the expression of a good-natured person who wants to be obliging while keeping himself to himself.

When I was small and we went to their old church, Grandma wore flowered skirts and high heels. Since then she has sharpened up her fashion sense. Today she had on a black jacket with an Aztec design and a teal-colored blouse. Her necklace looked like silver finger bones. She kissed the air in my direction.

"Hello, sweetie. Nice hat!"

"Look, we match," I said, getting in. My knitted beret with the brim happened to be the exact shade of Grandma's blouse.

I leaned on my fist and watched the fire station go by, and the public library where I borrowed my books a million years ago, and the lavender house with the yellow trim, next door to the orange house with the white trim. That's Takoma Park for you, the most original neighborhood this side of the Beltway. I always wondered who lived in those two houses and what they were like. Maybe I would knock on their doors one day without a hat on, and see what happened.

What is it with men and cars? Women are at least as good at driving, but if there's a man around, he gets the keys and she's the one who double-checks the traffic at intersections. Grandma didn't seem to mind. She had on her own half smile, completely different from Grandpa's. Hers said: Deep down the world is good and I want to be part of the goodness. She was humming. Maybe she was happy it was Palm Sunday. Or maybe she was happy to have me in the car. After all, I am her only granddaughter, and I was named after her. Madeleine Rose.

"Grandma," I said, sitting up. "Do you mind if I call you Rose?"

Smiling, she twisted around, her rimless glasses winking. "If you like." The thing about my grandmother is she genuinely finds me entertaining. "What brought that up?"

"Oh," I said airily, "I'm not a baby anymore."

"That's for sure."

"Besides, it's my middle name. I should be able to use it."

"Agreed," she said, turning back.

"What about me?" Grandpa demanded, catching my eye in the rearview mirror.

"You already call her Rose."

"Very funny."

"You can still be Grandpa, if that's what you mean."

"As long as I'm not missing out on anything."

"Don't worry." I patted his shoulder over the seat. "It's a girl thing. Isn't it, Rose?"

"Absolutely. Oh look, Maddy! A deer. Two of them!" Their big, unlikely bodies loped across the median strip and plunged into the woods on the other side.

"Whoa!" said Grandpa. "They cause a lot of accidents, you know."

"Can you imagine wanting to shoot them?" said Grandma. "I'll never understand wanting to shoot a beautiful animal."

"What if you're starving?" I asked.

"That's different."

Cars were backed up near the Metro station and we didn't move for ages. The first chance he had, Grandpa came off the highway.

"I need another coffee. If there's one thing I hate, it's sitting in traffic."

"HashtagFirstWorldProblems," I said.

"What?"

"Never mind."

He pulled up to the curb a few blocks later and got out and leaned into my window, speaking behind his hand in a stage whisper. "Your grandmother makes terrible coffee. It'll rot your socks."

"Why don't you make it yourself?"

He pulled a face and pretended to take off my nose. I watched him stride toward the coffee place, hands in his pockets, whistling. The hair on top of his head looked as though it could easily blow off. It gave me a queasy feeling, seeing him from the back. I trained my eyes instead on the dim sum restaurant on the corner, where Mom and I liked to go for Sunday brunch. The line was already down the sidewalk and around the block. I counted the people so as not to think about the back of my grandfather's head, or my grandmother humming in the front seat, fingering the strap of her purse, loving beautiful animals. It should be a law of nature that all family members disappear at the exact same time. Then no one would be left behind.

I had counted up to twenty-six, almost to the corner, when one person pulled apart into two. They had been kissing. Robin had his arm across Mom's shoulders. What a surprise! How funny to see them there. Her neck was bent, her shoulders shaking. As her head came up, I saw that she was laughing, not crying.

Go and have a day out with your grandparents! I have work to do. Unfortunately! That wistful wave from the porch!

My mother was holding on to his outstretched arm with both hands, not in the least worried about the wait. They had sneaked off the minute I was gone. They'd have the whole morning and part of the afternoon to themselves. A generous person would not begrudge them that. A generous person would be grateful her mother had someone. Whereas a person who had been unfairly singled out by the universe might think a hole had opened up into the future, where everyone was going about their business. Might even be willing Robin's good-natured self to go away and leave my mother to me, who had her first, who belonged to her completely, who needed her more.

My grandfather folded himself behind the wheel, chuckling about something or other. He'd insulted her coffee, but still Grandma was laughing and holding his cup aloft to prevent spillage, while behind their backs I could barely see my own hands, let alone the road or the cars, as we swung out into traffic, church-bound.

"Now, that's what I call a church, Rose." When I pointed to the steepled gray-stone on the corner, my grandmother's arm came along with mine. We had been joined together for the walk down Tenth Street because she's always loved linking arms, rubbing your back, resting her hand on your shoulder while she's talking to you. When I got sick, she started doing it nonstop. According to Mom, this comes from losing her own mother when she was ten, but I like to think it's me she wants to touch.

"No, that's Catholic. Ours is over there," said Grandma serenely. "First Congregational." What we were looking at was a box of blue glass floating on a concrete pedestal. The square panes formed a blade at the corner, and the clouds captured on their surface collided with the real clouds at odd angles.

"Wow," I said. "Very modern, Rose." The building gave off a violet shimmer that made me feel observed, like those sunglasses where the person can see your eyes but you can't see theirs.

"The church is in the two lower floors," said Grandma. "The upper part is offices we rent out."

"*You* rent them out?"

"The church rents them out. That's how it survives in this day and age. We built the building with that in mind."

"*You* built the building?"

She gave me one of her looks.

"So," I said. "The church is concrete and the offices are colored glass? Isn't that the wrong way around?"

"You're a quick study." She smiled. "Always were."

"We used to look more Gothic," Grandpa put

in. He was ambling along unattached on my other side. "The first church had a bell tower."

"When was that?"

"Eighteen sixty-eight."

"So you never actually saw it?"

"Ha! I'm not *that* ancient. We're on our third building now. Goes back to the Civil War. Services were once held in the Capitol."

"Why was that?"

I like to feed my grandfather questions. He's in love with information. Grandma is happy as long as she's holding your arm. Grandpa is happy as long as he's gifting you with facts, or digging up new ones.

"The first minister was chaplain of the House of Representatives. And did you know that the church built schools for freed slaves?"

Once we were inside, I made a beeline for the women's room. Splashed water on my face and rubbed my concealer stick everywhere I could think of. Red around the eyes and gray under them. Do church people scare easily? I touched both birds in the earrings Mom gave me for my birthday. They sat on a silver branch running across each hoop. The tiny birds gave me courage. *You look fine,* said the person in my head. *You will be fine.* Lo and behold, I was fine. Able to enter with jaunty indifference a room full of strangers.

I worked my way back through the adults, the

little kids, a few teenagers milling about. A lady handed me a program and a stalk of some sort.

"Oh, there you are, Maddy!" called Grandma, sounding anxious.

"I see everyone's got their palm branch."

"Frond," said Grandpa.

"Frond. I stand corrected." I rolled my eyes. Grandpa grinned and poked me in the arm. I elbowed him away.

"They're ethically sourced," said Grandma, taking my arm and tucking it to her side. After a minute I pulled away, pretending to search for something in my bag. I wasn't going to tell her about seeing Mom and Robin at the dim sum. There were plenty of other things for me to be crying about.

I followed them down the aisle of a sanctuary that was just as plain as the lobby. The blandness of the decor surprised me. Was there such a thing as taking humility too far? No carpet. No stained glass. Completely lacking in color except for a sea-and-sky quilt hanging behind the stage, where a piano and music stands were set up. In place of pews there were chairs, plus a set of polished wooden bleachers along one wall. My grandparents made straight for the second tier of the bleachers. People had left them a space and were turning to greet them.

Grandma glanced at me from time to time, on the verge of making introductions, but I lowered my head to the program. The picture on the cover was reproduced from some tapestry. Jesus, the crowd, even the donkey were wearing the same worried look you see on newborn babies. Wasn't this supposed to be the joyful day? The triumphant day? Couldn't someone come up with a cheerful picture for the occasion? There was no shortage of cheerful people on the premises, in spite of their varying states of health. I counted two wheelchairs, a number of canes, and five people with hearing aids. One was a small girl with sunken eyes and a peanut-shaped head. She was laughing and doing cartwheels in the aisle until her dad told her to stop. Maybe everyone has something wrong with them, even if it isn't visible. Maybe that's why we were here.

Sound of the Bell.
All Glory, Laud, and Honor.
Responding and Sending.

I stood up and sat down when Grandma did, and watched the ministers swish up to the lecterns, a bearded man and a woman with close-cropped hair. They had on black floor-length robes draped with purple satin. Kind of weird in an up-to-the-minute place like this that built schools for freed slaves. People must still want the ministers to look special, even if they make a point of putting their lecterns on the same level as the chairs. Or else what makes it a church and not just a bunch of people in a room?

The call to worship gave way to the silent prayer. Heads were lowered. Meek voices filled the room. I closed my eyes and tried to clear a special place in my mind. Sneak a look down. Nail polish coming off. Sneak a look sideways. Grandpa's brows were raised behind his glasses, while Grandma's were bunched in concentration. I did not want to see them like that. Sneak a look at the program. *No matter where you are on life's journey, you are welcome. Tough and Tender Days Ahead. Don't forget to validate your parking ticket.* My mother and I were prone to attacks of hilarity on the most earnest of occasions. I missed her. I needed her now. She could go to brunch with Robin whenever she liked. I closed my eyes and opened them again. The prayer was over. People were coughing, the offering plate was circulated by a boy in a baseball cap, while up onstage three musicians dressed in black took their seats.

I was close enough to see the musicians preparing their instruments. The pianist pumped his pedals. The clarinet player rotated his barrel and blew on the holes. The cellist drew her bow through a cloth and laid the cloth on the floor. She prodded her strings, fiddled with the keys, and brought her hand to rest on the slope of the wood. By some freaky coincidence was it Robin's C-Major Trio? No, selections from the first and third movements of the A Minor. All was ready. Tuning up had finished. The ministers had withdrawn to their chairs in the front row, the black tails of their robes sticking out. Fingers were poised. The bow hand was arched at the far end of the bow.

They began calmly enough. The cellist had a sweet idea. The piano, then the clarinet, considered it, took it over, gave it back. Before long they were playing with their whole bodies. The pianist hunched over, pulling his fingers reluctantly off the keys. Comically the clarinetist puffed out his cheeks. As the music zigzagged upward, one of his hands tried to fly off and conduct. I leaned forward, afraid for him. But no, he wiped the hand on his leg and replaced it just in time. The room swelled with music. The melody swirled and pranced, passing between the instruments, picking things up and, as the section drew to a close, setting them down.

They began again, quick and sharp. The pianist was in a world of his own, but the other two exchanged meaningful looks. Soon the cellist and her bow were in a frenzy, her black hair swinging side to side, beating out the time. Not gently, the cello's neck was gripped, the strings were pinned down by the dramatic vibration of her curved fingers. The melody loosened and tightened, climbed up and up, turned back on itself. The clarinetist had hold of a long sinuous passage. He was following it around to see where it would go, arching his back to make his body more available to the music, almost lifting off the chair. At the last minute he descended. The pianist finished with a stack of chords that made his hands pop off the keys. The cellist bent her head.

People exhaled and shifted their feet. No applause, no whistling, no standing ovation. To go through all that and get so little in return! I longed to rush up to the musicians and confess to something. The woman minister stepped to the lectern and said thank you on behalf of everyone, and thank you to the director who had made this possible, and the musicians tramped down some steps back of the stage. I sat in light-headed silence. Had I ever really listened to music before?

My grandmother gave me an everyday smile, covered my hand with hers, and mouthed, "Weren't they good!" My grandfather had removed his glasses and was peering at his program; music had never been his thing. Oh well. I was alone with it. I did not mind. I did not feel alone. I felt the opposite of alone.

The rest of the service passed me by. The final hymn I didn't even attempt to sing. I was thinking about my mother and Robin, kissing at the dim sum. That miserable girl in the car seemed like someone I used to know, who I felt sorry for but no longer agreed with. I thought about the keys and tuning pegs and strings, and the tender, practical way the musicians treated their instruments, like a kind of second body.

As the minister delivered the benediction, head down, one arm stretched out, I thought about the concentration of the musicians when they played. It was not like what happened during the silent prayer. They were practicing a different form of privacy. This is completely personal, they seemed to say, but we're all in it together. We urgently need to tell you something, and we are going to keep on telling you and telling you and trying to convince you that all of these sad, hopeful things we're saying are true, even though you won't understand it any more than we do.

I left my palm frond on the seat and led the way up the center aisle. What were the true things? One of them was this: Music can break free from the instruments and live a life of its own.

Right in front of us, in her father's arms, was the cartwheel girl. She stared at me from her small strange eyes. "Hey!" she yelled as if hailing me from a great distance. "What happened to you?"

My grandmother took my elbow from behind to steer me away, but I was smiling at the girl, my first real smile of the day. Let everyone look at me, or pretend not to. It didn't matter. It did not matter in the least.

Back home I found my mother curled up on the sofa, reading, her head tipped down so the cords of her neck were exposed. She looked at me with peaceful eyes. That's what a Sunday away from your sick kid will do for you. I laid my legs across her lap, wiggled my stocking feet to get her to massage them, and told her church had been awesome.

"What was so awesome about it?"

"Everything."

"Everything?"

"The music was out of this world. Epic."

She smiled, kneading my toes in her hands. What made me happy made her happy, even if it went against her atheistic principles.

"Arches," I said. Absentmindedly she obliged. "Ankles!" I barked when she made as if to return to her book. The pressure of her hands gave me the feeling that, for that moment at least, everything was all right. Everything was being held in place. It would have been a great unburdening to cry. For my tantrum on the way to church. For Brahms and the three musicians. For my mother's strong grip and the pleasure passing through me as if my body were as good as anyone else's. Instead I closed my eyes and vowed to the universe that I would be the kind of person who wished everyone well at all times, especially my mother, who didn't deserve any of this.

When Robin wandered in, I told him it had been the A-Minor Trio.

"I know the one," he said, seating himself a well-judged distance away from the two of us. "An unusual piece. Clarinet and cello. They say it sounds as if the instruments are in love with one another."

"Well, I loved it."

"Will you go again?" Mom wanted to know.

"Oh yes. I'll probably be born again."

"Not in that church you won't."

"Oh yeah? What if I'm planning to?"

"It's not that kind of place. I bet your grandparents were pleased to have you there."

"Thrilled," I said. "Ecstatic. I'd like to hear more Brahms."

"I've got the CDs," said Robin. "HashtagJustSaytheWord."

"Actually," I told him, "I want to hear it live."

After that, I went to church from time to time to confuse my mother and make my grandmother happy. I got used to the congregation and they got used to me, though I never grew to like the prayers. I closed my eyes and roamed around in my thoughts until the musical performance began. At home Robin and I organized our own concert series, for the good weeks between treatments. My requirement was that we had to be able to see the musicians up close. This ruled out the Kennedy Center and the other big concert halls, whose front-row seats were beyond our budget.

Instead we opted for chamber music at museums and libraries. We heard Beethoven at the Phillips Collection, and fifteenth-century French at the Shakespeare Library; at the Kreeger Museum it was Mendelssohn, and at the Renwick, Haydn's quartets.

Sometimes it was just Robin and me, sometimes the three of us went. Robin sat back with his arms folded, wearing this proud look. If my mother came along, she scanned the room to see if she knew anyone, and from time to time she squeezed my knee and whispered, "Isn't this fun?"

What they didn't know was that I came for the solitude. I always sat forward to see the musicians take care of their instruments before they played. When they were about to start, I was seized by the longing to be alone. It was like getting to the best part in a good book: I wanted no one in my line of sight. The others had to be present, but at a certain point I made them drop away, until, in the middle of a room packed with people, I might as well have been sitting there completely on my own. Waiting for the music to part company with the instruments. Wing its way out of time, out of reach.

Eve

6

W ho is Maddy?"
It was the kind of question all parents ask themselves, not only when the baby arrives, but forevermore. Where did she come from? How did she get here? Norma shaded her eyes at the lake. Of course that's not what she meant.

"My daughter," I said in a rush, afraid I was losing her. "Maddy's crazy about nail polish."

"I'd love to have a daughter," said Norma wistfully. "At our house it's all PlayStation and G.I. Joe."

"You might have gathered that Robin is not Maddy's father."

She glanced over. "He's not?" Clearly she had gathered no such thing.

"Maddy didn't have a father, growing up."

"But she has a stepfather."

"We've been together three years. It's amazing how well they get along. Considering how late he came into her life."

"In my experience," Norma said, from what I could see was a deep need to reassure, "children accept whatever situation they find themselves in. It's their normal."

"She used to miss him," I said.

"Who?"

"Her father. He left before she was born."

When we met, I was doing my master's in museum studies at GWU and Antonio was finishing his doctorate in neurobiology. He came from the north of Spain. He had the build and fairer coloring of the Basques, though he was born in the mountains farther east. He spoke four languages. Happy as he was to take advantage of our higher education system and to perfect his English, he never planned to settle here. I presume he now heads some world-famous research team back in Spain.

"Oh," said Norma. "It's pretty common, but sad." She checked my eyes to make sure she was on the right track.

Was *sad* the right word? We had known each other for a year and a half when Antonio passed his oral exam with no conditions. That night we washed down tapas with large quantities of red wine and collapsed into bed, high on his pass and on each other, and although the foil packet lay in plain sight on the bedside table, neither one of us reached for it. That was the beginning of Maddy.

When I told Antonio the news, in tones of incredulity bordering on joy, he slowly rubbed my arm with his thumb and said in a wondering voice: "But E-vie . . ." He had a sweet way of lengthening the syllables of my name. "I do not want to become a father by mistake. Of that I am sure."

We were in my apartment, facing each other on the sofa, our arms outstretched along the top of it. He was twenty-nine. I was twenty-six. His tone was scaring me. Flippantly I reminded him we were at an age when some couples are pushing out their second or third child.

"Yes, I know." He snorted. Antonio had escaped from such a family. "And I am not going to be one of them."

We talked that night, I cried, we talked the next morning. We talked for days. To everything I said—that he could stay and do his research in America, that we could both move to Spain, that our parents would be excited once they got used to the idea, that we had both allowed it to happen, that I was not prepared to put an end to this life—Antonio gave the same reply: "I know. You may be right. But I do not want to become a father." Sometimes it was "I am just beginning my career. I do not want to become a father." Or "I cannot settle here and become a father." It was as if the Antonio I knew had been replaced by an automaton. The accent I had once found sensual and charming was now a shield, a device to assert his otherness and keep me away. Woodenly he repeated himself, and in repeating himself he grew more and more distant. Had he wavered, or wept, or made propositions of his own, I might have felt different. I might have even been persuaded to abandon the pregnancy

73

in exchange for becoming parents one day in our own time. But the more Antonio said "I do not want to become a father," the more my defiance grew and the more insistent became the call of the life inside me.

"Never?" I pressed him on the last morning, at his kitchen table. "You never, ever want to have a child?"

He paused long enough to tell me what I needed to know.

"What you mean is, you don't want to have a child with me."

I waited for him to touch or contradict me. Then I stood up, tipped my coffee down the sink, walked out of his apartment, and began my life with Maddy.

Norma was waiting. Her gaze on my face was like a focusing of the sun's warmth, but I was determined to keep my replies short and hold her interest by connecting my story to hers. There's only so much a person wants to know about someone else's child.

"If you had become pregnant by accident, would Tanner have stood by you?"

"Yes!" said Norma. Then: "It never came up." Then, with the instinct women have to downplay difference: "Not that it couldn't have."

I could tell from the ironic tone she assumed when referring to Tanner that he was trying but decent, a lot like Robin, I suspected, though probably better-looking. He'd have just enough flaws to make him endearing and to furnish the self-mocking stories that shore up the sisterhood.

"Of course he would have. Especially coming from the South, as he undoubtedly does with a name like that." Norma's laugh told me I was right. "Antonio was just starting his career. He was a scientist. Very driven. He didn't want a baby."

"But you had her anyway."

"I had her anyway."

"Was that hard?"

"It's impossible to think of *not* having had her."

"Once they're here, they're here," said Norma. "Have you been in contact?"

I stared. "With who?"

"Her father."

I sat back. "No, never. Maddy always said she would hunt him down someday."

"You think she will?"

I looked past Norma to the open water. "Genes aren't everything. Though it's true that when Maddy was born, I felt as if I already knew her."

"Aw," said Norma.

"In the mirror I would see her features mixed up with mine. Did you ever get that?"

"Yeah," she said. "I got that."

"What, exactly?" I didn't want her to agree with me too readily.

"Well, once I felt around for a fontanel on my own head."

In those early days, the soft triangle that allowed the baby's skull to grow with the brain was a source of wonder and fear. I too remembered feeling my head for a fontanel, though I knew perfectly well they closed up by the age of two.

"So did I," I said a little grudgingly. I wasn't sure I wanted Norma to have had the same experience. That was the kind of thing you'd share with the baby's father.

"You should have seen us driving Luke home from the hospital! Tanner was going five miles an hour. With Benjamin we were calmer about cars."

After a moment, I said: "I would love to have had another child. Did your second son come between you and Luke?"

She considered this. "In a way, yes. The first year of Ben's life was the hardest thing I ever did. I kept thinking—This is impossible! How is anyone supposed to do this? Give them both *all* my attention? Luke and I already had our thing together. I felt like I was cheating on him. Tanner had no idea what I went through."

"That never happened to us," I said. "Maddy was all mine and I was all hers."

We fell silent and watched a canoe traverse the width of the lake near the north shore. Even at this distance it was easy to distinguish its long glide from the rapid joined strokes of a kayak. The canoe spun slowly in place before sliding back across with mysterious intent, barely wrinkling the surface.

The coming of Maddy had divided my life into before and after, the kind of line that I'd imagined could never be drawn again. The name? As a child I knew by heart the Madeline books—*Madeline and the Bad Hat*, *Madeline in London*, *Madeline's Rescue*; I loved their slanted drawings and cheerful orphans under the care of Miss Clavel, who allowed the girls any number of adventures but always tucked them up in two straight lines at the end of the day. The name Madeleine had a certain solemnity about it, but a playfulness too, particularly the diminutive form, which I soon started using.

By the time Maddy was four months old, she no longer had the look of a being from another world trying to enter this one. She was curious and for the most part serene, what people call an "easy baby." Even so, many nights I went to bed more exhausted than I thought was physically possible. I leaned on my parents a great deal, and on a Saturday mothers' group at the local library. Three of us started meeting in one another's kitchens, and jiggling one another's babies to sleep, and that first summer, we spent some weekends together at the lake house. I'd assumed at the time—why would I think otherwise?—that

Ella and Beth would remain my lifelong friends.

One long weekend in June, I decided to make the trip to the lake with Maddy on my own. I arrived with misgivings, but once we were there, just the two of us, I did not feel lonely in the least. The first morning, I walked around with her in my arms, reminding her of the layout of the rooms. On the terrace, we peered together into the hole of the wooden birdhouse my father had made in his cellar and nailed to the railing. It was late in the season for breeding, but the box was full of bulky life. We withdrew and watched from behind the sliding glass door. When the mother flew off—a tree swallow, judging from the small head and beak—we rushed out with a flashlight to get a look at her eggs. I lowered Maddy's face level with the hole so she could see them glowing in the hairy nest. That was the first time I ever heard her laugh.

The second day the eggs hatched. The two adults, one shiny blue, one green, took turns to enter the box, from which frantic peeping could be heard. Both parents were prepared to dive-bomb us if we came near; otherwise they gave no sign of being disturbed, and from the windows we were free to observe their coming and going. When both were away, I sneaked out with the flashlight. Naked pink mice with huge beaks, the nestlings took me for their mother and instantly started begging.

I sang to Maddy and lowered her kicking legs into the shallows, where she gripped the sand with her fists and feet. Temporarily I suppressed in myself what powers of perception Maddy did not yet have. The shining bowl of the lake had little definition for her, and so it had little definition for me. When she fell into her dream, her lips slick with my milk, I felt the presence of someone, half admirer, half guardian, who was watching me take care of my baby, and at the same time watching the tree swallows enter the hole in the box and do what they were driven to do there.

On the third day, I left Maddy sleeping and strolled out to the terrace in my bathrobe to check on the family. The lake glittered between the trees. All was quiet. The nestlings must have been asleep too. There was no need for a flashlight, as morning sun poured down from behind the house. I leaned over to get a closer look. Air and light had been sucked from the box. Inside, twitching slowly, coiled around itself and completely filling the space, was a thick, black rat snake.

Maddy

7

My grandfather came up with the idea. Or maybe I did. He said it first, anyway, but I was the one who led him there. We had gone to Meridian Hill Park, the best place near their house to walk the dog. I found it hard to climb the hill, so we drove to the entrance at the top of the park. Barney the golden retriever was straining on the leash. But first we had to pay a visit to the fountain, which in fact is more like a controlled waterfall. Thirteen shallow pools drop down to a huge one at the end made of old-fashioned stonework and arches in the style of an Italian villa. The water fills one pool, then spills into the next until some hidden system—Grandpa explained it to me once—pumps it back to the top.

When we got to the overlook, chambers of dingy concrete stared up at the sky. Nothing moved. This was its winter look. Funny how a thing like running water can be so important. Without running water the apartment building at the end seemed to be forcing its ugly way into the park.

"What's the matter with this place?" grumbled my grandfather. "The water's supposed to be on. Why isn't the water on?"

"Don't worry, Grandpa. I don't mind."

"Well, I mind."

We made our way back to the grassy stretch where we could let Barney off the leash. Strictly speaking, this was against the rules. When Grandpa knelt to unbuckle the leash, I felt honor-bound to say: "Isn't this against the law?"

"It's a weekday," he scoffed, still annoyed about the empty fountain. "There's no one around. Where's the harm in it? You have to keep your own counsel." That was one of his mottoes.

I threw Barney his tennis balls before we settled onto one of the weather-beaten side benches. He galloped off, doing his best to track the bouncing balls with jerks of his head. He preferred to catch them midair rather than to nose them out of the grass, but these days his jaws mostly snapped the air. He never seemed to mind. There was bound to be something foul and delicious to check out on the way.

"Have you ever read the Cat and Dog Diaries?" I asked.

"What are they?"

"This thing someone put online. The cat one goes: 'Another day in captivity. My guards give me hash and some kind of dry crackers, while they dine like kings on fresh meat . . .' The dog one goes: 'Waking up. My favorite thing! Food in my dish. My favorite thing! A ride in the car. My favorite thing!' Get it?"

"I think so." He smiled.

"Chasing balls with arthritis in my hips. My favorite thing!"

Barney came toward us with his lopsided gait, the balls tucked in the loose skin at the sides of his mouth where retrievers hold their birds. He made a detour to offer his services to a Frisbee game before dropping the balls one by one at our feet, grinning like a lunatic. Twelve years old and still a lot of life in him.

My grandfather scrubbed Barney's ruff with both hands. "Tell me about it," he crooned into the watery eyes. "Tell me all about it."

I picked up a ball and flung it, making a face. "Slimy disgusting tennis ball! My favorite thing!" Barney hurled himself away. It never crossed his mind that he was old. "And he tries to trip his owner," I said.

"Who does?"

"The cat writing the diary. 'Next time I'll try it at the top of the stairs.' "

"That's a bit extreme, isn't it?" asked Grandpa mildly. "Would your cat do that to you?"

"Of course not! Cloud luuuves me."

"Well, then."

"But she's still a kitten."

"Wait 'til she gets to be a teenager. Then watch out." My grandfather laughed with his narrow teeth and laid his hand on my head. I liked the weight of it through my baseball cap.

"Grandpa?"

"Yes?"

"How would you feel if you knew something didn't want you?"

"Didn't want me?"

"Someone, or something, was telling you *no*."

He studied my face for a minute. He said carefully, "Are you talking about your illness, Maddy?"

"What do you think I'm talking about?"

He turned his head, suddenly interested in the candy bar wrappers dotted about on the grass. "I wish they took better care of this place."

I swung my legs under the bench and waited. Barney had missed his midair catch again and was sniffing in tight circles at the edge of the shrubs.

"That's a subjective feeling, Maddy," Grandpa said at last. "I can understand you might feel like that. But it doesn't accord with the facts. We have to think scientifically."

"Facts!" I said with scorn. "The fact is there's *something* in the universe, or multiverse, or whatever you want to call it, that doesn't want me."

"Sweetie . . ."

"*No more Maddy,* it's saying. You can't argue with that. It's not saying no to you, is it? Or to Barney, even."

"Well, actually I *can* argue with that," my grandfather began, but I pushed on.

"You know what I think? I think it all started with my father."

Grandpa cupped his ear with one hand. "Beg your pardon?"

"I think that's where the idea came from. Originally."

I knew he'd heard what I said because he didn't ask again. He fixed his eyes on some picnickers sprawled on the ground amid the remains of their lunch.

"Know what I mean?" I prompted.

Grandpa's lips were a thin line and he was tense about the eyes. That's the way he looks when he feels out of his depth. I bet he was longing for Grandma to rise up out of the bushes and take over.

No one talked about my father much when I was growing up. There was nothing to say about someone who had bowed out so early. My mother always answered my questions because she believes in honesty and always tries to do the right thing. I know my father is Spanish, he's a scientist, he's named Antonio, and he has my height and eyes and hair. Or rather, I have his. They had never planned on having children together, and besides, he had to return home.

"What I want to know is why would a father not want to raise his own child?"

Grandpa spoke at last. "I wouldn't call him a father," he said reluctantly. "A father is someone who *does* raise his child."

"What am I supposed to call him? A sperm donor?"

"I would call him a young man sowing his wild oats who made a mistake. He was too lacking in imagination, or too weak—"

"He had to go back!"

My grandfather looked at me as if that was the first he had heard of it. "Well, whatever happened, the point is he didn't decide against *you*. You—Maddy—had not come into being yet. He decided against an abstract idea. He might have regretted it ever since. We don't know."

"But anyway," I persisted, "the fact is he didn't want me. As an abstract idea. And now it turns out the universe doesn't want me either. You can't argue with that."

But Grandpa was prepared to try. He launched into one of his long explanations about evolutionary change and variation and the way genetic accidents ensure that the species is strong in the long run.

"I get sick so everyone else can be healthy?"

"That's not what I'm saying. What I'm saying is it's not *personal*. There's not someone out there giving Maddy a disease just to be mean. It's the way nature works. It's chance. Some people have diabetes and some people have weak hearts. Some people get cancer."

He had said this before. I could never decide what I thought about it. I knew he meant it to be comforting, and I wanted it to be. But this idea of no one being responsible—not me, not my mother, not the doctors, not even God, if by any chance he exists—I found incredibly scary. I would prefer it if someone, somewhere, was making the decisions, even if what they decided, cruelly and maliciously or just indifferently, was to harm me. Otherwise, what is anything supposed to mean? Who is in charge?

"Okay, I get that."

My grandfather returned his attention to the litter-speckled grass, his nostrils flared in relief, or in further thought, or in contempt for slapdash park maintenance.

"Grandpa, would *you* have abandoned your daughter?"

Mutely, he shook his head.

"And if you *did* abandon your daughter, would you want to know whether or not she even existed? Would you want to meet her? Or would you think, Oh, that has nothing to do with me?"

Barney was at our feet again with the slathery balls. Neither of us picked them up. He pranced back and forth, trying to thrust one into our hands; eventually he gave up and lay down.

"Let's see," said Grandpa in a helpless kind of voice, stalling for time.

"I mean, men should have an idea how other men think, shouldn't they?"

He stretched his arm along the bench top. "I

suppose they should." He crossed his legs one way. "I suppose they should." He recrossed them the other way.

I was about to repeat the question when, with his eyes not on me but on the buildings beyond the park, my grandfather said: "Well, why don't you find out?"

"Find out what?"

"Find out what his thinking was."

"Whose thinking?" I asked cautiously.

"Your biological father's thinking."

"Antonio, you mean?"

"He did seem like a nice young man."

I stared at my grandfather until he was forced to turn his head. "You *knew* him?"

"We met him a few times. Your mother brought him over to the house."

"You're telling me you knew my father?"

"I can't say we *knew* him," he said hastily. "We met him, that's all, on a couple of occasions."

"Grandma too?"

"Of course."

"But why did you never mention it?"

My grandfather spread his hands on his knees. He leaned his weight forward on his arms, his shoulders up around his ears. "I guess because your mother had buried the whole thing pretty deep. He made his decision, and she had to make hers. It wasn't easy. In order to carry through with it and build a life for herself, she had to decide he didn't exist for her. So we followed suit."

"And what about me?" It came out shrill and babyish. "Didn't anyone think about me?"

"We *were* thinking about you. All the time."

"How could you, when I was only an idea?"

"Don't be hard on her, Maddy. Your mother's done a first-rate job. She did tell you."

"The bare facts of the matter, yes. I always said when I was eighteen I would track him down."

"How old are you now?" As if he didn't know.

"Sixteen and two months."

He gave me a long look.

"Sixteen and two months, with cancer," I said.

"So why don't you do it now?"

It was like a conversation in a dream. "Could I really do that?"

"You're asking me?" Grandpa smiled. "I thought you were the Internet generation."

"I mean could I do it, you know, with Mom and everything?"

After a while he said: "Your mother has enough to worry about. It would stir the whole mess up again for her." Another pause. "If she knew."

Some serious yoga was taking place in the center of the park. Two men in shorts were offering their bodies to the sky. All at once my grandfather's head swiveled around.

"Listen to me, Maddy." For an easygoing person, he could drop into command mode just like that. "This is very important." He raised one knotty forefinger. "Sixteen years is a long time. You'd have to be prepared for anything. *Any*thing. He could decide not to reply. He could be unpleasant."

"Got it," I said.

"He could be dead."

I didn't look away. "All right, already."

"He could have a family now and not want to hear from you."

That stopped me for a minute. I said severely: "Listen, Grandpa. Think about it. What have I got to lose?"

He sat back. "A lot."

"But you were the one who said I should find him!"

"You might have to give up an idea you have about him."

"Big deal." I snorted. "So I lose an idea? Add it to the list."

Now *his* eyes were watering. That I could not stand. I grabbed his arm and summoned my most encouraging voice. "But it might have a good ending! And then wouldn't it all be worth it?"

"Yes," he said. "I guess it would."

Silence thickened between us. Sensing a change of heart, Barney pushed his ball into my hand. I drew my arm back and hurled a long hard overhand.

"Good one," said Grandpa approvingly. "You don't throw like a girl."

"Hey!"

"Sorry."

"You'd better be. Look! He caught it." I made a fuss over Barney on his return. He had already forgotten what he'd done, but accepted the praise as his due.

My grandfather and I stood up at the exact same time. He snapped on the leash. "See?" he said with satisfaction. "No harm in a little strategic rule breaking."

On the way back, we took a detour between the yellow shrubs past the statue of Serenity. She sits on a low base, looking out over Sixteenth Street. When I was little, I was terrified of this statue. She used to appear in my dreams. Later on I made a point of visiting her. Still, I always approached from her right side, where she has a complete hand. The one on the left is gone; the wrist ends in a stump. Grandpa told me Meridian Hill used to be the most dangerous park in the city. Someone back then must have broken off her hand just for the fun of it.

It wasn't only her hand that was missing. Most of her face was gone. The eyes were blanks, and where the nose and lips should have been there was only pitted stone. It was a shame, because you could tell she used to be beautiful, and her gown still was, gathered at the waist and flowing between her knees. Her ruined features gave her a surprised look, but she had her bare feet planted apart in a proud, strong pose as if she didn't know she was damaged or else had decided not to care.

"Did you know there is a statue identical to this one in Luxembourg?" asked Grandpa, yanking Barney away from the pedestal, where he was lifting his leg. I sat down on the edge to rest.

"You mean with her face and hand gone?"

"No, silly. Same subject, by the same artist. It was bought at the Paris Exhibition in nineteen hundred. Apparently the sculptor used Isadora Duncan as a model."

"Why do you love facts so much, Grandpa?"

"Do I?" He sounded pleased that someone had noticed. "I guess because the more you know about something, the more interesting it becomes."

"But you don't like rules."

"Not when they're invented to keep us in line. Or show who's boss."

"To stop people from attacking statues, you mean?"

He laughed. "It's petty rules I don't care for. Small-minded officiousness."

"What about the rules for speaking English?"

"Well, yes. That's different. We wouldn't get very far grunting at each other and pointing, would we?" My grandfather gets this faraway look in his eyes when he's got hold of an idea and he's trying to separate out the parts. "And then there are family rules."

He removed his glasses and polished them. His eyes looked old and naked until he put them back behind glass. Once he's got the parts of the idea lined up in the right order, like cars on a toy train, he can pull the train forward.

"It might be: Don't keep secrets from each other. Or it might be: Don't give too much away. See what I mean? Rules can always be broken. Whereas facts," he said, bending from the waist to examine a patch of mold on the statue's knee, "you can't break facts. You can't disobey facts. They just are."

"Grandpa?" Even thinking it made my heart flap in my chest like something trying to get out. "Do you really think I should try to find my so-called father?"

My grandfather took my arm the way Grandma does, though without the same need. We turned our backs on the statue and followed Barney up the sidewalk to the car.

"Yes," he replied. "With all the aforementioned caveats, I really do."

"Why are you smiling?"

"I'm not," said my grandfather.

But he was. And we both knew it.

Two days later, in a voice that would not have carried past the living room sofa, I asked my grandfather what Antonio's last name was. We were alone in the front hall. My mother and

Grandma had gone into the kitchen. He glanced around and held out his palms in a helpless gesture that said: Don't involve me. My face went red hot. It had been his idea in the first place!

My grandfather put his hands in his pockets and bounced his keys and coins. I could see in his eyes that he wanted to encourage me while refusing to collaborate. Was it: If he didn't click the mouse himself then he would not be responsible for any ensuing disaster? Was it: Family business is women's business? Was it: He couldn't possibly tell Eve or Rose, so he should have kept his mouth shut on that park bench?

He was working his loose change hard. I waited until he looked at me. Then I trained on him such a long, injured stare that he drew me to his side and scraped his chin on my bare head and kept it there, hugging me close. Why do I always feel sorry for people when they are in the wrong? I wanted to hold out and get him to apologize, but then I thought maybe it was his clumsy way of telling me a search like this was something I had to do on my own.

I went to bed early and dreamed of blackbirds rising in a flock from the ground. When they crossed the horizon, their bodies turned into letters of the alphabet. Soon swarms of small black letters were crisscrossing the white sky, but they never formed any words.

After breakfast I switched on my computer. My screen saver had seaweed and sea horses in it, though, strangely, no fish. Even if he wanted to help me, I doubted my grandfather would even remember Antonio's last name. It's not the kind of thing men notice. I took a deep breath and typed "Antonio Spain scientist" into Google and clicked on Images. A grid of faces sprang to the screen. I scanned, clicked, and zoomed, as if I were shopping. What did a fortysomething-year-old Spanish scientist look like? Small pointed beard or a wraparound leprechaun one? Sharp eyeteeth? Shoe-brush hair? Gaunt? Jowly? The precise, alien quality of each image confused me. Antonios galore. More Antonios than I could ever need.

There had to be another way. I went to Georgetown's graduate student records, but when I put in the search box "Antonio 1994"—the summer I was conceived!—they asked for a last name and informed me that the online database only went back to 1998. I returned to the page of "Antonio Spain scientist" faces and clicked on one I liked the look of in the fifth row. No. He'd finished his PhD in 2000 at a university in Granada.

I abandoned that Antonio. I exited the bank of other Antonios who may or may not have been my father, and folded them up in my laptop, where it seemed to me they continued to lead a murmuring half-life. Sliding down in the chair, I tried to imagine what came next.

According to Miss Sedge, the particles that make up the solid world are not actual things but tendencies to exist. You can't be sure an electron is here and not there at any given time. No one understands it, not even the scientists.

I loved the idea of a jumpy, mysterious world inside the normal one. But what I didn't get was this: With all that uncertainty, a book or a tree or anything made out of atoms is always in one place and not another. So what if the particles behave in mysterious ways? In the real world, where it counts, there's no magic or flexibility whatsoever. You don't say my house was on Minter Place last week and this week it's on Greenwood Circle. You don't go downstairs in the morning and find the furniture's been rearranged or your white count has gone back to normal.

My father's tendency to exist seemed to increase once I started looking for him. But when I sat at my desk the next day and opened my laptop, my fingers hesitated over the keys. Chemo was starting on Monday. I was suffering from the faraway feeling that signaled I was about to be poisoned in order to be saved. Far away from Mom, far away from Cloud, far away from everyone and everything that mattered. Father, father, father, father. What on earth did that mean?

• • •

After church my grandparents arrived, and my mother cooked a special lunch of my choice, meat loaf with piquant sauce, as it would be a while before I could enjoy food again. These rituals gave impending chemotherapy the feel of an almost but not quite festive occasion, like Christmas without the lights or presents or fun.

As usual my mother could not settle down. She sat on the couch with her legs under her and beckoned me over to rub my back, as much for her sake as for mine. Robin shut himself in the music room. When passing me in the hallway, my grandmother laid the back of her hand on my cheek as though I was already running a temperature. Later on, when I was watching TV, Grandpa lowered himself heavily beside me. He stared at the screen for a while, jiggling his foot up and down, pretending to be fascinated by *American Idol*. I ignored him. Finally he leaned over and asked, in a double-agent whisper, "How's the search going?"

Slowly I turned and gave him a wide-open stare. "I thought you didn't want anything to do with it!" I put maximum reproach in my voice, although, being a sucker for sheepish smiles, I had already started to forgive him.

He pressed a finger to his lips and continued in his hilarious whisper. "I don't remember his last name, but I know he was a neuroscientist."

"Brain, right?" I whispered back. "Well, I can't find him in Georgetown alumni."

Brows up. "He wasn't at Georgetown. He was at GWU."

I whooped and high-fived him, knowing he would try solemnly to shake my hand instead. He used to get the high five wrong for real; now the handshake is one of our running jokes.

The noise brought Grandma to the doorway. She smiled from his eyes to mine. "What's going on here?"

"Deep, dark secrets, Rose," I said. "Don't ask."

I rushed upstairs. I closed my curtains, though it was the middle of the afternoon. George Washington University had better alumni records. In no time at all I found an Antonio Jorge Romero who had received a PhD in neurochemistry in 1994. I checked for other science PhDs that year received by anyone named Antonio. None.

I went to the window and pinched the hem of my curtains. My mother made them out of this cloth I found online. The design was like a musical score. With the sun coming through, the notes looked like birds on telephone wires.

After a minute I returned to my laptop and typed in "Antonio Jorge Romero neuroscientist." Up came a photograph of a smiling, brown-haired, tanned, intense-looking man. There was only one. He was on the faculty of University

College London. With a few clicks I confirmed the year and place of his doctorate.

I went to my dresser and made faces in the mirror. Mask of tragedy. Mask of scorn. Who do you think you are? Why should anyone care?

Back at my desk, the screen had gone blank. I jabbed in alarm at the tracking pad until his face lit up, still smiling, though not for me. I could breathe again, but for the life of me I could not look straight at his picture. I could take my father in only with quick sideways glances.

Warm eyes.

Lips-together smile.

Welcoming smile?

Something wrong with his teeth?

Eyebrows slightly raised. In humor? Arrogance?

Hair reddish brown like mine. Shoots of gray, like my mother's.

The closer I looked, the more the eyes withdrew.

I exited his picture and tapped a drumroll on the desk with my nails.

¡Coraje!

I went to Outlook and typed out an email.

Put it in Drafts.

Closed the lid.

Stared at the glowing bitten apple. Stared at the place in my arm where the needle goes in.

Opened the lid.

Opened the draft.

Unfocused my eyes so the words were unreadable.

Stitches in straight lines.

A winter's worth of birds.

¡Coraje!

¡Coraje!

Send.

Dear Antonio Jorge Romero,

You don't know me. My name is Maddy. I got your email address online. I hope you don't mind me writing out of the blue like this. I will get straight to the point. You were at George Washington University in 1994. Did you know a girl named Eve Wakefield? If you and Eve were an item at that time, you probably know what I am going to say. You might want to sit down. She is my mother. I am sixteen years and two months old. I know this might come as a big shock. Have no fear. I don't want anything from you except to introduce myself and hopefully for you to do the same. I was going to wait until I was eighteen to look for you, but due to various circumstances which I will not go into, I am doing it now. I sincerely hope this is not too much of a shock and that you will write back. Thank you for reading this, if you have read to the end of it.

Madeleine Rose Wakefield
(Maddy)

P.S. I haven't told Mom I am doing this.
P.P.S. If you don't reply, I might turn up on your doorstep.
P.P.P.S. Just kidding!

8

Until this happened I had hardly set foot in a hospital. Now, like it or not, the hospital was my place. The gift store at the entrance was my place. The receptionist who called me "honey lamb" belonged to me, and so did the lady with her glasses on a chain rattling her cart past the outpatient desk, and so did the cleaner in his two-toned blue shirt, kneeling on a pad to wipe the baseboards. I was drawn to the people who weren't in charge of life-or-death affairs, only these everyday tasks they were touchingly intent on doing no matter what.

We sat on the orange seats in the waiting room.

"Okay, Maddy?"

"Okay."

"We'll get through it."

"Yup."

"In a week or two you'll be a shiny new penny."

I held my mother's arm and laid my cheek on her shoulder as if I were a little kid in need of a nap. This made her draw me close and kiss the top of my head, which I wanted her to do because I was feeling bad about not telling her I was looking for Antonio. I especially felt bad when we were together just the two of us, with time to kill and plenty of silence.

She held me snug for a minute, then let me go and opened her book. The difference between my mother and me is that she can read when she's worried, and I can't. Her pixie cut was growing out. More gray than before. My fault. She raked her bangs back every page or so with two fingers of one hand. Her hair was getting shaggy down the back of her neck. Not what she should be aiming for, in my opinion. I didn't particularly want to have a shaggy mother.

You can take a lot in with sideways glances. A mother reading. A mother reading beside her sick daughter. A mother reading beside her sick daughter who the day before sent an email to her long-lost father. A secret does funny things to a person, and not just if you're found out. Inside your own mind, I mean. It's a delicious burdensome thing that takes up all the space so you can't believe that other people, my mother, for instance, shifting in her chair, blinking down at the page, and from time to time reaching out and giving my knee or arm a little press, could not tell. You want to show the secret off and you want to hug it to yourself. Should I have made that joke about turning up on Antonio's doorstep? He probably wouldn't reply anyway. Like Grandpa said, I had to be prepared for anything.

I jumped when my mother uncrossed her legs and inserted her bookmark. My mind was stuffed full of Antonio, and my mother's mind was stuffed full of other things, and neither of us knew what the other person was stuffed full of. She stood up and smiled at me, and I smiled back. Mine was a fake. She beamed her gaze deep into me in a way that used to signal a moment of humor and solidarity but that nowadays was likely to mean weariness or badly concealed fear. Maybe it also meant the guessing of secrets. Maybe through genetic telepathy she knew that I had emailed my father and she was trying to decide whether to bring it up or wait for me to. She always tries not to intrude. I turned my Tweetie-Pie eyes on her. Bring it up, Mom! Ask me!

My mother only stretched and went to get coffee. Drinking coffee is the one unhealthy thing she does. It is her daily pleasure. She won't give it up, no matter how badly she sleeps.

The bare skull of the boy sitting opposite had crisscrossing tracks of metal stitches and a purple map of skin above his ear. Eyes in dark shadows. Cheeks the only babyish part of him left. Head down, he was playing on his phone while his mother flipped through a magazine. All at once the boy swung his legs, and smiled right at me.

I stared to the side. It was a policy of mine not to meet the eyes of the other kids. My head was a boulder that received and transmitted nothing.

I pretended to be fascinated by the four-paneled

painting on the wall called *Each Day Life Begins Anew*, as if I didn't know it by heart. The four panels represented the seasons. Each girl started in one season and swung her feet into the next, except for the fall panel, where the swing was empty and run aground in mud. The last girl swung her yellow boots into a violet-colored winter, which proved only one thing—big deal!—that this so-called artist had studied the color chart.

"Do you like that picture?" The boy was as hoarse as an old man.

"Not very much."

"Why not?"

"Look at how crooked the swings are! I could do better than that. Her hands are like mittens."

"I think it's pretty," he said. "How old are you?"

"Sixteen."

"I'm ten. What's your name?"

"Maddy."

"Is that a real name?"

"Of course it's a real name! What's yours?"

"Torrence."

"Don't tell me *that's* a real name?"

He ducked and covered his grin with both hands. Kids that age, their teeth are too big for their mouths. His mother glanced up and straight down again.

"They said I'd be okay if I made it to three

years. I was so close! I only had two months to go. Then it came back. Are you getting chemo?"

I nodded.

"What do you have?"

"Cancer of the cells that are supposed to protect me." He wouldn't appreciate the irony. "Do you have any brothers or sisters?"

Torrence glanced sideways. "That's my sister."

So that was why she looked so young and bored. To head off the question, I volunteered: "I'm an only child," just as my mother took her seat, coffee in one hand and a hot chocolate for me in the other. "That's my mother."

The women exchanged guarded smiles and returned to their reading.

He held up his phone. "Summer gave me an iPod Touch. So I could play Angry Birds in the car."

I licked the whipped cream off the top of my drink.

"Do you know what Angry Birds is?"

"A game where these birds try to kill pigs who are stealing their eggs."

He pointed to a purple wristband he was wearing. "This is for Team Summer. I loved Summer. She died."

"Oh."

Torrence gripped the edge of his seat and swung his legs. "Can I give you something?"

"What do you mean?"

"That's how it works. Once you get a gift, you can give one to another kid with cancer. To cheer them up. What do you want?"

"Nothing," I said.

His look bordered on the scornful. "You must want *some*thing."

"Torrence," said his sister, warningly. "You know it has to be a surprise."

He lowered his head and swung his legs some more, and then I was called in.

My favorite nurse, Carla, was on duty. When she saw me, she crowed like I was her long-lost lover and gave me a smothering hug. Her frizzy hair was in a ponytail. Behind the glasses, she had the warmest eyes. Though I knew better, and though being embraced by Carla brought tears springing to my eyes, for a minute it seemed as if everything was going to be all right just because it was her giving me my chemo. Mom held my hand and rubbed my shoulder and exchanged smiles with Carla while she accessed my port and hooked me up and fussed with the valve, peering at the bag with a practiced eye.

Some of the kids I knew were there, Sandy and Rita, the dancer who'd lost her leg, but it was Torrence I couldn't get out of my mind. Tracks across his scalp. Covering his smile with both hands. Wanting to tell me things. Give me things. At least when I was ten I was carefree because I had no idea what was going to happen.

At least this part didn't hurt, like getting IVs did; with chemo the ugliness came later. I smiled at my mother and made a mental effort to welcome the liquid in. Some other girl was lying on the bed in my place. I was soaring over the hospital and the peaks of the trees and the traffic going around and around in circles. Above and beyond and away.

When we were leaving the hospital, I thought of Torrence again, though he was nowhere to be seen. He might have been there just for scans. We passed as always the stained glass windows of daisies and daffodils, the framed photographs of beaches, bridges, and peacocks. They don't let me out until my counts are up, but still the first week home is awful. Disappearing Girl. Monster Baby. I wondered if Torrence's mother took care of him when he was sick, or if he had a grandmother, because if you ask me, his sister would be chewing gum and waiting for the minute she could leave the room. It was possible Torrence didn't even *have* a mother. I couldn't bear to think about that.

I took my mother's arm and we steamed as fast as we could go to the parking lot, home, and my own bed. Antonio flashed into my mind. I banished the thought of him. He did not belong in this part of my life. I did not want him there. Good thing I had not told my mother. Together we followed the corridor around the courtyard, where the sculptures made of painted wood were visible from all angles. One had arms and legs jointed like a beetle's. One had a head like a giant pumpkin, under a hat from which a black feather protruded in the shape of fingers. The third character was seizing his skull with both hands, having been clobbered by a brick. His eyes were squeezed shut and he was roaring with laughter. Whenever I passed these sculptures, if you want to call them that, my question was: Is this supposed to be funny? Is this supposed to cheer people up? But today I was drawn to their dark goofiness. I stopped to examine the one hit by a brick. His head was nearly caved in, but he was laughing anyway, in this weird triumphant way, as if to say, Ha ha, you hit me, but you can't really get me! It almost made me want to laugh.

Each time, it takes a little longer to recover. That treatment was the worst yet. My port got infected and I went back to the hospital for two days of antibiotics. They had to call the IV team to get the needle in my arm. Even then it hurt like crazy. When I came home I was running to the bathroom all night long. My mouth was on fire from the ulcers, and I could only eat mashed bananas and smoothies. Food fit for babies. My feet were so numb, I couldn't even keep flip-flops on. Chemo does things to your nerves.

Dr. O says once the treatments are over, that should go away.

I lay facedown on my rug so I wouldn't come to hate my bed too much, pushing Cloud away whenever she came near; then I felt bad and tried to coax her back, but she'd had enough of me. All I wanted was my mother, and she was there, kneeling beside me on the rug, her singsong voice flowing all around the place, strong for me.

"Poor baby." Even before I got sick, she used to call me that if I was miserable for some trivial reason. All reasons before now were trivial.

"I want to be," I said to the rug.

"What?"

"A baby."

"Well, you started out that way, and you can be again. Whenever you need to."

"I don't mean a crybaby."

"You get that from me." I heard the smile in her voice. "I get it from your grandmother. Runs in the family."

"I mean a real one. That people take care of because it's fat and cute."

"You're not fat," she said, running her fingers down my spine, light as light could be; any harder and I'd be throwing up again. "And you're not cute. You're beautiful."

The blindness of mothers!

"Maybe I used to be."

She put her face near mine and whispered:

"People like us are supposed to cry. What would we do if we couldn't cry?"

"Okay, but why do *we* have to be the ones?"

I had her there. She kissed me in lots of places and left the room on some excuse or other before *she* started to cry, thereby disproving her point that crying was nothing to be ashamed of.

Little by little I got better until one day I was sitting up in bed, maybe not a shiny new penny, but not a grimy nickel either, when with a lurch of the stomach I remembered Antonio. Once my mother had delivered her lunch tray and gone back downstairs, I booted up my laptop and scrolled down all the boring ads and school announcements. Outside it was drizzling, but in here a giant bar of sunlight fell across my screen. Antonio Jorge Romero. There he was, waiting patiently in my in-box. Three weeks! Maybe he thought I had lost interest. Maybe he thought I was ghosting him. With a swift glance toward the mirror and another toward the door, my heart bumping like that of some elated creature who wanted to believe again in the universe and what it could deliver, I clicked on my father's name.

Dear Maddy,

Naturally I was very, very surprised to get your email. It's hard to know what to say and how to say it. It's true your mother and I were together in Washington in 1994. I left America the summer I graduated. You probably know that Eve and I have not been in contact since that time. Your mother is a wonderful person. I have thought about her a lot over the years. That is all I can say for now. Thank you for writing.

Antonio

OMG. Wow. When I saw you in my inbox I could not believe my eyes! I took a while to answer because I've been away. Most girls my age are on Facebook all the time, but I still use email like an old person (not that you're old). I think it's more personal and I don't always want everyone to know my business. I hope it's okay to email you again.

I'm not sure what I should call you. I am attaching a picture of me. It's one of my favorites. My friend Vicky took it last summer in the park. That's me on the left and Fiona on the right. You can see how much taller I am. I am a lot taller than my mother. I am in tenth grade. I play the piano (or I used to) and I love classical music. Robin, my mother's boyfriend, knows everything about classical music. We go to concerts, mostly chamber music. This is something else that most kids my age are not into, but Fiona says I am not like most kids and I guess that's a good thing, right? Being an individual etc. It feels so strange to be writing to you. I wonder whether I have made you up! My grandfather helped me find you. He's the only one in the family who knows. He said you might not want to hear from me and that I had to be prepared for anything. I think maybe I have lucked out . . . Please write back. If you want to.

Maddy

Maddy,

I am with you on the Facebook question. My children are too young for Facebook, but my wife makes fun of me because I do not even have an account. Thank you for the picture. It is so nice to see. This is very strange for me. Very strange! You can see my photograph on the UCL website. I am a neuroscientist. By the way, I think it's better if your mother knows we are in contact. Do you agree? If you want, send me her email and I will contact her myself. I'm glad she is with someone. Do you have any brothers or sisters?

Antonio (you can call me Antonio)

9

I printed out our exchange so that something of Antonio would occupy the same space as me. I put the printouts in a folder and slid the folder down the wall by my bed. Under my bed is one place in the house where no one ever goes. There are things under there with half an inch of dust on them. A fairy wand that used to light up, a Lalaloopsy doll, a collage I made in third grade, a plastic diary you unlock by punching in a code, a book called *Sexwise*, and probably lots of other things I can't see. I know because when something drops between the bed and the wall, I have to shine a flashlight down and fish it out with barbecue tongs. The edges of the lost things are gray and furry like the objects that could be seen through the portholes when they found the *Titanic*. I was about to do a huge clearing out of my bedroom when I got sick. Now I'd rather just leave things where they are, along with the tongs and the folder of emails, where I'll put the new ones when they come in. *If* they keep coming in.

Luckily my counts weren't high enough for the next treatment, so I had a few extra weeks of feeling good. Next time I went to visit Jack, I met his father. Coincidence! Two fathers in the same week. Maybe finding a father is such a big event it's like a magnet that drags other fathers into it.

Jack and I were on his laptop browsing when I heard the front door open and footsteps on the stairs. It made me jump, although we were doing nothing worth being jumpy about. Mr. Bell is stockier than Jack, but with the same broad face and narrowed eyes that give you the feeling he's thinking deep thoughts, or at least amusing ones. He shook my hand as if he had bald girls in his kitchen every day of the week and said: "I guess you've been having a hard time."

"Dad!"

"Sorry. Did I say something wrong?" He searched my face for signs of offense. "I'm always embarrassing my son." He slapped Jack on the back. "It's in the job description."

Jack shrugged his hand off. "Be like your hairline, Dad. Withdraw."

His father winked at me. I hoped he would see through my weak smile and ask me more specific questions about the hard time I was having. But he didn't, so I hugged myself as if I were cold and picked threads off my sweater.

Mr. Bell draped his suit jacket on a chair and loosened his tie. His case had been postponed, he said, which was why he was home early. He asked me some polite questions about my mother, where we lived, and so forth, and then the three of us talked about the campaign. He stood with his feet apart like a sheriff in a Western, rotating an invisible ball in his hands to make his points. He had a lot of points to make. Jack elaborated on whatever his father said, and I could see that underneath, he was full of admiration. Even if they didn't give it a second thought, the time they'd spent together was obvious. Correction. The time his father had spent with him. Because let's face it, children are stuck in one place, taking whatever comes. It was Jack's father who had bothered to be there all along, so that now he could clap his son on the back in that fake hearty way and Jack could shrug off his hand. That was a true father.

Having changed, Mr. Bell went out to Office Depot for paper and print cartridges—so he informed his son, who crossed his eyes to let me know what he thought about that level of detail.

"Your father's so nice." For some reason Jack and I always spent our time in the kitchen. When we weren't looking at something together at the breakfast bar, Jack liked to stand with his back against the counter, as he was doing now.

"My father's a pain."

"Yeah, right."

Sheepish smile. "Sometimes."

"What happened between your parents? If you want to talk about it."

"They split up. I was ten. My sister was already in college."

"Why did they split up?"

" 'Irretrievable breakdown.' I used to put my headphones on at night when they were arguing. Apparently my father wasn't exciting enough for her. My mother's with someone more exciting now." He caught sight of my face. "Don't worry. I'm used to it. Back then all I wanted was for them to get back together. I tried everything I could think of."

"Like what?"

"Oh, I broke my leg jumping off the porch roof."

"Don't tell me you did that on purpose!"

He grinned. "Not really. But after that we were together every weekend for a while. Then the summer after seventh grade I ran away from camp with Freddy Cook. We were in the woods all night before they found us. We said we were trying out our survival skills, but my parents didn't buy it. That's when we went into family therapy."

I nodded, smug because *we* had never had to go to family therapy. Then I remembered that to go to family therapy you have to have a family.

"This guy George." He tucked his chin into his neck and harrumphed: " 'So how do you feel about that, Jack? Your mother doesn't love your father anymore, and you don't ask your friends over because you live in two places and neither of them feels like home. Any thoughts you'd like to share with us about that?' " Jack laughed. "I liked George, actually. I forget, has your mother always been on her own?"

"She's not on her own. She's with Robin. He's like a stepfather to me. I love Robin!" I was being a little too emphatic, but boys aren't tuned in to that kind of thing. After a minute I said: "I never knew my real father, if that's what you mean."

"Oh." Jack glanced at me. "Well. I liked your mother. She was fun. Do you remember that game we played where she used to roll us up in towels? We'd hatch or whatever cocoons do, and go tap her on the shoulder and she'd turn around all surprised, and then we'd be butterflies and dance around the room."

I stood up, stretched, and sat down again. Now was not the time to go down memory lane. Couldn't he see I had something to tell him? High board. Dive in.

"Know what, Jack?"

"What?"

"You're not going to believe this." I was trying not to smile. "I found my real father this week."

I didn't blame Jack for thinking it was a joke. "No way!" He stared at me, ready to start laughing if I gave a sign.

I told him the story of the search, my grandfather's turnaround, my email, Antonio's reply. Jack kept very still, leaning against the counter with his arms folded, his eyes fixed on my face. It was the most complete attention he had ever given me. Maybe it was an exotic thing, not knowing your father, finding him online.

"He's a scientist in London," I said. "He's sometimes in the news." Didn't scientists write for magazines? That's the news.

"What kind of scientist?"

"Neuroscientist. Brain."

Jack was eyeing me with curiosity. "You seem very cool about this."

"No, I'm not!" I didn't know how to tell Jack I would pretty much take anyone's father over the one I had. A mean one, or one who got drunk, or was old or divorced or way too strict. "It's just kind of strange."

"So what are you going to do? Try to meet him?"

"Meet him!" I echoed. "I only found him on Sunday. My mother doesn't know. My grandfather doesn't even know. You're the only one who knows."

He was silent. "Seriously?"

"Seriously."

This fact had a strange effect on Jack. From where he was standing at the counter, he flicked me a couple of puzzled, grateful looks, like I had just given him a surprise present. The barstool I was sitting on was one of those retro diner ones with a red padded seat. It could swivel all the way around. I pushed off the floor with one foot and started the stool slowly spinning. The stainless steel refrigerator went by . . . the window filled with lawn . . . the five-ring stove . . . the rack with hanging pans of every size . . . Any second he would come into view and I would have to reckon with Jack again, with having told him about Antonio.

Two things happened at once. The empty counter swung by with no Jack leaning on it, which meant he had gone away and I would never see him again, and Jack was behind me, reappeared as if by magic in a new form. Big and near. Turning me. I tilted up my face and shut my eyes. But no one kissed me. Instead I was gripped by what felt more like wings than arms and my face was squashed into his neck. Being so close that I could feel the heat of him and smell his grassy smell was as good as anything that had happened to me in a long time. But why didn't he want to kiss me? Lost his nerve? Afraid of catching what I had? Seconds ticked by. Do something!

I laughed and pulled away.

His arms dropped. "What's so funny?"

"Nothing!"

He went to the fridge and held the door open, peering into the lighted interior. It was lonely having him so far away again. I went over and touched his arm that was propping open the fridge door.

"Nothing's funny, Jack."

He shrugged my hand off, a little more gently than he'd done to his father. "Hungry?" he asked, letting the door swing shut.

"Not really. I might need to go."

"Right."

"I wasn't laughing at you."

"Right."

"At myself, more like."

"No need for that," Jack said stiffly.

I was afraid to touch him. "Friends?"

A fake smile was all I got back.

Hi Antonio,

I know Mom would be basically fine with the idea of me writing to you. But I REALLY don't think we should tell her right now. The thing is, one of her best friends has cancer and my mother is very busy and stressed. I think it would be better not to give her one more thing to worry about (not that she especially would, but you know what I mean). I am an only child. I have a Ragdoll kitten named Cloud. I really wish I had a brother or sister. I especially wish I had an identical twin. Then you would have two surprises on your hands instead of one . . . ! Mainly there would be someone else on the planet like me. And if one of us got lost, Mom would have a spare! Just kidding. I have two cousins, Denny and Joe, but that's not the same. They live in California. We live in DC. Well, Takoma Park, Maryland, to be exact. My grandparents live right in the middle of DC, on Corcoran Street. Sometimes I wish I belonged to a huge family. But I like mine the way it is. How many children do you have?

Maddy
P.S. Estudio español en la escuela.

Hello Maddy,

Bravo on learning Spanish! I come from the north of Spain, a little place in the mountains. I moved to London eleven years ago to take a research position. I met my wife, Erica, here. She is English and I ended up living in London without really intending to. A lot of things in life happen without you intending them. We have two sons. Oscar is 6 and a half, and Daniel is 4. I don't know what your mother has told you about me.

I am so sorry to hear about your mother's friend. What I am worried about is that Eve will feel left out when she knows we have been writing to each other. I'm so happy you wrote to me, but I think it's better if we stop for now, until you decide whether you can tell your mother.

Saludos,
Antonio

Antonio,

Well are you going to tell your family about me?

Maddy

10

The week after the disastrous non-kiss, I texted Jack to say I wasn't feeling well and couldn't come over. He replied *K,* which was worse than no reply at all. For two days I did not get dressed or leave my room much. I had to stop Mom from calling Dr. Osterley. I told her I might be seriously ill but she had to respect the fact that I was a teenager with hormonal ups and downs. I said she should consult her book on the adolescent brain. I said did she think it was fair for my emotional life to be public property just because I had cancer. She backed off. Which left me to stew in my room. Which I had to admit had its downside.

In a fit of cooped-up frustration, I pulled out the sketchbook she got for me and started sketching my shirt hanging on the back of the chair. I drew in jagged, careless lines so anyone watching would know it was an idiotic thing to do and my heart was not in it. My heart was back in Jack's kitchen, obsessively and pointlessly going over who said what when, replaying the stool-spinning scenario to edit out the moment I closed my eyes, expecting something to happen, and the moment I laughed.

Little by little, what I was doing overtook

what I was thinking. The pencil scratched into the silence. My thoughts dropped away. All my attention was taken up by the folds of the shirt. They fell from the shoulder seams in soft columns. My job was to brighten their curves and deepen the crevices between them, to give each one its own peculiar shape. A long triangle squeezed in the middle. A tube. A canoe with slanting ripples. The lower edge of the shirt gathered all the folds together and made sense of them. I tried to show this by going over the hemline twice. Tipped my head. Too heavy? Too dark a stripe at the bottom? I erased it and redrew it more gently, compared the shapes again and feathered the shadows so you could hardly tell at what point they turned into light. When I stepped back, there it was: a second shirt hanging in a second, silvery world that appeared to be newly made but might in fact have been there all along.

I found my mother downstairs, slowing to a dignified pace before entering her study. She smiled, not so much at the drawing as at my face.

"Sorry, Mom." I went up close so she would hug me.

"For what?"

"Nothing. Just sorry."

The next day I drew Cloud curled up on my bed. She ruined it by turning over. I drew that pose instead until she moved and I had to start again. After lots of attempts, I gave up and rubbed her stomach, thinking about her miniature organs inside, all in perfect working order.

Draw another shirt? No. Something alive that would keep still. I held up my left hand. Index finger pointed at the ceiling, the others curled into the palm. With my right hand I started to sketch. The hand of the Serenity statue must have looked like that before it was broken off. Elegant gesture. Terrible drawing! I scribbled it out. Maybe shirts were all I was capable of. I got up and crossed the room. Coming back, I encountered my faraway self, straining to see out of the mirror to where I was. Corner of your room? Clothes hanging in your closet? Dare you to draw yourself. Dare you! *Too hard,* somebody whispered. *Too sad.*

I dragged the chair to the mirror and began before I could talk myself out of it, thinking this time about Antonio's smile in the photo. Warm, like his emails, but not giving anything away. What if Antonio could see me now, a bald girl with hoop earrings drawing a bald girl with hoop earrings? If he could see me now, he would know. I didn't want him to know, and not because I hadn't told my mother about him yet. I just didn't want him to. Couldn't I be a normal girl for once? Besides, if he felt sorry for me, I would never know what he really thought.

Once again, the rhythm of looking up and down and matching the shapes left no room for my thoughts. My mother had an annoying habit of being right. Drawing made you think only: Things are what they are. The light falls where it falls. The shape of my forehead is what it is. The trick in doing a face, according to Mr. Yam, is to pretend it's an object like any object in the world. The other trick is to keep the overall look of the thing and the tiniest details in mind at the same time, or to be able to flip back and forth between them. Once I started, I remembered that I had always been good at both tricks.

This time when I showed the drawing to my mother, she shook her head slowly while blinking fast. I guess it was her child with no hair, trapped inside a mirror. We were sitting on the couch. I felt something pass between us, by way of the drawing.

"That bad, Mom?"

"It's a superb drawing, Maddy. Extraordinary. You look . . ."

"What?" I demanded. "What do I look?"

Eyes on the picture, she said: "Beseeching . . . but also defiant."

"What's beseeching again?"

"Beseeching is: Please help me. Defiant is: Don't mess with me."

"Feisty, you mean?"

"I guess."

"That's a good thing to be?"

"In your case, yes. You've always had that side to you."

"And the other side?"

Her eyes filmed over. "Understandable." She kissed my forehead and tried to sound breezy while holding on to me for dear life. "Completely and totally understandable."

Back in my room, studying the drawing, I decided it was my forehead and eyes that said "Help me"; my mouth and chin said "Don't mess with me." I liked the fact that those qualities leaked onto the paper without me exactly putting them there, and I liked the fact that my qualities were apparent to other people. In any case, it was a good drawing; anyone could see that. I pretended Antonio was looking over my shoulder. Bet his children can't draw like that. His other children.

Antonio,

I will think about it. But she is truly upset and worried about her friend, which is a much bigger thing to worry about. At least I think it is. And I'm the one who has to put up with her when she's stressed. ☺

Maddy

Vicky and Fiona came once or twice a week now instead of every other day. Fiona had drama club and Vicky had a lot of homework to catch up on, or so she said. Her homework was mostly Wade. Though I gathered the romance was not exactly going according to plan. She sat in my desk chair and unbuckled her gladiator sandals. "These are killing me." She gave me a searching look. "How's Maddy today?"

I liked being talked to in the third person. She only did that with us. "Doing fine," I said. "About the same." I had no intention of telling Vicky about Antonio. He was an astonishing fact that did not feel like a fact yet. "But how are *you?*"

"Oh, you know. Surviving. Wade's being a dickhead. I tell him, Girls are like fires. You don't tend them, they go out." Vicky's marimba ringtone went off. She rolled her eyes. "That'll be him." Glanced down. "No, it's Billy. Do I answer it? He went out with Carina Butler last night."

"Answer it," said Fiona. Billy Quinn was this boy we had a soft spot for. He had narrow shoulders and a mournful face, and he was incapable of deception or spite. We were like his big sisters.

Vicky nodded, keeping her eyes on Fiona and me. ". . . Just say her bone structure is giving your bone structure . . . Kidding, Billy. *Kidding.* Hang on a sec, I'm putting you on speaker. I'm with Fiona and Maddy." She held the phone over the bed, equidistant from all of us.

"We can help," I said. "How did it go?"

"I think she wanted to kiss me."

"*Wanted* to?" Vicky googled her eyes at us. "Wanted to kiss you?"

"I got the feeling she did. She was standing pretty close."

"Did you kiss Wade on your first date, Vic?" I said.

"Course not." She grinned. "Leave some excitement for next time, Billy."

"How do I do that?"

"Put your hand on her cheek and lean in," said Fiona.

"Hug her," said Vicky. "Then your faces will be close. If she gives a sign, you'll know it's all right to go ahead."

"Thanks, guys," he said. "You're the best."

"But if you take too long, she might go for it herself."

"Oh, shit . . ."

"No, Billy, that's a good thing! It shows you're a gentleman."

"Girls like that."

When we'd hung up, I lay back. It was exhausting having to care whether Wade was good enough for Vicky, or whether Billy had kissed Carina or not, or whether she would dump him and destroy his confidence forever.

"How's Jack?" asked Fiona.

"Great. There's this publicity drive for the march we're working on."

Vicky was at my dresser giving herself a cat eye. She turned around, one eye winged. "I think it's great you're into all this. I really do. But to be totally honest with you? I can't get excited about it."

"You don't want to think about the end of the world as we know it?"

"She does it to be with Jack," put in Fiona from the beanbag.

I did not like being talked about as if I wasn't there. "Not *just* that."

Vicky gazed at me for a moment, eyeliner wand poised in her long fingers. "Take asteroids." She turned back and raised her brows to start the second eye. "There's a hundred percent chance the earth will get hit by an asteroid. Hundred percent. Sooner or later. Boom. Finito. So why sit around and worry? You can't move someplace else. Same with the climate. We might as well live it up now. That's my thinking."

"Do you want your children to grow up in a desert?"

"What children?" said Vicky to the mirror. "I'm not having any boring kids. I'm going to have fun."

"Well, I want kids," Fiona announced.

"Same," I said. "And I'd want them to have polar bears and trees."

"Go right ahead." Vicky's hair lay across her shoulders like a thick black shawl. Italians know

135

how to make hair. Nothing like Fiona's cotton candy or my reddish brown waves way back when; hair-wise the three of us could belong to different species.

"Where are you meeting Wade?" Fiona wanted to know.

"He's picking me up. Four-thirty. Remember he got his license?"

"You're abandoning us at four-thirty? What happened to chicks before dicks?"

"Sisters over misters!"

Vicky kept a cosmetic silence. I used to think people wanted to be around her because she was beautiful and her parents were rich, but it was more than that. She was always completely herself. She was funny and kind in a distracted sort of way, and she never threw shade. Watching her stroke the eyeliner out to a witchy point, I could see right into the future. Vicky would have adventures, and mishaps, and three or four husbands, at least, with divorces to match. I glanced over to see if Fiona was thinking the same thing, but she was on the floor, arching her back into the Upward Facing Dog.

"This position," she said to the ceiling, "elongates the spine."

"God knows yours needs elongating," said Vicky.

"Hey!" Fiona used to envy me my height. I don't suppose she does anymore, but she is still desperate to gain some inches. She came out of the pose and sat cross-legged, rubbing her thighs. "I keep getting these growing pains, but nothing ever happens."

"Poor baby," I said. "Don't even think about it. Short is the new tall."

Fiona would stay sweet and petite and have a houseful of oddball kids and she would stand by her man no matter what. In their different ways, the two of them would get what they wanted. Whether it happened tomorrow, or next year, or some other time, or not at all, made no difference. The future for them was a huge misty field they couldn't see the end of.

"By the way," I said, "there's nothing going on, you know. With Jack."

"Well, I can tell you he doesn't post anything interesting on Facebook," said Vicky. "It's all icebergs and fund-raising links."

"How do *you* know?"

"If you're not going to stalk him, we are! See if he's leading you on. Believe me, he has some hot girls after him."

"A philanderer? Jack Bell?" Fiona was across the room now, squatting down. "Nice guy, but not exactly—"

"Fine by me," I cut in. "We're *friends*."

"Friends," said Vicky with distaste.

Fiona stood up, my sketchbook in her hands. "Hey, what's this? Don't tell me you drew this?"

"Okay, I won't."

"Oh my god. It looks exactly like you. *Exactly*. Maddy, you are such a good artist. Isn't she, Vic?"

Vicky turned around, both eyes winged now. "Whoa," she said. "I could never do that. Not in a million years." People who look out for themselves don't mind giving praise.

"You've never tried," I said, to be generous back.

Fiona was flipping through the pages. She came to the half-finished sketches of Cloud. "This is cool. Squint your eyes and look from one to the other."

"It's like she's moving on the page," said Vicky.

"Alive, almost."

Maddy,

Sorry I have gone quiet. I have been busy and also taking time to think. This is a complicated situation for everyone, ¿no estás de acuerdo? If you still want to keep writing I guess I am okay with it for now. I will try to answer any questions you have.

Antonio

Eve

11

Norma reached up to tighten her ponytail and I thought she shuddered a little in the heat. I'd ended up telling her the story of the snake without exactly deciding to.

"I told Maddy when she was old enough."

"What did she make of it?"

"Oh, even as a child, Maddy liked the . . . Gothic, shall we say. She never shied away from frightening things. She wanted to know what was out there, I guess."

"Is she still like that?"

I steepled my fingers. "Oh, yes."

"Mine are scaredy-cats," said Norma. "Maybe they'll toughen up when they're teenagers. Isn't that when kids get into horror movies and gore and whatnot?"

"I guess so," I said. "It's strange. I haven't thought about that snake in years."

I could not read Norma's silence, so I pointed out the family of ducks that every day made their way from the peninsula to the fallen tree on the lot next door. They proceeded with a mechanical, jaunty confidence, as if protection of the young is a matter of getting everyone in the correct position. We followed the ducks' progress until they disappeared one at a time through the gap under the trunk.

"Do we actually hear those ducks swimming," I said, "or do we only *think* we hear them?" Sound or imagined sound: the distinction is not as great as one might think. What I imagine is also part of the world.

Norma cocked her head. "I don't think I can hear them."

I considered this a very cryptic reply. "Even if they're too far away to hear, we invent the sounds." Nearby, in the shadows of the overhanging branches, bronze shafts of light plummeted down. "Maddy tells me there are three worlds in a lake. The surface texture. The mud, weeds, and rocks underneath. And the reflection. The trick, she says, is to hold all three worlds in your mind at once."

Norma nodded in an encouraging way that made me suspicious. Why had she stayed this long, gamely listening to my nonsense about lakes, snakes, and turtles? She laced her fingers and straightened her arms, palms out, a gesture often accompanied by a yawn. Any minute she would stand and make her excuses, lower herself into the kayak as clumsily as she had disembarked, and paddle back to her life.

The dock trembled underfoot. I turned. Robin was standing by the moored boat.

"I've got to go," said Norma, rising from her chair.

"No, no!" he protested. "I don't want to break

anything up. Just came to say hello." He was looking back and forth between us, smiling a little, trying to gauge the moment. "You're from across the way?"

"New kid on the block. Norma," she said, extending her hand. They looked comically mismatched. Norma was from fair, big-boned, northern stock, while Robin, who had a Greek grandfather, was slight of build and deeply tanned.

"Eve says you're making a new room in the attic?"

He showed her his stained palms.

"You've hurt yourself," I said, moving closer to touch his knuckle. I'd always thought Robin's shyness was visible only to me, but maybe it was plain to everyone.

"I'm afraid there's a long way to go." He returned his hand to his pocket.

"My husband's an optimist when it comes to remodeling," said Norma. "My personal rule of thumb is to estimate how long it will take and multiply by four."

"That's about right." Robin laughed. "We'll get there in the end. Come in and see what we're doing sometime." The two of them had warmed to one another, I could tell.

"And you come over to ours," said Norma, kneeling to untie her kayak. "I'm dying to get to know people."

Together we watched her plunge in and set the thing rocking. Robin held the mooring rope until she had arranged her legs, and she shoved the dock away with her paddle and raised it to wave, like someone who was convinced that the world was a magnificent place and we were all lucky to be here.

Maddy

12

I still had a moment of amazement, when opening the front door, that a teacher was coming to my house. She wore her tan belted raincoat and large-framed glasses, and carried her cloth tote bag. I've missed so much school that the only hope of me going into junior year is to continue with the home tutoring. Even then, I might have to repeat a year. It depends.

"Do you know we've raised four hundred dollars selling your cards?" said Miss Sedge once we were downstairs. She was there to get me through biology, but the campaign was taking more and more of our time. She had a gruff way of speaking, like there were stones in her mouth she had to talk around. I hardly noticed anymore; it was just part of her, like brown was the color of her hair. If you'd told me a year ago that I would admire Miss Sedge and look forward to her visits, I would not have believed you. I guess if you'd told me a lot of things a year ago, I would not have believed you.

On her laptop was the image Jack and I had Photoshopped of the White House underwater. We'd named it *The Picture Postcard Zone*. "It's a fabulous image. We'll definitely use it on the posters. And signs on the day."

"It was my idea," I reminded her, though Jack had already given me the credit.

"I know it was. You're a star. You both are. Now we need to think of something else. Something to go with the speeches. I don't know exactly what."

The doorbell rang. I jumped a mile. She pretended not to notice. I had made sure she arrived first because I wanted us to be deep in conversation when Jack got there so that he would be the odd one out. I wanted him to see I was someone to be reckoned with, even if I didn't know what to do when a boy grabbed me out of the blue and then forgot to kiss me.

I heard Jack talking to my mother in the hall, and my mother directing him down. I had resolved to be looking elsewhere, but my eyes had a mind of their own. He joined us at the table, booted up his computer, and opened a blank document. I took it as a good sign that he could hardly look at me.

"Let's brainstorm," he said, as if we'd been waiting for him to come along and save the day.

"You can't say *brainstorm* anymore."

"You can't?"

"It's insulting to people with epilepsy."

"Ha!" said Miss Sedge. "If I had epilepsy, I'd find it insulting to be patronized like that."

She was not one for correctness, political or any other kind. True, she was an overly strict hall

150

monitor, but Jack said that was to keep on the right side of the school authorities. They didn't like the fact that she'd gotten herself arrested in the last campaign.

"Is this even legal?" I asked.

"Is what legal?" she said.

"Inciting minors to activism and civil disobedience," said Jack.

"Is it legal to destroy the earth we all live on? Is it legal to poison the atmosphere? Is it legal to melt the polar ice caps?"

"It's probably *legal*—" Jack began.

"Who cares?" I jumped in to cut off his technical point. "Change the laws."

Miss Sedge gave a throaty, approving laugh. "Precisely. You can't do the civil disobedience part, but you can work behind the scenes and go on the march. It's you young people who should be up in arms. It's your world." Under her breath she added: "My ambition at that school is to resign before I get fired." I liked the way she answered questions by not exactly answering them.

"What could we make?"

Jack said what about a video montage of melting icebergs? I said too obvious. What about a hot-air balloon slowly bursting? He wasn't sure. A cartoon? A song? Busily he recorded all the ideas, darting glances at me now and then but keeping his eyes mostly on Miss Sedge. She was younger than she looked at first, not much older than my mother. Would I change places with her? To be sitting in some high school girl's family room chatting about my favorite subject? To be a person for whom Jack was just another smart sixteen-year-old boy?

We went over the list. The hot-air balloon was too literal, a cartoon too glib.

"Not a song . . ." I made my goofball face. "A song would be so extra."

"Less is more," said Jack.

"Whatever that means."

Miss Sedge leaned back in her chair. Unsettling as her silence could be, we could trust what she said because she never tried to flatter us.

"The structure of the benzene ring was solved by a dream. The problem had been preoccupying Kekule for a long time. Then one afternoon he fell asleep and dreamed of a snake biting its own tail."

Were we doing a science lesson now? Jack and I exchanged a tiny shrug.

"Though there's no proof," she went on, "he ever had the dream. His accounts of it over the years were inconsistent."

"Then why believe it?" said Jack.

"Consistency is overrated," said Miss Sedge. "Einstein would listen to music when he came to a dead end in his thinking. He said that usually did the trick. Alvarez was studying something else—magnetism—in the geological record when he figured out what happened to the dinosaurs. He and his father came up with the idea that the earth was hit by an asteroid."

"Funny," I said. "My friend Vicky was talking about asteroids. Is it true one is going to hit us?"

"Sometime in the next two millennia. It could be a hit or a near miss." Miss Sedge removed her glasses, rubbed her eyes, put the glasses back on. "There are competing theories, of course, about the dinosaurs. What I mean to say is, solutions often come from outside the domain of the problem."

"Thinking outside the box," said Jack. "Blue-sky thinking."

"If you want to go for the clichés."

"Well, what would you call it?" I asked, feeling sorry for Jack, though I agreed his cliché habit let him down.

"I'd call it 'creative thinking.' I'd call it 'roundabout thinking.' I'd call it 'making use of all of our talents,' including ones we aren't in control of. Velcro!" Jack laughed and I laughed. "An engineer was hunting in the Alps and noticed his clothes covered with cockleburs. He found they had tiny hooks that stick to the loops in fabric. Voilà! If you go straight for an answer, you get something you already know. If you go the crooked back way, you have a chance of getting something more interesting."

"So what are we supposed to do?" Jack didn't like being in the dark about anything.

"Well, what are you preoccupied with these days?" Miss Sedge was addressing both of us, but I got the feeling she was really talking to me. "What do you wake up thinking about? What's important to you?"

Jack leaned forward, eager to speak.

"And don't tell me what you think I want to hear."

Now was my chance. I went upstairs, got my sketchbook, and handed it over without a word. Miss Sedge said nothing. First she held each page an arm's length away, then she removed her glasses for a close-up. She examined the shirt, the incomplete versions of Cloud, and the drawings of myself in the oval mirror. Since Monday I had made five more drawings, some with hats, some without, and with different expressions from pouting to neutral to fierce. Jack was looking over her shoulder. He whistled and glanced swiftly up at me.

Miss Sedge put the pad down. She aimed a look straight into my eyes until I almost felt like the beggar in the temple about to be healed.

"These are good," she said. "You know that, don't you? What are you going to do with them?"

"Do with them?"

Miss Sedge was gazing through me now. "I'm getting an idea." She woke up her laptop and

154

typed something into Google. Scrolled down. Clicked on a YouTube clip. In a few seconds an image rolled into the black box. Jack and I leaned toward the screen so that our arms were not quite touching.

It started with waves on a shore. Water, sand, and sky were made out of charcoal lines that had been set in motion. The shore crackled in place; waves shuddered over it, withdrew, shuddered back in. A dog appeared. Two dogs. A cow. Children gathered; ran around; stroked the dogs; stroked the cow; ran away. The animals lay down. The shallow waves came and went around them. Birds winked on and off in the sky. The dogs and the cow melted away until all that was left was a light patch where they had been. No people, no children, no animals returned to the sand and no birds to the sky. The waves came and went, came and went, until everything froze and we were staring at the play triangle.

I hit the triangle and replayed the clip.

Jack said, "He made it all from drawings, didn't he?"

"Incredible."

"It's jerky, that's the only thing. Couldn't he have blended them better?"

"No!" I clapped him on the arm and he didn't pull away. "I love the way even things that are supposed to be standing still are moving."

"I guess so," he said.

"Each thing has a ghost around it, from where he erased the last drawing. Everything looks like it's made out of mistakes."

Miss Sedge said nothing, just sat there smiling openly like she had spent a long time winding up a special toy and was getting a kick out of watching it go. I'd had no idea she knew anything about art.

"That's what you can do with your drawings, Maddy. Animate them."

Antonio,

English and art are my favorite subjects. I like science too, but mostly because I have the most amazing science teacher, Miss Sedge. I'm doing some serious biology this year. Plus I am interested in the environment. I am going on a march against the Keystone Pipeline in October.

I don't know what I want to do, I mean as a career or a job or whatever. They had these career advice sessions last year at school that got me panicked. How are we supposed to know? I have lots of questions for you, though. For example: How tall are you? What are your hobbies? What are my grandmother, grandfather, uncles, aunts, cousins in Spain like? What are Oscar and Daniel like? What are you trying to find out about the brain? How do you do the research—in a lab, or by examining people? Have you read *The Man Who Mistook His Wife for a Hat?*

Maddy

Dear Maddy,

As a scientist I am gravely concerned about what we are doing to the earth. We need young people to get involved. It is your world we are destroying. You are right, we need to rethink our place in the natural world with a little (a lot!) more humility. We can't count on science to get us out of trouble. It is dangerous to think we can. The earth will survive, no matter what we do to it, but we might not be here to enjoy it!

I am a good scientist and a terrible artist. I like to read, mostly nonfiction. Biographies and history books. I play the guitar, classical and also folk. I am six feet, two inches tall (just over two meters). Oliver Sacks does great work in observing the dysfunctional brain as a way of drawing conclusions about the normal brain. I am part of a laboratory that is studying memory and synaptic transmission. If we can understand better how neurons normally talk to one another, we might find out what happens when things go wrong. We do this by studying living cells from rat brains under the microscope. So yes, it is laboratory work.

Speaking of work, I'm afraid I have to go!

Antonio

13

Jack found out from Mr. Yam what software to use and had it installed on my laptop. His dad bought us a copy stand and we fixed his camera to it in my room, where we had some privacy. Once we had something to work on together, things eased up between us. I almost forgot about that embarrassing day in his kitchen. We played around together with the frame rate and resolution on practice sketches that I erased or blocked out with white paint. Like everything else, it was harder than it looked, and we hadn't yet decided on the image sequence.

"Are you sure you want to use yourself?" he kept asking.

"It was my idea, remember?"

"It's not too . . . close?"

"The closer the better."

"Well, if you're sure."

Then the next day: "You're sure you don't want to use something else?" until I got fed up and told him to stop. People think when you have disaster in your life that you don't want to think about it. They don't realize you think about it all the time. The animation gave me permission to think about my situation and at the same time make something from it. I tried to explain it to Jack, but

159

I'm not sure he got it. I thought my head could be wrapped in a cloth, then slowly unwrapped, or I could gradually go bald. Jack said no.

"Why not? Do you hate me being bald?"

"Too obvious. What about little by little you're covered with human habitation, starting like from the beginning of the Anthropocene? Caves, mud huts, cities?" We felt no closer to a solution, but we didn't want to consult Miss Sedge. "What do we wake up thinking about?" said Jack. "That's what she said."

To be honest, I did not want to tell Jack what I woke up thinking about. First thing in the morning was the worst. My mind worked away all night long, examining my life from every angle with no one to cover up for me or say comforting things; then, just when I was coming to, my mind gave me its conclusions before I had a chance to think. At that time of day the conclusions were always if not sad, then scary or bleak. Who wanted to hear about sad, scary, and bleak?

"Well, what do *you* wake up thinking about?"

Jack would not say.

Between treatments, we took an Uber to the Mall, to visit my favorite monument. No statues, no marching buddies, no pillars or famous speeches, just the black stone getting wider and thicker with names as we walked down, and at the bottom it was like some kind of soundproof room with everyone staring at the names of people who would never be seen again. Thousands and thousands of them. I could look in the book and see exactly how many, if I wanted to. Which I didn't. Our reflections were caught on the polished surface, Jack in his Georgetown sweatshirt, me in my baseball cap, with the names stamped across us and those personal notes taped to the stone. I used to like reading them.

"I don't know." I steered Jack back up the slope. "I don't think this will help us with what we're making. Do you?"

It was by chance that I hit on the idea. If you believe in chance. It was the day I took Jack to meet my grandparents. We sat around in the kitchen drinking lemonade and admiring my grandmother's ceramic pots, and Jack answered her questions about school and laughed at my grandfather's lame jokes, and then we horsed around in the back with Barney.

"It's so different out here," said Jack. Where we lived, we had lawn on all sides, and the backyard was as nice as the front. Here, the houses were dignified and orderly from the street, but out back the wooden porches and fire escapes and additions of different sizes and states of repair looked as though a kid who didn't know any better had thrown them together. An idea was circling in my mind, trying to land.

"Want to go to Meridian Hill Park?"

I stopped on the way, pretending to admire the nonexistent view down Sixteenth Street. Why weren't there any benches on this side of the park? Jack took my arm, and once we arrived at Serenity, I was happy to perch on her pedestal and lean forward, hands on my knees, to catch my breath. "The Mall belongs to the government and the tourists," I told him. "This is just a little park, but it feels like mine." He was so busy fussing around me, bending over to check my eyes, that he didn't notice the statue at first. When he did, he was instantly putting the camera to his face and twisting the lens, getting it from all angles.

"You mean you've never been here?" I wanted him to remember who'd found it in the first place.

"Don't think so." He stepped back, focusing and snapping. "I love things like this. Last year I was obsessed with peeling paint."

"Been done," I said.

He gave me a fierce look. "I don't care if it's been done! I'm doing it, okay?"

I held up my hands in self-defense. Why do I say things like that just when we're having a nice time?

"Sorry." He gave me an anxious smile. "Do you know how she got this way?"

"Vandalism, I think. It's been like that ever since I was little. The Park Service never gets around to repairing it."

"I hope they never do."

$\bullet\ \bullet\ \bullet$

All news is graded. Terrible, not great, not too bad, and okay. After my last treatment, the scans were not great. They started me on a stronger combination of drugs. When I got back from the hospital, I was lower than ever. I did a lot of crying. This would go on and on and on. I would never be free of it. Grandma sang me lullabies, Grandpa made hushed inquiries outside my door, and my mother stayed with me night and day. All of that helped. But drawing was the only thing that really, truly helped. As soon as I could sit up, I started drawing the worst possible me on my most desperate days, puffy and bruised, scary, scared, and hopeless.

By week three, the magic week, the new poison had done its damage and I could finally eat and go outdoors and feel human. My mood came bobbing up, as though I had on a life preserver that wouldn't let me stay under. I'm lucky that way.

I studied Jack's photographs of Serenity and drew her in my sketchbook. I got a sneaky pleasure out of drawing the statue. Not that I wanted her to crumble. But considering that she *had* crumbled, she had been damaged by something she had in no way asked for and could in no way change, I wanted her crumbling right out in the open, for everyone to see. I made drawing after drawing of myself and drawing after drawing of the statue's gouged-out face, knowing I couldn't show these to my mother. Could I? I just had to keep going and see what happened. Nowadays that was my motto: Keep going and see what happens.

I called Jack to tell him I had an idea. I didn't want to tell him over the phone, so we arranged to meet at his house after school. As it turned out, something better happened that day, and weeks went by before we thought about the animation again.

Hello Antonio,

Back again! We were away. Do you always email me from work? Your research sounds amazing. Although—poor rats! Do you also try to discover things like why music is so emotional when it's just sound waves going into our ears? Or what happens after you die? Or is that just not possible??!! You didn't answer my questions about your (my) family. But I guess I didn't tell you what you wanted to know about Mom, so we're even. I'd still like to know, though.

Are the boys glad summer is coming? Is London always rainy and cold? I don't think I could stand that. I love hot weather. Though in DC it gets incredibly hot and everyone stays indoors in the AC.

Maddy

Maddy,

Music has a profound effect on us. Most things that have a profound effect on us gave us an evolutionary advantage at some point. My research is very specific, about the biochemistry of the brain and maybe a bit boring to the average person. But it is really about some of the most interesting human questions. Like, how can we remember a phone number or recognise an apple? How can a memory last a lifetime? And eventually, what's happening in the brain when we listen to music or feel happy, sad, etc.

I think what happens when we die is not something science can research. Not all scientists are atheists but I myself am an atheist and I have quite a pragmatic approach to these matters. You will discover your own ideas as you grow older.

I hope you had a great holiday. I guess American schools are more relaxed about kids going on holiday during term time. Here it is almost a criminal offense.

Antonio

14

It rained so hard between my house and Jack's, it was like running through a waterfall. Getting rained on improved my mood. Anything out of the ordinary did. I turned up on his porch drenched. He gave me a gray T-shirt and a pair of gym shorts to put on, and in his bathroom I peeled off my wet things and toweled down, keeping an eye on myself in the mirror.

I would be perfect for an anatomy lesson. My collarbones had their own shadows. A lot of girls would die to be this thin. Which kind of misses the point. I guess I looked okay under the circumstances, especially if I turned sideways so you couldn't see the bump on my chest that was my port. Long neck, not-quite-human head. Better from the side, hand on my jutting-out hip. Front view. Port bump visible. Nipples staring. Hip bones. Lips. Who thought that up as a body part? At least there was one upside to chemo. No need for a Brazilian! Which Vicky tells me hurts like crazy but the boys expect you to have.

Jack Bell? Please would you go up to the model and locate the clavicle?

No problem. The clavicle is right there. It is also called a collarbone.

Go ahead and touch the model.

The collarbone goes from the shoulder to the neck . . . here . . .

Excellent, Jack. Now, can you point out the pelvic girdle? Quickly! She's getting cold.

Well, the pelvic girdle attaches to the spine approximately here . . .

"Are you okay, Maddy?" His hesitant voice came through the door. "You haven't fainted or anything?"

I plucked his clothes from the toilet seat. "Out in a sec!" How long had I been in there? The T-shirt smelled of laundry soap and, under that, the grassy smell of Jack. Even with the elastic waist, his shorts were loose on me. They could fall down. And I had no dry underwear to put on. Oh well! Que será, será. I rolled up the waistband, coughing to fend off the giggles. No laughing. No laughing this time.

Jack was in the kitchen in his usual place, standing with his back to the counter, hands poised on either side of him. He didn't move when I came in. I stopped in the middle of the floor to let him get a good look at me. I wanted him to see me wearing his clothes. I tried to keep a slightly superior expression on my face. Who said I wanted to kiss him? That hug he gave me the other day had just been a moment of solidarity about fathers.

"I had this idea for the animation." Now that I was here, with air in my shorts where air did not usually go, did I really want to think about sad skulls and crumbling faces? "We don't have to do it now."

"Okay," said Jack. He went to the fridge. By now he knew I didn't like beer, so he kept wine coolers on hand. When we'd drained our drinks, Jack got up and, without asking, got us two more. He held on to my glass a little longer than necessary before letting me take it. I saw the pulse beating in his neck. Some kind of showdown going on behind his eyes. I was pretty sure then why we were not getting down to any work.

On my way back from the bathroom I stumbled on the leg of the stool. Jack caught me from the side and stopped me from falling. Someone's heart was thumping, maybe his, maybe mine. That was the moment he could have let me go. I could have pulled away. Instead, we straightened up and started to kiss. I was shocked at first by the greedy, fishlike movements of our faces. But soon I didn't want to stop. I had never kissed a boy, but once we started, I knew exactly what to do.

I pulled back to see his eyes. The shy, proud look in them, and the sense of Jack morphing from one thing to another and back again, made me laugh. This time I knew he didn't mind. It was a completely different kind of laughter, aimed at both of us because of the outrageous thing we were doing. Jack's hands were on my back, pressing me against the bulge in his jeans. I felt myself teetering on the edge of empty space, and there was nothing to do but start kissing again. The universe might not want me, but Jack did.

He backed me down the hallway, our fingers laced together. I maneuvered us around so that I was steering him instead. The kissing made me daring and free. Jack had on this dazed expression, but he was with it enough to glance at his watch.

"When's your father back?" I whispered, tightening my fingers.

"Late. I don't care. Do you?"

I did, but I had to say no. Had to hope Jack knew what he was doing in relation to the work habits of his father. We reached the doorway to his bedroom. Maybe he hadn't planned this in advance? Maybe he didn't wish to tempt fate by being prepared, for instance, by disinfecting his room? It smelled of feet and old apples. Half-closed curtains created a maroon twilight. Single unmade bed against the far wall. I gave him a playful shove to the chest. We tumbled onto the bed, wrestling. When he was on top, he peeled up my T-shirt, and seeing I had no bra on, he stopped and murmured something I did not catch. It was a one-syllable word he kept repeating in a confused, slurred voice, before he lowered his head to kiss me where I had never been kissed. "What?" I demanded, to keep him talking. "What?" Though by that time I didn't need to know.

When he raised his head, our eyes met. That was hard to bear and we could not keep it up for long, but for me it was the defining moment that made sense of our bare skin, the shock of his mouth on my breast, the sensation that I was levitating off the bed and at the same time sliding down it. Jack looked as if he couldn't quite place me. Now was the time to put my hand on his zipper. He shimmied his jeans and boxers down, yanked off his socks and shirt, and came to a halt on his knees in front of me, where his features were instantly seized by the terror of being naked and in plain view. More buff than he looked in clothes. Thing flipped up tight to abdomen from nest of hairs. I had seen erections online and in this book I had, so I was familiar with the overall design. Even so. Strange beyond strange seeing one in the flesh, attached to someone who chewed his pens flat and could solve quadratic equations.

He hunkered down next to me, making loud shivering noises, pretending to be cold instead of shy. His skin was hot along my legs. Into my ear he whispered, "Do we need to use . . . you know?" I shook my head, and as I shook my head, a thought intruded that pretty much brought things to a halt. Had my mother and Antonio really forgotten in the passion of the moment, or had they secretly wanted me?

I shifted so we were no longer touching, and Jack froze, alert to the tiniest change. We stayed that way for a long agonizing moment, me with my knees folded to one side, Jack trying at the same time to stay clear of me and to hide himself, no easy trick on that narrow bed, each of us gazing into the fearful eyes of the other person. Then his leg slipped and lodged against mine, and the weight and heat of his leg said to me: Why not? Why not do this if I wanted to? So I reached for Jack and his brand-new components, and in no time at all I was looking into the most joyful face I had ever seen. Reason enough to keep going, in spite of everything.

We lay together under the sheet, Jack on his back, me with my head on his shoulder. This was pretty uncomfortable and I had to twist my neck to see his face, but I didn't say anything because it's the position they assume in movies after sex, and I could tell he was proud to be holding me like that. He was radiant, in spite of his shrunken state. Like he just won the lottery. Olympic gold.

I felt proud too, for different reasons. Whatever happened, I had done it. Bronze maybe, not gold, but I had experienced it. How could I not be happy about that?

He rubbed his cheek on top of my skull. Now that he was allowed to touch it, Jack seemed to genuinely appreciate the feel of my head. At least I thought he did. At one point he'd held my head with both hands. This was one of the heartening things about the afternoon. Another was his sincere effort to touch me. He gave up too soon, but that might have been because it felt so good I lost my nerve and jumped a mile as if to say—Hey! Why do you think it's called "privates"?—and set about attending to him instead. He kept asking me if it hurt, which was sweet of him. It hurt, but not that much. No one barged in on us. He didn't fall asleep. I lay there, warm through and through. This body that had betrayed me was good for something.

"We should talk about it," Jack said in his normal voice, which took me by surprise. "If we want to," he added hastily.

"That's what it says in this book my mother gave me when I was fourteen."

I'd reacted, of course, with fake operatic indignation: one, that she would get me such a thing in the first place, and two, that she would suggest with an impish smile that we discuss it and look at the photographs together. She knew full well I would hide the book, devour the book, find roundabout ways to bring up the book, take the book as not exactly a green light but an understanding of some kind between Mama mia and me. Which I did, thinking: Wow; disgusting; thrilling; bizarre. One day, one day.

"It's supposed to get better," Jack informed me solemnly, and his face did this thing that made me scoot up and kiss him in different places. As if he knew anything about it!

"It was great," I said, and sank back down with a sudden pang. "You were great." Late afternoon was my least favorite time of day. Neither one thing or the other. Unnaturally still. Dingy light. When? When, for me, was it going to get better?

"Your mother gave you a book about sex?" asked Jack. "My mother would never do that."

"What about your father?"

"My father gave me The Talk. Once when I was ten, on a camping trip. One a few years later. Final one last year. That one covered contraception and STDs."

I raised my head, smiling a little. "Did it cover the female anatomy?"

Jack reddened and looked away. "Are we supposed to be talking about our parents at a time like this?"

I nestled down and kissed his neck to fend off the late-afternoon feeling. You'd think having nothing between you but skin would bring you to the true center of a person. You'd think. But the fact was, I felt closer to Jack kissing in the kitchen than I did later on. Mouth first, I had all of him. I would not tell Vicky this, or even Fiona, but it wasn't just having something inside me that belonged to someone else. It wasn't that the setup was obviously five-star for him but how on earth was it supposed to work for me? No, the thing was this. When he was pressing the mattress on either side of my head and whimpering in ascending notes that made me think of a blind dog scaling a cliff, it was as though Jack went away and left me and I had no idea if he would return or what he'd be like if he did. True, he was lying there now speaking to me in his everyday voice. But once they've emptied themselves out like that, isn't it easier for them to walk away?

Jack tightened his grip on me and kissed my forehead in slow motion, exactly as you might if you loved someone but couldn't tell them. I felt an upsurge of longing for my mother. She was home waiting for me, but I couldn't turn to her now. I hid my face in Jack's shoulder and he laid his head on mine, tender as could be, unaware that I was no longer with him. I was standing on a lone rock jutting out of the sea. Recklessly I had scrambled out there, wanting what everyone wants, doing what people do on sunny mornings. But now I could see the black water stretching out in front of me to the horizon, and behind me, in silence, the tide had come in and closed off the way back.

15

From the road, my house looked like a replica of itself. Not smaller, exactly. Purple paving stones curved as always up to the three porch steps. Pointy dormers, black handrail, red shutters were just the same. But still the house was different. Complete without me.

My mother was unloading the dishwasher, her back to the kitchen door, making such a racket she didn't hear me come in. Humming, she stacked the cupboard, raked her bangs with one hand, and bent down again, her denim hips too slight and girlish to belong to anyone's mother. Clattering plates is the loneliest sound ever.

"Mama?"

She stood and turned, eggbeater in one hand, wineglass in the other, smile at the ready. "Oh, there you are! I was starting to—" At the sound of her voice I could not control my breathing or the shape of my mouth. My mother veered toward me. "What's wrong, Maddy? What's happened?" Eggbeater bounced to the floor. Glass hit the counter's edge and shattered, leaving her holding a jagged cartoonish stump.

"Did I scare you?"

"Are you okay?"

"Careful!" I said.

"Careful!" she said.

I took the remains of the glass from her, dropped it in the trash, and reached for the dustpan. My mother's clumsiness was legendary. Tools for dealing with it were always close at hand. "Don't move. I'll get this." The breakage had momentarily knocked the heartache out of me. When I stood I felt something slithering down, deep inside.

"Mom, you're bleeding!"

"Am I? It's nothing." She was trying to look into my eyes.

I dabbed with a dish towel at the back of her hand. She was right, the cut was not deep. Her hand was strangely meek in mine. The bones were close to the surface and so were the veins. She let me press the towel until the blood no longer seeped back in when I took it away.

"What is it?" she asked again, drawing me near and murmuring the usual things. "You've been at Jack's?"

I bowed my head and made myself as small as possible. "We're working on the animation. I got caught in the rain."

"Your clothes aren't wet," she remarked.

"Used his dryer."

"Are you cold, Maddy? You don't want to catch a chill."

"I'm fine." I burrowed into her again. "Mama?"

I began in the voice of someone outdone by the events of the day.

"Ye-ess?" crooned my mother as if she knew what was coming.

"Why did my father leave?"

I felt her arms go heavy and still. "What brought this on?" When I didn't answer, she said at last: "Well, I don't know why. Not really."

"He had to go back home?"

"Yes, I suppose he did. One way or another."

"But he could have stayed?"

"At the time I thought he could have."

"Or come back."

"Yes."

"Why didn't he?" It was like talking across an echoey tank. "Didn't he want a baby?"

Silence across the tank. "I guess he didn't want one with me."

"You? He didn't want *you?*"

"Not enough, anyway."

Shivers went up my back that my mother's patting hand could not reach.

"Were you mad at him?"

"At the time I was. Mad and sad."

"Are you still?"

"It was a long time ago, Maddy. It's his loss. Think of everything he missed out on."

"This?" I pushed away. *"This?"* Gesturing at the whole of my sorry, invaded self.

"You!" she cried. "He missed out on you."

I don't know what my face was doing, but my mother's had expressions darting across it that I had never seen. She didn't want to be having this conversation, but one of her principles was that a mother answers her child's questions truthfully. Maybe that's why I had never asked her so directly before. We always referred to Antonio in a certain way, as though he were a fairy-tale character whose actions had already been accounted for.

"Well, I am," I said.

"You are what?"

"Mad and sad."

"I know you are!" came the instant reply. "Of course you are, Maddy! I've known it all along."

"I wasn't so much before," I said. "I didn't used to think about it. But I do now. All the time."

I could have told her then, one or both of my secrets. It was the logical thing to do. Antonio was already with us in the room, and there was time to put Jack out there too, like a troubling dream to be aired and given a daytime shape. My mother had that look again, of someone being forced to stare into harsh lights. I held my nerve, swallowing down the dread that filled my throat like laughter. Was it possible? Could I really? It seemed like another girl standing there thinking these thoughts, daring to withhold and to go without.

That was the moment Robin picked to wander

in. When he saw us, he did a speedy U-turn, glancing back over his shoulder. My mother told him with her eyes to vamoose and leave the kitchen to us. What I did then was a surprise to me as much as to anyone. I went over and dragged Robin in and propped him up between us as if he were a prize stuffed bear I had won. The astonishment on their faces was gratifying, and so was the sturdy feel of his forearm, which in truth was only pretending to resist.

"Far be it from me," said Robin, "to intrude on a female moment."

"You're not intruding. Is he, Mom?"

"Not at all." My mother broke away and went to the drawer by the sink where household items end up that have nowhere else to go. Eyes down, she began flinging things out. Screwdrivers, broken earrings, a carrot-shaped magnet, a flashlight with no lens, rubber bands, candle ends, fuses, and pens tumbled together and came to a stop as though the kitchen floor had always been their true resting place.

As if hypnotized, Robin and I watched her stretch the excavated Band-Aid, a blue Disney one, across her hand, which was not even bleeding anymore, furiously blinking away tears before they spilled down or were noticed. One of the things I hated most in the world was to see my mother cry. I longed to rush over and win her back. It was a miracle I stayed put.

Even if Robin had not come out of his trance to tenderly gather up the objects and check the floor for shards; even if he had not made cooing sounds and offered her one of his short-man hugs, causing her to turn and hide her face in his shirt, I would have stayed put. Because *I* had someone with me now, or that's the way it felt, and together we were going around silently closing windows and shutting doors and gates I didn't even know could be shut and closed. Whether my mother saw it this way or not, the fact was, keeping a secret or two would be better for both of us in the long run. I have to think about the long run now.

PART II

Eve

16

The day after Norma rowed over to us, a storm moved in. I went down to the dock every morning as usual, even in the rain, but she did not appear again. Three days later, Robin and I drove home.

When we pulled into the driveway, crickets were ringing the summer's end. It could have been any August night from my childhood, returning from the cool lake to the hot city. On Corcoran Street, my brother and I would race each other into the house. Now I didn't want to leave the car. Robin braced his arms on the steering wheel for an elaborate yawn, exactly as my father used to do, while I observed that the measures we took to make the house appear inhabited while we were gone—arranging the dormer blinds at different heights, setting the porch lamp on a timer—only drew attention to its emptiness.

Inside, I slapped my shoulder bag on the dining room table and flipped through the mail that our neighbor, Mrs. Platt, had left in a neat pile when she came in to water the plants and feed the cat. Robin scooped Cloud up like an infant, yodeling "You Are My Sunshine" to her sulky face, until she struggled from his arms and stalked off.

When I first got her for Maddy, she'd been a tiny parcel of bodiless fur. Now she had an adult's swinging gait and the smoky features of her breed. I didn't care if she was annoyed at us for locking the cat door and leaving her at the mercy of Mrs. Platt, who in our absence maintained a dry prison diet. I just wanted to find her there when we returned.

Robin smiled wearily at me, his forehead scored with sunburn. When I first met Robin, he had been under this very table, on whose surface I was tracing spirals with my fingertips. I had come back from shopping the morning of my fortieth birthday to find two men assembling the gift from my parents, hand-crafted from English walnut. I don't remember the assistant—he has a different one now—but I often think back to that version of Robin, when he was a wiry stranger supine on the floor, his hands gripping the slab to position it and screw the legs on from underneath, squinting in concentration, his raised arms causing his T-shirt to untuck from his jeans and flap over the shadow of his waist. In his low nimble commentary he told me he had moved to northern Virginia to apprentice to a Japanese master craftsman and eventually set up his own business. He'd rescued the wood from a construction site near Culpeper where trees were being felled and burned; the slabs had been drying in his workshop when Rose and Walter went to see him about a commission.

"Nice people, your folks. Nice as they come." On his feet again, he stopped and studied me for the first time, to see whether niceness ran in the family.

I called him back a few weeks later to tighten a wobble that had developed at the crossbars. We went out for lunch. He called me when he was next in town, to check on the repair. I asked him for a quote for a built-in bookcase in the family room. When he came to fit the bookcase, he took me out to dinner. Six years my senior, Robin was industrious and softhearted, with an indulgent smile that I thought was reserved for me until I saw him bestow the same smile on checkout girls, waiters, and car mechanics as he coaxed them into conversation.

Robin slowly tunneled into my life until it seemed he'd always been there, holding forth on wood grain, sonatas, and wildlife. It was not in Robin's nature to force things, and I had to be on my guard until I could judge the consequences for Maddy. But she was growing up and needing me less, and after the first weeks, during which she refused to smile at him, she grew more and more open to Robin's presence in our lives, even urging me, as she put it, to "seal the deal."

"Seal the deal? What do you know about sealing the deal?"

"More than you think."

One Saturday when Maddy was at a slumber party, Robin came over to eat fish tacos and enjoy our newly repaired fireplace. At that time, the empty house held an erotic allure and we moved from the living room floor to the bedroom, and soon we were spending most of our weekends together. We each had one child— his was a twenty-three-year-old son in Cincinnati whom he didn't often see, the product of an early disastrous marriage—which meant that there was no pressure on us to procreate. Robin found a nearby garage to rent for a workshop, and with little ceremony, he moved in. I remember thinking at the time that life was as good as it had ever been. Maddy was diagnosed seven months later.

I couldn't stop my fingers tracing spirals on the wood, circling in one direction, then the other. Nothing about this table was symmetrical, apart from its uniform thickness. It was made of two lengths of golden red walnut, straight-cut across one end, tapered to curves on the other, and fastened together with inlaid butterfly joints. A long crack at the straight end was part of the design and its charm. The table was one of the few possessions I would go into a burning house to save. Maddy, though, had never liked it. She found it lopsided and unfinished.

Robin came over and stilled my hands with

his own. He wrapped his arms around me. "Turn down the AC. I'll unload the car and call Mrs. P. We'll go straight to sleep."

I hauled my bag as far as the landing upstairs. Then before I could decide not to, I turned the handle to Maddy's room, went in, and sat on her bed.

In the months when I could bear neither to stray too far from the house nor to keep myself too busy, I would look into Maddy's room from the door. It felt intrusive to enter when she could not invite me. Now I was in full view of her posters, her shaggy rug, her white dresser with the oval mirror, objects that were regarding me with the level gaze of things that could be converted to other uses.

Experimentally I leaned back against the triangle cushion, circling one wrist with the fingers of the other hand to survey the room the way she did, queen of her world. While I was in this position, my cell phone slid from the pocket of my shirt and fell between the mattress and wall. I poked my hand down. Box. Book. Cardboard. Some kind of folder, furry with dust. I had to smile. Maddy had inherited my approach to housekeeping. Nowadays Mrs. Walsh only ran the vacuum around the rest of the house.

It was too much trouble to find a flashlight, so instead I knelt on the bed and pulled out enough objects to make space for my hand. I blew off the dust and held each one for a moment. A collage of a city street she'd brought home in third grade. Her eager, bashful face. The *Sexwise* book I had given her. I hoped its no-nonsense advice had served her well. I tried a matter-of-fact smile: so far, so good. Next was the pink plastic box, half diary, half keepsake holder, a Christmas present from Rose. To open it you needed a four-digit code, long forgotten.

What a comical performance! In my presence she had made a point of punching in the code, to remind me that she alone could gain entrance, and then elaborately shielded the contents of the box from my gaze. If I turned away too readily, she offered to let me see; if I declined, she followed me around, growing more agitated and finally insisting that I look at her private things. Of course the catch could be forced, but I was pleased to note I had no desire to break in to the diary of a nine-year-old, or to know what trinkets she had seen fit to hide there. Last item: a green file folder with one word scrawled across it. *Antonio.*

Even as a teenager, Maddy had roundly childish handwriting; the *i* was dotted with a circle. I saw myself as if from above, kneeling on the bed. My hands felt weak, numb almost, while what they held was twitching with life. I wanted to lift the flap. I could not bring myself to lift the flap. Slowly I lifted the flap.

Dear Antonio Jorge Romero, I read. *You don't know me . . . Dear Maddy, Naturally I was very, very surprised . . .* I flipped through the pages, scanning. *I'm not sure what I should call you . . . As a scientist I am gravely concerned . . . Do you always email me from work? You can never trust an English summer . . .*

I replaced the pages and closed the folder. Kneeling on the mattress, I slipped it back down between the bed and the wall. I stood on Maddy's rug, shame thumping its way through me. I could walk away. Pretend I'd never come in. Forget what I'd seen. Instead I rushed to the bed, snatched the folder from the crevice, and holding it in front of me like a shield, made my way downstairs, calling for Robin.

He sat on the piano bench, swiveled around to face me. His sand-colored hair was still springy enough to do a convincing comb back; its thinness was visible only from above. Another five years, if we lasted that long, he would join the rest of the domed population. He'd fare better than most because he had so little vanity and such a characterful face. He read the two pages I handed over and whistled through his teeth, waiting for me to come to him.

"I'm going back to the lake. I need to be alone," I said. "I need to think."

Our intimate life had pretty much ground to

193

a halt once Maddy fell sick. There were times, when she was at church with my parents, or at Jack's, when we managed it, generating a precarious hope that lasted for days. But mostly I couldn't bear to indulge in the comedy of sex; I couldn't stand joy.

Robin reached for my hands and swung them. "Can't you think with me? I'm not just a pretty face, you know."

I whipped my head side to side.

Robin let go of me and stretched his arms out, tinkering behind his back with the highest and lowest keys. When he'd moved in with his Boston upright, we'd demoted the old piano Maddy had learned on to the basement. Her lessons had dropped off by that time, and once she was ill, she had no interest in practicing, or in acquiring knowledge about music or composers. She wanted to go to concerts and to lean forward, carving out with her shoulders a private space to remove herself to. She hushed me if I tried to speak to her. To the music itself she gave a hungry attention I could only observe from the corner of my eye, shut out of her world and sick with pity and fear.

"You don't have to hide away, Eve."

"Maddy wrote to him for months and I never knew! She never told me."

He slid over on the bench to make room. I pressed my cheek to his unyielding shoulder. If it's true that underneath we all seethe with lunatic notions, irrational beliefs, and bizarre wishes, fear knocks them out into the light. Over the year of Maddy's illness, I was by turns remote and accusatory with Robin. It was my child who was under threat. It was my child getting thin, my child being punctured and invaded, my child who might never grow up. Robin's son was a standoffish young man named Vince who worked as a hospital orderly and was uninterested not only in his father but, from what I could tell, in any normal human contact. At night, lying in the dark, I could not banish the thoughts. The world could do without Vince more than it could do without Maddy. Why not him? The shame of it distanced me even further from Robin, who had done nothing but stand by me, observing my anguish from afar with a look that said: Let me in.

"I know it's hard on you," I said.

"What is?"

"The way I am. What's happened. Everything."

He squeezed me a bit roughly, I thought. "I don't like you going up there on your own. Why don't you see if Beth or Ella will go with you?"

I looked at him in surprise. "They bailed on me."

"Is that what happened?" It had grieved him when my friends and I had parted company.

"You know what happened! We drifted apart."

"Well, can't you drift back together?"

"It's too much for you, isn't it?"

He crossed his arms. "All I'm saying is, being isolated is never a good thing."

After a minute, I added cautiously: "Who knows? Maybe Norma will be there."

"Our new neighbor?"

"It would be nice if she is."

"Well," he said, "I'd rather that than you being alone."

17

After the last of the factory towns, the road ran through mile after mile of cropland fitted to the earth like carpet, broken only by corrugated sheds and farm machinery lined up on paved lots. Every so often there appeared a barn in such a perfect storybook shape, painted such a perfect red, that it seemed to have come off the cover of a brochure. But don't ask me; I'm not the one to gauge the truth of appearances. These days the outside world strikes me as either a backdrop or a façade, with brushed-on highlights and hidden seams that I could expose if I looked closely enough.

My week back at work had passed in a daze. After summer vacation at the lake, the encounter with Norma, and the discovery of the letters, it was hard for me to believe I was assistant director of anything, let alone the education service of an award-winning museum. I drew up the fall schedule for the interns, debated with my boss the pros and cons of evening workshops, led tourists, amateur artists, and retired people from gallery to gallery, while my mind was fixed on Friday afternoon, when I could leave early, go home, pack my overnight bag, and set off. Now, with the light draining from the day and Bach's two-part inventions ringing around me in the car, time seemed to be moving forward again in fits and starts.

More cropland, more stalled machinery, more unlikely barns. In the eastbound lane a twelve-wheeler slid past, heading for the lower lakes, where fracking was under way. They wait until dusk to send unmarked trucks through with their cargo of water. Tawasentha was the highest of the trio of lakes, and thus far the association had stood firm; but the payment offered was eye-watering, and at the last meeting a quarter of the members had voted in favor. For all I knew, it was only a matter of time before landslides and poisoned groundwater came to us too.

I should be the ideal activist, inspired by how Maddy had faced the unthinkable. Courage could be taken from courage. Imagination could be brought to bear. Where was my imagination? Where was my bravery?

I turned left at the country store and began the claustrophobic ascent up the mountain through National Park forestland, coming to a stop at the single bar gate, the entrance to the lakeshore road. Up rose the thick, spicy scent of the ferns. A bearded man appeared on the stoop of the caretaker's bungalow and, as he swung open the gate, I was overcome by misgivings I should have been prey to all along. Was I out of my mind? I did not want to see anyone. She was probably not even there. But I could hardly turn around now, so I stepped on the gas and drove through with a wave. The caretakers came and went. Who could live for long in that exposed place, close enough to smell the lake but not to see it?

In the morning I boiled an egg and ate it on the terrace, then I took my coffee down to the lake. Without Robin in the house behind me, the dock felt like a boat whose moorings had been cut. I oversaw the lifting of the mist, observed the water's surface become pocked by little competing breezes, and searched for signs of life in the yellow monstrosity opposite. I even stood up and did some stretches and deep knee bends. Without binoculars I could not confirm whether the movement I thought I saw was people or foliage. There was nothing to do but shoulder my bag and set off down the lakeside path. Narrow as an animal track, it snaked around between the tree roots, pine needles giving way underfoot to spongy moss. It was this path that kept the perimeter of the lake passable, fulfilling another bylaw of the Tawasentha charter: The shoreline had to be accessible to residents at all times.

I had to admit that up close the yellow of the house was more dignified than from a distance, an ocher shade that was almost Venetian. Stealthy as I was, I still managed to alert the dog, a curly brown terrier, who bounded out from behind the woodpile and bayed stiff-legged by the overturned kayak.

Norma appeared at the ground-level door to see what the commotion was. She stepped out, scolding, "Shhh! It's okay, Homer. Friend, not foe," and stood there, looking surprised. "Oh. Hello!"

"Sorry to disturb you."

"Don't worry. He's just showing off. He's a big baby. Aren't you, Homey?" She bent to stroke him. The cartoon name sounded strange in Norma's soft voice.

"I was walking around the lake."

"That's nice." She frowned at the sky. "It's a good day for it."

I spotted the bumper of a pickup truck in the driveway. "You must be busy."

"Always." She straightened up, grinning her can-do grin, her gray sweatshirt spattered with paint. Today a tortoiseshell headband held her hair back from her face. She looked more self-contained than I remembered. "Want to come in? See what we're doing to the house?"

Now that my aim was in reach, I said: "Maybe another time."

"Sure? It's no trouble. The boys are at my mom's. I don't want them around when we're doing the floors. Some nasty chemicals."

I shaded my eyes and studied the lake. I did not especially want to enter Norma's house. Tanner might be in there. I doubted he was, given the unguarded way she was speaking, but even so I did not want to be ambushed by the trappings of happy-go-lucky family life.

"We could have coffee out here," Norma offered. When I turned back, she bestowed on me such a hospitable smile that I had an urge to say something unpleasant, just to see what it would do to her face.

"Okay."

Their dock was larger than ours but in worse shape. The top of the T was roped off. I saw from the chalky mounds on the boards that the ducks used it as a rest stop. The whole lakefront, for that matter, could do with attention. Even in the shallows there was none of the fine white sand my father replenished every year that made swimming a pleasure. Norma's lake floor was all muck and sticks, and the ground was swamp, I could tell, from the shoreline to the house. Up close I could see no obvious signs of tree felling. Had I been wrong about that? Maybe they had just trimmed back the branches.

Norma parked me at the wooden picnic table and went to make coffee. That gave me a chance to look around and make friends with Homer, who assumed a sphinxlike dignity at my feet. It was a different lake from here. Whereas we had a view down the entire length, they could see only the stretch of water between their cottage and

201

ours, the rest being hidden by the promontory that separated this lobe from the main body of the lake. It gave them greater privacy but also an oppressive sense of enclosure. Across the water all that could be seen of our house was the point of the roof through the trees. Our dock made a pale line under the green dabs of the chairs. It would be hard to tell what someone was up to there; I could see why Norma had interpreted my arm waving as a call for help.

She appeared with two cups on a tray. We exchanged small talk about the recent cold snap. The sun dipped in and out of halfhearted clouds. A breeze lifted the reddish frizz at Norma's forehead, causing her to reach up and try to tuck it under her headband. Scattered over the ground were a wagon, a ball and bat, and an assortment of water toys.

"How are the boys?" I asked, wanting to be reminded that she presided over a world unconnected to mine.

"You know. Angels or criminals. Nothing in between." She sighed. "What would I do without my mother? She's fantastic with them. They're a handful. Especially Ben, of course. But then he gets Luke going."

"Why especially Ben?"

"Benjamin has a lot of issues," said Norma easily. "Did I mention that? He's on the spectrum. Pretty far over on the spectrum."

"Oh," I said. "I didn't know."

Norma smiled in a practiced way, to let me know there was no need for awkwardness or pity. "We tried the public school. School doesn't work out for Ben, at the moment, anyway. There's a place he goes to half the week."

"That must be tough."

"It's been awful." She corrected herself: "Quite a journey."

It was a word I particularly disliked, one that had been employed by a number of people over the last two years to describe my situation. "Is that the way you see it?"

"Well." Norma studied me. "Better a journey than an affliction, right?" She smiled her sunny smile. "So how are things with you? How's Maddy?"

The moment had arrived, with little effort on my part. Norma was not a friend, but she was warm and wholesome and free from contamination. I'd had friends and I'd lost friends. What I needed was another stranger.

"Maddy didn't make it," I said.

"At her age, I'm sure she has other things to do. At least you and Robin are free to come and go." She wrapped her mug in both hands and looked down at them, thinking, perhaps, of the freedom that she and Tanner might never have.

"No, I mean Maddy didn't make it. She died last November."

Norma's head jerked up.

"She had cancer."

It was a relief to have said it, to have given it to her to hold; also a triumph, a shame, and a burden. Her light blue eyes filmed with tears. I had turned a coffee morning into a tragic drama, an acquaintance into a confessor. Would I have to carry Norma now too?

She was searching my eyes for a last-minute sign that I was joking, knuckles jammed to her lips. "You didn't say!"

"It's not easy!"

"Of course not . . ."

"I'm sorry," I said. "You've got kids. It must be a shocking thing to hear."

Did I invent these thoughts for her, or did I read them in her eyes and the set of her shoulders, the tiny changes that flickered like light across her features? The desire to know everything. The desire to compare my life to hers. The desire to look away. The desire to rewind time, to withdraw into her own troubles, to never have kayaked over to my dock in the first place, because now she and I were roped together by what I'd told her, and a person as kind as she was would not know how to detach herself.

"In case you're wondering," I said, "I'm not crazy." Norma made a noise but I hurried on. "I don't particularly believe in anything. Do you? But now I think: Maybe it's arrogant to be so sure. Who knows if she's still somewhere? No one does. Even if they think they do. *Especially* if they think they do."

Norma nodded mutely.

"So sometimes it helps to act *as if*. There's nothing wrong with *as if*." I saw now that everything anchoring me to what was correct and in the scheme of things had gone with Maddy's death. There was no long run. There was no last analysis. *As if* was not just a matter of survival, of getting through in any way possible. It stood for the fact that my relationship to meaning itself had profoundly changed.

Slowly, wonderingly, Norma whispered: "The snake . . ."

"Strange, isn't it?" I winched what bound us together a little tighter. "I hadn't thought about that in years. The fact is," I said, "I get some comfort from the snake."

"You do?"

"It's as though it was already decided. As though nothing could have prevented it."

A year ago, had I given it any thought, a coincidence like the snake would have struck me as cruel and irrelevant, another sick game the universe was playing at my expense. Now all I had were the patterns I could make, the metaphorical resonance I could find. Perhaps that was all there was to have.

I let Norma ask me questions. I told her

about Maddy's exhaustion and weight loss, the symptoms we mistook for teenage recalcitrance and sleep deprivation, the demands of a new body and a hectic social life; my absorption with Robin at the time and my sense that Maddy was on the eve of a new life and so was I; the misdiagnosis, which meant that the illness had been relatively advanced by the time it was discovered.

"Do you know how strange it is to have to think about the inside of your child's body?"

She shook her head.

"A child's supposed to be a child. Not an arrangement of matter in better or worse shape."

I told her about the music, the campaign, Maddy's determination to fit as much as possible into what time she had. I told her about my friends who organized a team of standby drivers, cooks, networkers, and consolers, and a rotation of people to stay with Maddy when Robin and I went out. I told her about our hopes for the new drugs, the relapse, the rapid decline. Maddy's death I passed over in one sentence.

"You'd think, if the worst happened, that all your friends would be there for you forever? Instead of which, they seemed to withdraw. Even my close friends. Maybe especially my close friends. Ella was in the middle of moving, but Beth . . ."

Norma looked aghast. "They abandoned you?"

"Not exactly. Well, I don't remember much about the first few weeks. I know people were there, helping. But after a while, something changed. It was like I was radioactive. No one wanted to come too close."

"I guess no one knows how to do it," said Norma. "What to say."

"Maybe it's me. Robin thinks it's me, I'm sure he does. Whenever Beth came by with her kids, I was rude, or I made some excuse so they would go. I couldn't stand it."

I bent down and rubbed Homer's neck. I felt the quiver of his skin under the fur, the sun's heat on my back. Norma was watching the white flake of a sailboat out on the lake, her hands around one raised knee. I straightened up.

"Something else happened this week."

She turned to me the troubled eyes of someone who had never known Maddy and was incapable of missing her.

"Do you want to hear? You can say no. I've dumped a lot on you already . . ."

She shook her head and then nodded, dazed with secondhand calamity.

"Remember I told you about Maddy's father? I hadn't seen or heard from him since I found out I was pregnant?"

"He's contacted you."

"No."

"You've contacted him."

"No."

"Well, what then?"

"Maddy did. I found the emails this week."

Norma's hand moved across the tabletop and covered mine as easily as she had examined my nail polish the week before.

"Why didn't she tell me?" I said. "Why did she have to go behind my back?"

"Is that the worst thing? That she didn't tell you?"

Wasn't it obvious? The past and Maddy's part in it were a sealed box. She would not be following me around, begging me to open it and look inside.

Norma tried again. "Well, what were the emails like?"

"I don't know," I said sullenly. "I was too shocked to take them all in." This was true, but I had seen enough. The salutations and sign-offs, the familiarity, the occasional cajoling tone, left no doubt it was an exchange over many months: a two-way street, a relationship.

"Well, do you have them with you?" asked practical Norma.

I gave her an aggrieved look. "Yes."

"Well, do you want to look at them now?"

Did she have to start every sentence with *well?* There was nothing to do but open my bag. The zipper made a tearing sound. Homer stirred; Norma patted him down. I set the green folder on the table between us. Norma's hands stayed in her lap. I pulled out the top page and handed it to her. Then another, and another and another. I gave her the first six letters. They did not take long to read. She laid the last one facedown on the table and raised her glistening eyes. I was as dry as could be.

"You get the gist. Her last one was in September. I don't know if he kept writing after that."

"Did she tell him she was sick?"

"I don't think so."

"Oh!" Norma moaned. "What a terrible punishment!"

"He's probably thinking she'll contact him again one of these days."

She touched the papers. "Was he a nice guy? He sounds like a nice guy."

"Nice enough. I was crazy about him at the time." I paused. "Well, he can't be *that* nice if he abandoned a pregnant girlfriend."

"No."

"And never tried to contact me."

"Did you want him to?"

"I'd have shut him out if he had. My unforgiving streak."

"Did Maddy know about your unforgiving streak?"

"What do you mean?"

"Is that why she didn't tell you?"

"How should I know!"

Norma did an "okay, okay" thing with her palms and gazed off at the dock.

"See, that's the problem," I began in a conciliatory tone. "I can't ask her. I can't even—"

A workman stood before us, thumbs hooked in his tool belt. He glanced from Norma to me and back again. "Could I borrow you for a sec? It's about that corner cabinet. We could've measured wrong."

Norma got up, shooting me an apologetic look. "Be right back."

In her absence I studied my fingernails. I had not repainted them. The color had shrunk to an island of white-flecked purple in the center of each nail. Picnic table benches were hard to relax on. I adopted a number of stiff positions while gazing off, pretending to enjoy the view; our cottage looked far away and closed up. I would call Robin when I got back.

I didn't hear Norma until she was sitting down again.

"There is a way to find out," she said. "Two ways."

"Did they measure wrong?"

She looked blank.

"The cabinet."

"Oh. They did, as a matter of fact. But it's salvageable. I'm not even calling Tanner."

"Find out what?" I asked.

"Didn't Maddy say her grandfather knew she was contacting him?"

"True." I had not allowed myself to consider this yet.

"Your dad didn't tell you what was going on?"

"No," I said shortly.

"Wow," said Norma. "What a secretive family."

"What's the other way?"

"Find Antonio," she said.

I snorted and my foot collided with Homer. Gamely he rose and stretched. "I'm not doing that! I raise his child, and then he starts something with her behind my back? No thanks."

"Maddy wrote to him first . . ." Norma ventured.

"Are you taking his side?"

Considering me for a moment, she said mildly, "Well, since you can't talk to Maddy, at least you'd get his point of view."

Beyond Norma's roped-off dock the open water resembled wet stone. I was warming to her idea. Something had me in its grip, and what it promised was far more primitive and gratifying than knowledge, or the mirage of closure.

"You know, I think you're right," I said slowly. "I might just do that. Put him in the picture."

18

Back home, I reread the first few letters as dispassionately as I could and scanned the rest, saving them for when I was stronger. It was not easy to hear Maddy's voice on the page, her schoolgirl exclamations, her wise-wistfulness seeking to gain favor, love even, from someone who did not know she was dying. *Wow . . . I could not believe my eyes! It feels so strange to be writing to you. I wonder whether I have made you up!* Each page had one email printed on it, with date and time information at the top. Some were only a line or two long. They were in exact sequence. Maddy may have been an indifferent housekeeper, but she had inherited her grandfather's passion for documentation and order. That, or else the messages were of such crowning importance that each had to be given its own page, pampered with white space, meticulously filed, read over and over and stored in their slot by the bed to keep them close to her and safe from me for as long as she was around.

Nor was it easy to hear Antonio's voice on the page. *You will discover your own ideas as you grow older . . . I am maybe finding out how different girls are . . . A lot of things in life happen without you intending them . . .* The even spacing and nonnative order of his words, his lightly rolled *r*'s and soft *b*'s were like a lullaby gone bad, working the spell not of comfort but of loss. Reading Antonio's emails, I was the young woman besotted with his gentle lecturing, his humor, the natural authority and charm radiated by speakers of other languages. I was the one who wanted Antonio and Antonio only to be the father of my children, and I was the one consumed with red-hot fury at him for forsaking us. He had entered Maddy's life just as she was leaving it. *Whereas I like my own company!* Yes, Antonio. You always were sold on your own company.

An ambush outside his office. Follow him home. Spring myself on a family dinner. I indulged in such scenarios for several days, perfectly aware that they would never take place. It was not my style. Another idea, however, was forming. I spent a week composing an email, rewrote it, left it to simmer in drafts. Finally I clicked it on its way in the spectral manner of electronic messages, thinking this was all wrong, that such a letter should generate hideous grinding, scraping, crashing noises.

Dear Antonio,

Remember me? I recently found out that you and Maddy have been in contact. I think it was a bid for independence that led her to keep this from me. Suffice it to say, she has always had her own mind and of course I am proud of that.

At first I was annoyed at what seemed like underhandedness on your part. It is natural for a sixteen-year-old to want to keep secrets, but it is harder to understand an adult going along with that under the circumstances. I can't help thinking if you had really wanted me to know you were communicating with my daughter, you would have found a way to tell me. But then I guess you have gone all these years without choosing to contact me, so maybe it's not so surprising. I'm sure you have your reasons.

I am not sorry Maddy found you. I would never deprive her of something that is her birthright. She needed to fill in the missing pieces of her heritage, if that is the right word. I'm glad you saw fit to respond to her in such a friendly way.

I am writing to see whether it would be a good time for you and me to meet and talk. To state the obvious, regardless of how it ended between us, we will always be connected through Maddy.

I work for the Bryce Collection in DC. I may be going to London soon on business. I know you have a family. I would not want to upset them. I want to talk to you, that's all. I will leave it up to you how we could best do that.

Looking forward to hearing from you,

Eve

My letter was, in the end, longer and more formal than I intended. When I read it over I thought I came across as uptight. Had I been uptight back then? Antonio would not remember me that way. Maybe if he met me now, he would think I had grown up. Or maybe—I steeled myself against the thought—uptightness had, in his eyes, been one of my crimes. Anyway, I hoped I had pitched it right: frank without giving too much away, candid enough to hint at grievance, friendly enough not to scare him off. At the last minute I replaced *bothering to contact me* with *choosing to contact me*. The fact that Antonio had been willing to enter into such a warm exchange with Maddy gave me hope that he would agree to see me. I didn't know what I would do if he turned me down or did not respond.

I tried to put it out of my mind. My laptop beckoned and repelled me at the same time. Ten days later I was checking a work email and there was his name in my in-box, his message having arrived as stealthily as mine had departed.

Dear Eve,

I can't tell you the number of times I thought of writing to you after I left the U.S. Well I don't know the number . . . Believe me, it is a high number!

Imagine my shock when Maddy wrote to me. We emailed back and forth for a few months. She stopped writing quite suddenly in September. I guess some doubts must have got to her. Of course I respected her wishes and did not push her to change her mind or explain. I really hope I did not offend her in any way. Maybe the situation was too much for her, especially doing it on her own. Maybe when she is older she will want to talk to me again and, who knows, maybe meet each other someday. I have to be honest and say that it was an amazing thing getting to know Maddy, even that short time. I guess it is not every day you find out you have a child you didn't know you had. And Maddy is such a charming and interesting person. Congratulations, Eve, for raising her like that. Really, I mean it.

I'm not sure why Maddy was so against telling you she was writing to me. Believe me I did try to persuade her. I can hear you are somehow angry. I apologize. For my part, my wish is that you would have found a way to tell me of Maddy's existence.

If you are coming to London of course we must meet. Has Maddy told you something about me? I am a researcher and lecturer at University College London. I have two boys, 6 and 8 years. Erica, my wife, does not have any idea about this part of my past or even the slightest idea that I might have another child somewhere. Even I never thought this. Which is why it is a strange dream for me. I will think how we should best meet. We can keep in contact by email if that is okay with you. Thank you for writing.

Antonio

I read Antonio's letter with an absurdly racing heart. By the time I reached the end I was weak with disbelief. *Imagine my shock . . . a strange dream for me . . .* How awful for you, Antonio! Who would have guessed that pregnancy leads to the birth of a child!

I nursed my fury, laced though it was with compassion as the rhythm of the words called up the Antonio I had once loved. I countered these flashes with the memory of his robotic voice, his locked-up eyes that gave nothing away, allowed nothing in, until the final bitter knowledge: "You don't want to have one with me." What it had cost me to walk out of his apartment, and what it had cost me in the ensuing years going it alone! Only a saint would have returned his call the next day; only a martyr would have fed his need to justify himself and be forgiven. I could not have borne a minute more, just as I could not bear the spin he was putting on it now. *My wish is that you would have found a way to tell me of Maddy's existence.*

Antonio, the wronged party! Antonio would have liked an annual report on the child he abandoned! If something in the tone of his letter troubled me, I thrust it out of my mind. The idea of meeting him began to work on me from inside, twisting out of shape every other relationship in my life.

19

My father crouched in the hallway, snapping the leash onto Barney's collar. His hair was completely white over the pink of his skull and still held the ridges of the comb. I moved toward the door. I did not like looking down on my father's head. It was Sunday afternoon, and the annual Blessing of the Animals was taking place at the National Cathedral. When my brother and I were small, we'd gone on a yearly pilgrimage to this conference of creatures. I had taken Maddy as well, though not consistently and not for many years. I proposed to my father that we go for our walk there while Rose was at her monthly book group.

"They had an iguana last year," he said, heaving himself upright and ignoring my offer of a steadying hand. "What'll it be next, stick insects?" He bent over again to retrieve something from the floor. "Vultures!"

"Oh, they can't allow birds of prey."

The leaflets hit the wastebasket. *"We have buyers for you! We want your house!"* I'd been a baby when my parents moved into what was at the time a run-down neighborhood near Dupont Circle. During the middle-class flight to the suburbs they had stayed put. My father taught high school social studies, my mother mostly fourth grade; ten-year-olds were her limit, she said. When the middle class returned, it was only a matter of time before there were sidewalk cafés and a farmers' market. Burned out twice in the riots, Fourteenth Street was now a boomtown for condos and restaurants; overnight a laundry had been turned into a Belgian brasserie, its ceilings installed prestained with cigarette smoke. Rose and Walter's house remained largely unchanged: the same unadorned brick, stout black door and arched portico, whose lining, I noticed as I followed my father down the steps onto Corcoran Street, had started to crumble.

Three doors down, workers were hosing the hostas of the house with the face on it. The green man was the work of a hammered-metal artist and had been there for as long as I could remember, inserted in the recess of a small window. Smile half hidden in his beard, he gazed knowingly down at us as we passed. For young Maddy, the face had been a source of awe. She never went by without stopping, hands behind her small back, to face him. "He's mad at me, Mom." "He's so sad today. He wants to come down from there." "Does he ever go indoors?" "Does he know what I'm thinking?"

We put Barney in the car, parked behind the elementary school in whose playground Maddy, aged six, had fallen off the jungle gym and broken her arm, and drove up Connecticut to Tenleytown.

"It's a long walk from here," I pointed out. We could have parked further on, but my father said why take the dog for a walk if we're not going to walk? He stopped frequently on the long incline up Mount St. Alban to catch his breath. I did not like to hear my father's labored breathing. I stopped whenever he did, pretending to admire the view, and took the leash from him, although Barney's impatient straining was no doubt a help on the hill.

The steps of the church and the courtyard swarmed with animal life. Twin black terriers, white and pink puppies, golden puppies, brown puppies, beagles, mongrels, retrievers like Barney, and cats, mundane and exotic, sat in strollers and quivered on leashes. There were monarch butterflies, frogs and salamanders in glass boxes in their owners' arms, and crates bearing pets we could not identify from where we stood. The white-robed ministers were all women. They dipped their sprigs into bowls of holy water to bless the animals with beatific smiles: long life and good health to all. Choral music poured from the cathedral face, piercing to the part of myself where spiritual yearning was stored.

"Dad?"

He was righting Barney's ear. "Going on fourteen and you wouldn't be caught dead in a stroller, would you, old man?"

"Dad."

He straightened up and gave me his attention.

"I wanted to talk to you about something I found in Maddy's room."

"What's that?"

I pulled a manila envelope from my bag and removed Maddy's first letter to Antonio. I had only brought one. It was the fact rather than the content of the exchange that mattered. I handed it to my father without a word. *Dear Antonio Jorge Romero, You don't know me . . .*

I waited while he read it through, tapping the paper from underneath with his finger. "And he wrote back?"

"About thirty times." He looked at me then, trying his best not to smile. I had planned to be direct and unemotional, but my voice trembled with accusation. "Why didn't you tell me?"

My father's silence was maddening. He never rushed into anything. "We were in the park one day," he said at last. "She brought it up. She thought her father rejecting her had something to do with her getting cancer."

"How could she think that?"

"It wasn't logical. She had this idea about the universe not wanting her. I was glad she could say it out loud."

"Well, it's upset me." I blinked hard. "As you can see."

He didn't move or come to my aid. "It's understandable, isn't it? She had to find him before it was too late. I helped her out a little, that's all." The implication was clear: *I* had not helped Maddy look for her father, had I?

"But why didn't you tell me?"

I had seen my father's face deformed by hilarity and by grief, but seldom by guilt. After a moment, in his reasonable voice, he said: "Don't you think you had enough to face? We were so worried about you, Eve." He let me pluck the letter out of his hand. His voice was hoarse. "We still are."

I waved the paper at him. "Did it never occur to you I would want to know about something like this? How terrible it would be to find out later?"

His eyes traveled up and down the façade of what Maddy used to call "that big, sharp church," resting on the rose window set deep between the towers. "I guess," he said at last, "it was something she had to do on her own."

I kept my silence, willing the animals to be gone. I could not bear so much soft, creaturely life in one place. No water could wash that away.

Eventually my father said: "She didn't tell you?"

"*Obviously* she didn't tell me! Did Mom know?"

"Of course not. If I'd told your mother, I'd have told you."

"It was just between you and Maddy."

He nodded. "She never showed me the letters. As things got worse, it wasn't exactly at the front of my mind."

A clergywoman approached; her smile faltered when she caught sight of our faces. That was when my father tried his one-armed sideways hug on me. The woman took it as her cue to flick her holy water on Barney, and as she did so, I slipped out of my father's embrace and stood apart on my own patch of sunlit stone. I was not beholden to my parents anymore. I no longer had to bide my time or hold my tongue because I needed them for Maddy.

"Shall we go?"

My father plunged his hands in his pockets and bounced his change. "What was he like? Was he kind to her?"

"Kind enough."

"Oh good! It meant a lot to Maddy, the idea of Antonio. I warned her he might not want anything to do with her. She was very determined. She was annoyed because I never told her I met him, way back when."

"Well, Maddy was nothing if not determined. We all know that."

Still my father did not move. "So," he ventured, "it was a good thing she found him?"

"How would I know!"

He blinked at me in surprise. His eyes were wet.

"Probably," I rushed to say. "Probably it was."

When I stayed home from school as a child, I waited all day long for my father's step in the hallway. Until he spoke to me and laid his hand on my forehead, my malaise was not wholly real or authorized.

I took his arm and scolded him. "You should have told me!"

He did not yield to my touch or my lighter tone. "Don't you think," he said at last, "it was up to Maddy to tell you?"

Outside the Metro, I handed my father the leash. I was taking the train north to Takoma Park.

"Are you sure you'll be all right, Dad? Want me to come with you?"

He dismissed the idea with a flap of his hand and bent over to pry a paper cup from Barney's jaws. He tossed it at the trash can, missed, tossed again, and then he stood very straight, looking up and down the street, smiling the composed smile of someone whose life was mostly behind him. Joggers pounded past, their faces tense and faraway. Was it possible that my parents had made a recovery of sorts? After all, she wasn't their child.

"Did you know," he said, "they've started piping classical music into the Metro stations?"

"Oh? Why is that?"

"To discourage gangs from congregating." It was the kind of story my father thrived on.

"Does it work?"

"Of course not. We'll just end up with a generation of highly cultured youth!"

He offered his face for me to kiss, flooding me with remorse. He had supported me without question in single motherhood. He had come to Maddy's aid and guarded her secrets. I may not have given Maddy a father, but I had given her a grandfather, and their relationship had been closer and more open than mine with him would ever be. He would never get over it. He would never be the same.

I waited for him to lay his hand on my head. Instead he gripped my upper arm and released it, his other signature gesture of affection, and set off down the sidewalk after Barney, taking with him the larger part of what he felt about Maddy and about me. Half a block away, he waggled the fingers of one hand behind his back. He knew I would be watching.

Maddy

20

It was true, if a little misleading, to say Jack was helping me with the animation. Depends on what you mean by *help*. He took the pictures of Serenity, he found some images of cities and forests, he supplied the camera, the copy stand, and the moral support. But the drawings were all mine, the ideas were mine, the head was mine. I made the decisions about how the images changed one into another. So I would say I was the artist and Jack was my assistant.

Once I got started, all I wanted was to be alone in my room. I had the copy stand on my desk with Jack's camera aimed down at the paper taped to the base. The drawings and photographs I was working from were pinned to my bulletin board. With Cloud on the bed for company, and my mother out of sight but close by, I could continue for sometimes an hour at a time before I had to lie down. The days I was too exhausted to work, I lay in bed and tried running sequences through my mind, imagining the changes I would make. That didn't get me anywhere. With drawing, the point is to *see* what you're thinking.

For the smallest movement, I had to plan the beginning, middle, and end, and then draw all the steps in between, taking shots as I went along.

The program gives you a ghost image of the last frame to help you line up the next one. "Onion skinning," it's called. I came to love the words. Onion skinning. Project windows. Time lines. I got good at guessing how much to erase at once and where to draw in the new position. You had to do lots of stages even just to get the eyes to open. Thirty-six frames for three seconds of movement!

Once I had done the erasing and redrawing for a particular change, I couldn't insert another stage. If it was wrong, I had to start over. I made some pretty hilarious mistakes, like shutting one eye before the other so she looked like she was winking. I found out the hard way you can't make the tiniest change *here* without making the tiniest change *there*. You have to work on the whole thing at once.

The biggest lesson I learned, and the one that it took a while to get used to, was that you have to give up the real drawing in order to make the animation. You have to make each mark as if it's the most important thing in the world, and then you have to cover it up and never see it again for the sake of something that seems alive but isn't really, it's just a mirage. But a beautiful one. The drawing you can hold in your hands is ruined. My head hurt thinking about it.

The best thing was, I could do whatever I wanted. Speed it up, slow it down, open the eyes, close the eyes, populate the head, clear the head, add a whole new sequence if I felt like it. I hummed and sang while I worked. And when did you first get interested in animation, Miss Wakefield? Call me Madeleine. Oh, it was years ago, when I had some time on my hands. Did you ever think you would become one of the most famous artists of your generation? Never! Not in a million years . . .

My mother's step on the stairs. Silence. That was her listening outside my door.

"Come i-innn!" I called, extra-brightly to hide my frustration. If I got interrupted, I might leave my thumb in the shot, and a retake was not so easy because you had to reverse all the changes.

"Working again?" My mother threw a hungry glance at my copy stand but came no closer. She set down the tray with her latest snack idea— scrambled egg on rye toast. Slice of avocado on the side, carved into the shape of a sleeping cat.

"Thanks, Mama." With a pang, I watched her tug my bedspread and round up the wastebaskets. "The sketchbook was a great idea. I love drawing."

"I'm so glad."

Her eyes traveled over the pictures pinned to my wall. Luckily I was working on the ones for the campaign, not the private ones. Even so, my skin prickled all over, like in those dreams where you find yourself in the school cafeteria with no clothes on. Maybe she knew about the other animation I was doing. She'd always known everything about me. Even things I didn't know myself.

"I could help you with your drawing," said my mother. "If you ever need a second opinion. Just say."

Sharper pang. "Sure, Mom." She hugged me from behind and kissed the top of my head. "Are you okay?" I asked.

"I'm fine. Are *you* okay?"

"I'm fine."

She seemed in good spirits, considering. No wobbly voice. No staring into that too-bright light. My mother was happy I had something to do. Art is her thing, after all. She doesn't do it much anymore, but she looks at it and teaches people about it, and some of that must have rubbed off on me. I don't think it came from Antonio.

Almost time to change the paper. With all the erasing and redrawing, you get rips and smudges and the surface becomes a lot more interesting. Eventually it gets so interesting you can't use it anymore. Then you start again with a clean, boring sheet.

Wherever my mother was, in the laundry room or the kitchen or tapping on her computer in the study, there were these invisible strings running from her to me. I could feel them tugging. Here I am. If you need anything. Please need something I can give you. She knew I was up here making an animation but she would never ask to see it, no matter how much she wanted to. If she asked, I would show her. I might even show her the other one someday. If I thought she could stand it.

Hi Antonio,

Me again. How are you?

Did I tell you I have a boyfriend named Jack? He is almost as tall as you, and he's already got his driver's license. Science is his favorite subject. He has that kind of a mind. Since I met him, I have gotten more interested in how things work. Like how the heart pumps the blood around and how many complicated reactions are going on all the time to keep everything on track. Did you know that your heart beats 100,000 times a day!!! I don't even like to think about that.

I used to draw a lot and I've started drawing again. Jack and I are making an animation for the campaign. It's going to be cool.

Maddy

Maddy,

Yes, the more you learn about the natural world, the more miraculous it seems. Did you know that the odds against any particular person with that person's exact genetic makeup being born are astronomical?

Boyfriend! That's great. I hope he's good to you . . . I didn't have a girlfriend until older than you. Eighteen, I think. I was very nervous with the girls. I remember feeling excited about the future but also incredibly scared.

Oscar likes football and wall climbing. The younger one, Daniel, is the artistic one. He has always loved to draw too—cartoons mostly. We go camping together in the summer holiday, and we usually go for two weeks to Spain.

I would love to see your drawings one day, if you ever want to show me, and your animation. I'm not even sure how you make an animation. Maybe you can explain it to me.

Antonio

21

Dr. Osterley is always telling me to live as normal a life as I can, and at the end of June my mother let Jack and me drive up to the lake house, just the two of us, in his father's Nissan. He'd passed his test the minute he turned sixteen. Me, I'm going to learn when I have more time. My mother insisted on being a passenger with him a few times before she said we could go. Even so, she had to lecture him on the evils of speed, the stupidity of other drivers, and the tendency of the teenage brain to downplay danger. I could see her point. After all she'd been through, to lose me in a car crash would be really annoying.

"You're a great kid," she said to Jack on the morning we left. "But you have to remember your frontal lobes are not fully developed."

"My what?"

"Your frontal lobes."

Jack laughed. "There's nothing wrong with my lobes! Way above average, these lobes." When we were small, he liked my mother because of the games she played with us, and he liked her now for the same reason.

"I have no doubt," said my mother, "yours are more highly developed than most. The same goes

236

for Maddy. But you *are* sixteen. Your brain is a work in progress."

"Everyone's brain is a work in progress."

"I've got a book if you want to read about it."

Jack shot me a grin. "Your mother's got books on everything."

By now, it was plain that Jack and I were sleeping together. He even stayed over one night, and my mother let him stay in my room. She appeared surprisingly cool about this, though I was pretty sure she hadn't told Grandma. Aren't mothers supposed to object, on principle?

The trip seemed longer than usual, and the fields and barns were like fields and barns in a dream because I was in a car alone with Jack, driving to the lake. I kept reaching over and pressing his leg, and he put his hand snug over mine, until after a minute I said, "Two hands on the wheel," and he took his back.

I slammed the car door when we arrived and breathed in the spicy Tawasentha air. "Have you ever smelled ferns like that?"

Jack climbed out and stood there, sniffing respectfully. I was proud to be in possession of the key to the house. The flimsy lock in the doorknob would not keep out anyone who decided to get in. But no one ever did. Tawasentha Lake was one of the safest places in the universe. Not that I was safe anywhere. The door jammed as usual and then crashed open all at once and we were met by a whole other set of smells, including mouse droppings, mildew, and air freshener, cinnamon flavor.

"Wow, nice," said Jack, though we were in the mudroom, where all he could see were light switches and a bench for taking off your shoes. Despite my new rights to his body, the sight of Jack in the mudroom, tossing the car keys and catching them in a sideways swipe with his strong fingers, made me shy. The house was empty. No one was coming. Nothing stood in our way.

"Remember to call your mom," said Jack.

My stomach turned over when I heard her voice on the phone. She was in one of her playful moods. "How many speeding tickets did he get?"

"Jack's a good driver," I said. "You'd be impressed. What's Robin up to?"

"Just got a big commission."

"What for?"

"A corner unit. It's hideous, apparently. Have you been down to the lake?"

"Not yet."

"Go on. Enjoy yourselves."

"Mama?"

"What?"

"Oh, nothing."

When I'd hung up, Jack reached for me and I burrowed my face into his neck, trying my best to relax. I had spent every summer at the lake house since I could remember. I was as much at home there as at my real house. My child self was at the window looking in at Jack and me hugging, and she was feeling a little left out. For her sake, I pulled away, leaving small placating kisses on his face.

Jack followed me to the utility room. I turned on the electricity and showed him the back bedrooms, leaving the living room for last. The front windows were so huge, the lake might as well have been right inside the house. This time I was the one who reached for him. It was easier to relax when there was something to pay attention to outside of ourselves.

"Want to go down to the dock?"

"Can we eat something first?" said Jack. "I'm starving."

We made peanut butter sandwiches and ate them at the kitchen counter.

He waved his sandwich at the hall ceiling. "What's that?"

"Oh, there's a pull-down ladder. It goes up to the attic."

"What's up there?"

"Just attic stuff. It was going to be a playroom, but Mom never got around to having it converted. Robin says he's going to."

"You don't need a playroom anymore," Jack pointed out.

"No, but it could be some other kind of room. I always wanted a secret place up in the trees."

"Sounds cool."

"I doubt it'll ever get done."

After our snack, we went down to the dock. The air was warm. We settled in the green chairs. I was glad we had arrived at that time in the evening when there was still plenty of daylight left and the lake was turning into a calmer, more secret version of itself. Jack was quieter than usual, looking out at the water as if he were alone.

"Do you think," I asked him, "I would be the same person if I hadn't grown up with this lake?"

"You couldn't know without rewinding your life and doing it again. *I* didn't grow up with a lake."

"And you survived."

"You just have to guess," said Jack.

"My guess," I said, "is that after all these years the lake is inside of me. Not as in—cut me open and find a lake."

"No."

Out in the middle, a dark bar drifted on the silvery surface. I knew what that felt like. You laid your paddle across the canoe and stopped trying to steer or control it, or wonder which way to head next. Let the water decide.

"Do you know what it's like here in the winter?"

"Awesome, I bet."

"It is so, so beautiful. You should hear the

sound the lake makes. It's the most unbelievable sound. Like this enormous thing, like an airplane, is under the water trying to turn over."

"Is it the ice cracking?"

"Not cracking. I don't think it's cracking. Shifting, maybe? Or trying to break away from the shore?" I knew it would be impossible to impress on Jack the sound made by the frozen lake. You had to hear it for yourself. "Next winter you have to come up."

"Sure," said Jack. "Let's." A bird went by, so high it didn't make a sound.

"Do you ever pretend," I said, "that you're looking at yourself from outer space?"

"Sometimes, yeah."

"Or else looking at yourself from the point of view of something under a microscope?"

"A thought experiment, you mean?"

"Well, from outer space we are just this slime on the surface of the earth. And to, say, an atom, we are these irrelevant giants."

We held hands between the chairs, watching the lake turn different shades of violet and black. After a while, without looking at me, Jack said:

"Maddy?"

"What."

"Do they ever tell you exactly what's going on?"

"With my treatments, you mean?"

"Don't talk about it if you don't want to."

"We have to be optimistic," I said, copying my mother.

"I was just wondering." High up, a piece of moon was showing through, not yet brighter than the sky. "Did you know," he said, changing the subject, "that all the water in the world is all there will ever be?"

"Meaning . . . ?"

"Meaning that water is constantly turning from one state into another. Ninety-seven percent is in the oceans. Only three percent is fresh. There's surface water, there's ground water underneath, there's what's stored in ice and snow and in the air—"

"In the air?"

He made his lips a circle and blew. "Breath is mostly water. We're made out of water. But the thing is, there's a fixed amount. It can't be added to or taken away. It just changes into another form."

"Okay . . ."

"We drink the same water the dinosaurs did."

"Okay. So when the earth heats up four degrees," I said, "and the ice caps melt and the trees and animals die, the water in them eventually ends up in the oceans?"

"And the air."

I thought for a minute. "Is that comforting? I don't know if that's very comforting."

"It is, in a way. In the long run."

The lake looked strange all of a sudden, as

though the trees had turned to liquid and the water to rock. I wanted to smash its shiny surface. I did an experimental hoot, like you do to test an echo, and something took the sound away from me and stretched it out into a scream. Every awful thing that had ever happened to me, everything I was furious with or desperate about, got sucked into the scream, and it got louder and louder like a siren getting closer and closer, until it filled the sky, scaring even me.

"What the—!" shouted Jack.

"Sorry," I said cheerfully. Let him think that screaming at the lake was something we did all the time, just for fun.

He was staring at me, not sure whether to laugh.

"You know what, Jack? I could end up raining on you. Or in your bathwater."

"Maddy . . ."

"Coming out of your faucets. I could end up in your coffee. Not that you would know it was me."

"Anything is possible," he said in a weak voice.

"Or maybe you *would* know."

We were silent for a long time.

"Jack?" I said at last.

"Yeah?"

"I want to still be *some*where."

His retort was instant. "They can do amazing things. They know so much these days! Don't talk like that, Maddy. Please."

I noticed that the more worked up Jack got, the calmer I became. Maybe there was only a certain amount of fear to go around, so we took turns holding it.

"Just say it does happen. Just say. Wouldn't it be sad if you and I never talked about it?"

I had never seen him look so scared.

"Jack?" I said. "Don't take this the wrong way."

"Okay."

"Why do you want to be with me?"

His eyes opened to the whites. "Don't you think we're good together?"

"Of course I do! *Obviously*."

"All right, well." He made as if to pout.

"Is it because I'm sick?"

"No!"

"You have a thing for sick girls?" He looked so affronted I poked him in the arm. "Just say it, Jack! It doesn't matter. Don't think too much. You always think too much!"

He stared at me as though I had uttered some profound, prizewinning thing. "That's just the point! I do think too much. I can't help it. I like people who think. Most kids are hung up on sports or looks or being popular. It all seems so trivial."

"And I'm not trivial."

"No . . ." His voice went low and teasing. "You're definitely not trivial . . ."

"I'm not?"

"You're deep . . ." He tipped his head sideways between the chairs and kissed me lingeringly to let me know he liked me for much more than my lack of triviality, which, by the way, was not only the result of a random thing that went wrong in my immune system. But I wasn't going to give in yet. I made him look at me.

"Listen, Jack. In the future? If I'm not here?"

"Yeah?" He was ready to fight again.

"Anything good happens to you?"

"Yeah?"

"It's me."

Jack looked as if he might burst out laughing or crying, and couldn't decide which. We went up to the house, arms around each other.

Strange at first, doing it in the lake bedroom with the life preservers hanging on the wall and the shelves full of board games and stuffed animals I'd never bothered to get rid of. We left the curtains open. There was something thrilling about that, even though no one was out there to see us. Maybe it was being at the lake house. Maybe it was the conversation we'd had on the dock. But that time was the closest and the best. The way it's supposed to be. So it was the saddest time too. The books don't tell you about that.

I rolled onto my stomach and Jack ran his hand up and down my spine. His dampness was squashed against me, his legs giving off a lazy kind of heat. It's true that men literally empty themselves out. I felt emptied out too. With my free eye I could see the line of silver through the trees, fringed by my lashes. Night took a long time to fall here. The water held on to the light. My eye slowly closed and slowly opened, giving me the silver line again. Where would that line go? Where would the lacy trees between me and the line go? Where would the moss go that was in so much shadow now you couldn't see it, you just had to know it was there? What about every idea I'd ever had about the lake? Everything that had ever happened to me at the lake? Where would that go? I could feel the answer like some sorry thing circling around and around itself, unable ever to lie down and rest, and the answer was: Nowhere. The lake would still be there. But *my* lake wouldn't be there. Whatever I felt, thought, saw, heard was sealed up and attached to me and only to me, and it would go wherever I went.

I pulled the sheet up and tried to keep the sadness from taking over. If I let it take me over, then sadness was all I would ever have. I unrolled my length beside him. It was a miracle, when you thought about it. If Miss Sedge hadn't put us together for the campaign, I would not be here in the lake house bedroom with Jack. I would not know what it was like to lie next to a perfectly warm body that was naked just for me, and feel the ripples from his hand fanning out.

"Jack?"

"What?"

"I love this place."

I made him keep stroking my back and listen to every last detail of every story I could think of about the lake. The year my cousins and I rescued dragonflies trapped in the spiderwebs under the dock. We picked the sticky stuff off with tweezers. If their wings weren't too damaged, they flew away. The first time I swam across, with Mom and Grandma alongside in the canoe. Singing on the dock before a storm. Picking blueberries at the air force base. It was my job to remove the hard green ones and the leaves and twigs that got mixed in. My grandfather's birdhouses, walks down the glen, the perfect silence in the woods when it snowed.

"There," I said.

"There what?"

"Let's get up."

I let Jack go first. I liked watching him put on his clothes. He was still shy about me seeing him naked, but this time he didn't seem to mind dangling around the place right in front of me. Puckered and saggy. Bruise-colored. So different from the rest of his body. So different from the one in bed with us, which had a mind of its own. I didn't close the curtains, though I'd never liked them being open once it got dark. Jack did some shadowboxing and threw his underpants in the air and caught them with his foot. I lay on my side, laughing in the right way.

The thing was this. Once upon a time Jack might have thought of me as this girl he built planetariums with, or this girl he talked about the ice sheet with, or this girl he made an animation with. But now, whatever happened, he wouldn't be able to pass over me too lightly. I would always be the first girl he did it with. That's not something you forget.

Hi Maddy,

About time it warms up. London climate is not the best, especially compared to Spain or America, that's for sure. You never can trust an English summer. You have to always take a jacket when you go out. I miss the heat of my country. But I guess I am used to it by now. I want to ask again about your mother. How is she? And her friend who is ill?

Antonio

Dear Antonio,

I would love to travel to Spain or London. Anywhere, really. I've been to California and twelve other states, plus Montreal. I guess that's not too bad. I bet there are kids who have never been out of DC. Jack and I drove up to our lake house, just the two of us.

My mother is an atheist like you. Maybe that's what attracted you to each other? My grandmother is a Christian but not the yucky kind. She is really smart and she has an open mind, as much as you can have an open mind and still believe in God, prayer, heaven, etc. My grandfather goes to church but he never talks about it. I don't know if he really believes. Do you think it's possible to believe in life after death without believing in God? Vicky is a Catholic and she goes to church but I don't think it has much to do with God, it's just what Catholics do, like eat fish on Fridays and speak Italian in the kitchen. I wish I could take it so lightly. Fiona's not the religious type.

Mom is okay. Her friend is hanging in there.

Maddy

Maddy,

I come from a Catholic family, and church was part of my life growing up. I didn't really question it until I got older—thirteen years maybe? My parents didn't like it when I stopped going to church. My mother especially. They are simple people. I guess I wanted to make a point. Once you look at the concept of religion with a scientific frame of mind, it seems less and less plausible. Though I would NEVER rule anything completely out because part of keeping a scientific frame of mind is being open to being proved wrong. A lot of discoveries came from scientists entertaining ideas that seemed ridiculous at the time. Do you know what a paradigm is? A paradigm is a view of the world that organizes our way of thinking, and even our perception, what we see and don't see. Scientific revolutions don't just add new facts, they change our entire worldview.

I do find it very hard to conceive of an afterlife. We are animals. Smart animals, but even so, animals don't go to heaven, do they? I suspect it is a story people tell themselves because it is so hard to accept the idea of not existing. You also have to look at the damage religion has done. So many wars fought in the name of it. People thinking they don't have to make the most of their life because they have a spare one. In my way of thinking we must believe we are given one life. I know you have an inquiring mind, and that is such an important thing. But I wouldn't worry too much about it for now!

Antonio

Eve

22

had taken to arriving at work before everyone else, when Roland the security guard was eating donuts in his office on the mezzanine. He knew I liked the run of the place before the day began. I snapped the switches one by one as I made my way through the dark building. Light leapt ahead to create the space as I needed it: the lower gallery with its shrouded piano, the paneled staircase, the glass bridge that linked the original house with the airy modern half of the museum.

After Maddy died, I'd preferred going to work to staying at home. I let go of the young people's programs, but retained my managerial responsibilities and still led sessions with adults. Lately I'd been spending a lot of time alone in the galleries. I felt thrown back to a time when art had seemed thrilling and necessary; but when I stood in front of the paintings I loved, they were like old friends I had fallen out with, trying to tell me something I couldn't understand.

Today I headed for the wax room. This was an alcove the size of an elevator, located off the gallery that held Renoir's *Luncheon of the Boating Party*—the collection's most famous painting. I felt for the switch. The little empty room sprang to life, its pitted coat of beeswax glowing like skin. Many a visitor stepped in and out again, complaining, "There's nothing in there!"

When it was first installed, I had found the wax room oppressive; underneath the sweet smell of birthdays and Advent, something lay in wait that was feral and indifferent to the human world. Strange that I was drawn to it now. My sensory life had been reset in so many ways that I often found myself seeking out what used to repel me. I positioned my folding chair in the corner. Aside from anything else, the empty room was somewhere to think.

"Wasn't it was up to Maddy to tell you?" My father had ventured the question cautiously, because he knew it was the crux of the matter. Maddy had chosen to find Antonio independent of me. There was no getting around that. I was starting to see that you can lose someone not just once, but over and over again. All these men who wooed her away from me! Jack, Antonio, and in a complicated way, my own father. Of course she needed the counsel and approval of men; of course she craved their love. I knew that. I accepted that. No doubt as adults she and I would have reclaimed our female solidarity and laughed together at the foibles of men. No doubt eventually I would have told her the full story of Antonio. I always planned to do that. We always planned to track him down once she turned eighteen. Plans!

When I emerged from the wax room, the main gallery lights were ablaze and Alison Ward, one of the attendants, was sitting on her hands, practicing her scowl for the day. Just before going on compassionate leave, I had put Alison on probation because of an incident in when she'd argued aggressively with an intern giving a public talk. Since my return she'd had the air of a child flaunting impeccable behavior while biding her time. Then last week a visitor had complained about Alison to one of the docents.

She saw me carrying the folding chair and raised her eyebrows. My watch said nearly ten. I had been in there longer than I'd intended.

"Good morning," I said brusquely. "The cleaners told me something spilled in the wax room. They aren't allowed to touch anything in there."

I went straight over to her, glad that I was standing and she wasn't. She knew I was making excuses. She knew what everyone knew about my life. Her face was round and pale in a boxy haircut, self-inflicted, by the look of it. She watched me from narrowed eyes, shrewd in the way a mistreated cat is shrewd. The contrast with the stylish merrymakers of the painting beside her was comical. Not to mention the contrast with Maddy.

"Was it?" asked Alison in her scratchy voice.

"Was what?"

"Was something spilled in there?"

"If so, they cleaned it up," I said. "Alison, I have to tell you there's been a complaint."

"I thought you said the cleaners weren't allowed in the wax room?"

I ignored that. "Not official, but a complaint nevertheless. From a member of the public."

"A complaint about what?"

"A visitor told one of the docents that you spoke to him in an 'extremely rude manner.' Something about a Matisse."

"People don't like being told what to do, no matter how polite you are."

"And how polite were you?"

Alison had a way of appearing to be looking at me without actually meeting my eye. "If it wasn't an official complaint, what are you telling me for? They can say anything they want."

I gave her what I hoped was the piercing look of a line manager. I no longer had any confidence in my own authority.

"He was this big loud guy. He went right up and put his finger on the Matisse. I said, 'Please don't touch the artwork.' He said, 'But it's behind glass.' I said, 'If you touch the glass, the glass touches the painting.' He gave me a dirty look, and when he thought I'd turned my back, he did it again. Where do people get off, damaging works of art?"

"How long have you been here, Alison?"

"Year and a half."

"Weren't you planning to start a master's?"

"I was going to." She made a face. "Want to know why he was provoking me?"

"We take visitor complaints very seriously, you know. It's a disciplinary matter."

"The guy was wearing a backpack. He must've sneaked up the fire stairs. So I said to him, 'You can't bring that in here. Can I ask you to go check it in the coatroom?' He said in this nasty way, 'You can ask me, but I'm not leaving this in any coatroom. Do you know what's in here?' He went like this . . ." Alison made the hand sign for a pistol. "Pointed his finger straight at my head like he was taking aim, and laughed. Asshole."

"Did you call him that?"

"Of course not."

"Phew."

"I called him a redneck jerk."

"You can't call visitors names!" I sighed. "You know that."

"Should I have called the police? It's against the law here, carrying a gun."

"Alison, in this kind of job you have to keep your cool. You could have looked for Roland, or any one of us, to back you up."

"I told him I was going to get security and he swore at me and stomped downstairs. So I guess I scared him off. I bet you're putting me on probation again. Great. Send me away for keeping some maniac from destroying a Matisse."

"Well, he would have pushed my buttons too." I tried not to smile. "People can be exasperating. How old are you, Alison?"

"Twenty-four." For the first time she looked straight at me through the ragged edge of her bangs. "How old was your daughter?"

"Sixteen," I answered automatically.

"I'm sorry," she said.

"Thank you." There was an awkward silence in which I blinked away the threat of tears. "Well," I concluded, composing myself. "I won't take this any further. But next time I suggest you breathe deeply and count to ten—no, one hundred—before you bring out your big guns."

We grinned at the same time. I exited the gallery in the direction of the offices. Though I had never been partial to *The Boating Party*, the blurred, candy-colored brushstrokes actively annoyed me now, the men striking poses in their undershirts, the woman in the bonnet ostentatiously kissing her little French dog. Not a sharp angle in sight.

The office area was large enough to be divided into separate rooms, but that would have gone against the spirit of the place. We each had a long table to ourselves, with bookshelves and bulletin boards creating zones of partial privacy while retaining a sense of collegial openness. The interns shared a table by the window.

"Claire," I said, coming to a stop by her desk. We had the place to ourselves. "I have an idea." Claire Tivington was director of education. I was assistant director, which was the way I preferred it, second in command. Her eyes lingered on her screen; we had a financial audit coming up. "I could do with a new project."

She gave me her businesslike face. Fifteen years my senior, she was a no-fuss lesbian who dressed in pantsuits a little too tight and short in the leg; to the relief of the staff, she had finally let her eggplant-colored hair go gray. The instant Maddy was diagnosed, Claire had given me as much compassionate leave as I wanted, persuading a retired colleague to provide cover. Though we had always kept a professional distance, I was immensely grateful for her kindness. Now Claire folded her plump hands on the desk.

"One year is coming up, isn't it?"

"I'm thinking it might be a good time to revive the England trip."

"Okay," she said. "Let's look at dates and figures."

"I was thinking early December."

"That soon?"

"End of November is, you know, the anniversary."

She gave a sage nod.

"It's an interesting moment over there. They're serious about merging education with commissioning, curation, forms of display . . ."

"Yes, I know," she said.

"I could do a series of interviews, like we discussed. Find out what's happening on the ground. Write up a report. A book, even." I paused. "I'll need someone with me."

"Let's not get ahead of ourselves." She checked my eyes. "Well, it does sound good. We might be able to spare one of the interns. Melissa, maybe? Anyway, there's a lot we'd need to figure out first." She unclasped her hands and one of them inched toward her mouse. "Funds, for a start."

Melissa was a confident, demure intern who dressed in short skirts and over-the-knee boots. She gave bland visitor tours and was starting to write content for the website. She was liked by staff and public alike. She never put a foot wrong. I balked at the idea of spending two weeks in London with Melissa. But it was a good sign that we were already talking about details. With Claire being the bighearted person she was, I thought there was a chance my request would be granted.

"Dig up the proposal," she said. "We'll see what we can do."

I ran across Alison frequently after that, as though our encounter had rendered her visible.

She spent her lunch breaks in the galleries, or the ground-floor shop, flipping through books. One day I came across her, arms folded, in front of *The Silence That Lives in Houses*. She glanced at me suspiciously.

"Do you like that painting?" An inane question. I'd banned the word *like* from my teaching sessions.

"I think I know what he meant," said Alison.

"Who?"

"Matisse!" she snapped. "Who else?"

I left a long pause. She had no idea how to talk to a line manager. "What did he mean?"

"Well," she began, "it's bright and noisy outside the window, but what you want is to be indoors, where you can look at your book and your globe and *think* about what's out there. See, the trees are solid but the interior is all outlines. The people are outlines. They're facing away from the window. They're facing the vase of flowers. The book they're looking at is blank . . ." She stopped. Her voice lost its animation. "I don't know," she said, sullen again.

"You really love this, don't you?"

Alison pushed her glasses up with one finger. "When I started here, I thought, Oh, it'll be great, I'll be near the art. What a joke. It's just a customer-service job. I might as well be working in a drugstore."

"In my day you could work your way up. There

were federal positions. My master's was run out of a town house in Foggy Bottom. Now, to do anything interesting, you have to have at least an MA. And even then—"

"Maybe I like the art too much," she cut in. "I don't want to have to dream up nonsense about it."

"Is that how you see what we do here? Nonsense?"

Maddy had once said, about a wall panel I wrote: "I don't understand a word of this. Sorry, Mom. Not one single word." I had taken her to too many Fun Days at museums. It had been a great relief to me when she started drawing again.

"Can't you let people think for themselves?" asked Alison.

"Like the man with the backpack?"

"What was he doing here, anyway?"

"Everyone has a right to look at art."

She snorted. "Someone like that isn't capable of looking at art."

"I wouldn't be so sure."

"All they do is read the labels. Maybe if the words weren't there, they might have to actually look at the art for more than two seconds." She crossed her arms again. "You should have to pass a test before you're allowed in here."

"Oh yeah?" I smiled. "And what would you put on the test?"

"What about: 'If you could own any work in

the collection, which one would you choose and why? Anyone who mentions how it would look over their sofa is banned for life.' " Alison gave a hoarse laugh. "We'd have the place to ourselves." Slyly she added, "You'd like that, wouldn't you?"

I let two weeks go by before raising the London idea again. To my surprise, Claire had already looked into dates and finances and found someone to cover for my absence. She'd contacted a British colleague I might be able to stay with to keep our costs down.

"It's a good moment, as you say. No telling what might come from something like this. And it will do you good to get away."

"You can say that again." I gave her a hug. "Thank you, thank you, thank you, Claire!" Stepping back, I said casually, "I was wondering if Alison Ward could come with me."

"Alison?"

"She's had a rocky time recently."

"Have you followed up that complaint?"

"This guy threatened her with a gun, believe it or not. She apologized. What I realized is that she knows a great deal about art. Not the obvious choice, I know."

"Don't you think an opportunity like this should go to someone more . . ."

"Presentable?"

"Experienced. Alison's an attendant. She's very young."

"She's planning to do an MA in museum studies. At Johns Hopkins." When had I become so adept at improvisation?

"Oh, I see."

"It could be a good way," I said, "of showing that we value our staff at every level."

At this Claire laughed out loud and fixed me with a square look that said: Let there be no nonsense between us. I did not normally try to put anything over on her. I could see she was mentally scanning everything she had read about bereavement.

Eventually I said: "I don't know why, but I feel drawn to young women these days. I want to be in their company. I want to help them out."

Claire tipped her head to one side and gave me one of her deep, regretful smiles. I knew then that the London trip was in the bag, and that Alison would be allowed to go with me.

23

From work, I took a meandering route to Corcoran Street, feeling the need to be in my mother's company. My afternoon teaching session had gone well. The group had been more attentive than usual, and Ben Shahn's *Still Music* seemed again to be eloquent and full of possibilities.

Now that the London trip was taking shape, Antonio was everywhere. He'd been an invisible presence in the gallery, observing the way I drew knowledge out of people they didn't even know they had. He accompanied me down the streets we had once walked together, past the mansions built by turn-of-the-century shipping magnates, now luxury apartments and military museums, past the block-long embassies on Massachusetts, some of which, Robin said, must be worth more than the countries they represented, past the hotel famous for the sting operation that brought down the mayor. Incarceration did him no harm in the long run; when Antonio and I first met, the mayor had just been elected for another term.

When I turned onto R Street, though, Antonio dropped away. I had the sensation of Maddy's small hand in mine. My steps had brought me past the little brick house with the purple door. A former garage nestled between two brownstones, it had acquired the local nickname Hobbit House. When Maddy was small, she always insisted we detour past it, so that she could study the faux-medieval ironwork and the gas carriage lamps, and solemnly inform me that's where she was going to live forever and ever.

I quickened my pace to my parents' house, and rang the bell before letting myself in. The heavy door gave way all at once, delivering me onto the fur-choked mat. Would they never fix their locks or replace their doormats?

"It's me!"

Coffee, wet dog, old wood: essence of home. Maddy had loved that smell. She'd loved everything about their house: the pictures crowding the stairway walls, the piles of books, the handmade pottery squatting on shelves, and the bulging cartons on the back porch that had been there long before recycling became fashionable. My own childhood and my memories of Maddy had a way of merging together. The place still half belonged to her.

"Mom? It's me-ee!" I called again, though, being an expert in empty houses, I no longer expected a reply.

I was in the kitchen starting a note when I looked up to see my mother making her wordless way down the stairs. She had on jeans and a yellow sweater embroidered at the neck. Her hair was flattened as if she had just woken up. It struck me that this place, the stage of my childhood, had become the house of an elderly couple. In her slow progress toward me, I saw stair lifts, walkers, and home help, a high bed installed in the bay window. I saw my mother and my father leaving the house they loved and the neighborhood that no longer particularly loved them.

"Hello, dear," she said.

"What's wrong, Mom?"

Her eyes slid out from under mine. "Oh, just one of those days."

"Where's Dad?"

"Hardware store. Something to fix the back door. Rain got in and swelled the wood."

"Kind of late in the day to go shopping."

"I think he wanted to get out of the house. This is a nice surprise. On your way from work? Cup of something?"

"Yes, please." Once we were seated with our herbal tea, I asked again what was wrong, confident of a buoyant response; then I could tell her my news. Instead my mother's eyes brimmed with tears she made no effort to hide.

"What is it, Mom?" I went over and hugged her from behind. "What is it?" I repeated, with foreboding.

There was in my mother a well of darkness she was determined not to see. She stepped around it and gazed resolutely past it. This gave her a sunny temperament, twice-yearly migraines, and a low tolerance for bad news. When my brother and I were small, my father had cut disturbing articles from the newspaper before handing it over. She read around the holes scissored out of the pages. Through the years this story had been relayed as fact; recently I'd begun to suspect it was a family myth, or a onetime stunt recalled as a regular occurrence. In any case, it was a cruel irony no one had the heart to point out that the person who'd lost her own mother at the age of ten, the person who most feared calamity, would have to face the death of her only granddaughter.

"Lightning strikes twice."

"What did you say?"

She angled a weak smile up at me. "Lightning strikes twice."

"I was just thinking that." I passed her a tissue. We both kept one on our person at all times. I returned to my chair to give her some privacy.

"I've been thinking about my mother," she said slowly. "I don't know why."

"Has something happened?"

"Everyone loved her. My father never recovered, you know."

"Of course not. Of course he didn't."

"My mother never met you. She never had the pleasure of being a grandmother."

"No."

"*Never* is an awful word, Eve. I hate that word."

"Me too," I said.

"It's a great pleasure, you know, being a grandmother."

"Yes," I said. "I was looking forward to it." My grandmother had been bedridden for a year and died of a lung ailment she would no doubt have survived today. "It must have been terrible for you. Beyond terrible."

"Oh, I had Aunt Jean." That's what she always said when the subject came up. "Aunt Jean was wonderful to me."

"Yes. You said." A vision of Maddy came to me, ten years old, in her sky-blue leotard, ponytail swinging to her unself-conscious twirls and jumps. At least she'd had me right to the end.

"I didn't lose a child," said my mother. "I never lost you. Or Chris. That would have been unendurable."

The air was thin as mountaintop air. "I've endured it."

"You astonish me," said my mother. "How you've faced this. How you've survived." She paused. "It just makes me sad you don't have that comfort."

"What comfort?"

"The comfort of faith."

She had said this before in different ways. I was accustomed to indulging her. I had not minded taking Maddy to their church when she

271

was small. I let her make what she would of the language and the imagery. Belief belonged to my childhood, after all, and I was grateful for the sense, so deeply part of me, that what we can see is not all there is. Through the nightmare of Maddy's death, I had leaned on my mother and let myself be soothed by her devotional murmurings. What counted was the tone and the intention. If my mother was held up by God, she could hold me up. I did not care. I could not judge.

"It doesn't matter," said my mother hastily.

My heart was beating in my ears. "Maybe it does, Mom."

"What I meant was, I wish that was something you and I could share."

"I know you do," I said. "Sorry."

My mother only smiled a little, running her thumb and forefinger around the handle of her mug. "You were such a curious child, Eve. Always turning your head to see another side to things. 'Open the curtains,' you'd say. 'The nighttime wants to come in.' You found your father's cap out in the rain. 'Look! It's Daddy's old, dead hat!' "

"Maybe," I said slowly, thinking of that sepia person in her shapeless dress, hair crimped into earmuffs, smiling the enigmatic smile of early death, "what gets pushed down comes up somewhere else."

"What do you mean?"

"I can't imagine losing your mother and having to pretend it's in your best interest."

"I'm not pretending."

"*Believe* it's in your best interest."

But even as I spoke, I could feel the tangle of my own erroneous logic. By the lake with Norma it was: Maddy's death was preordained! The snake got the baby birds! There's nothing wrong with *as if!* In the presence of my mother, it was: Drop the wishful thinking! No higher meanings! No mysterious patterns! And back again: Had we brought this on ourselves? Was she taken away because we didn't deserve her? Once a thing happens to you, you become the kind of person that things happen to.

"I can't explain it, Eve. I don't know what it's about or how it affects anything else in my life. All I know is, my faith is something essential to me. It's in a box over here"—with both hands she set down her invisible box—"and I need it. Selfishly, for myself."

"Well!" I said. "I can't argue with that."

She smiled at me. "Maddy found some solace in it."

The beating started up again, gong-like in my ears. "How do you know?"

"She came to church with us. It meant something to her."

"Of course it meant *some*thing to her. She liked going out with you and Dad."

"I'm so glad."

My eyes settled on the ridges and gullies of my mother's hands curved around her cup. Eventually age brings all the bones to the surface. "It was the music, Mom. Maddy loved the music. Did you notice she only went to church when there was a concert?"

She shook her head, keeping her body unnaturally still.

"Maddy had her own mind. But she liked to please. She didn't want to disappoint anyone. Just don't tell me you know what she was thinking. Do you remember that time we stayed overnight and you were talking to Maddy about God?"

Rose nodded vaguely. Maddy had been six. From the landing I'd listened to my child's reedy voice and my mother's resonant one singing "All Through the Night," a lullaby I too had been raised on. I heard Rose explain that she loved Maddy and so did God, and He would watch over her while she slept.

"Mom . . ." Maddy said to me afterward, "what happens if you don't *like* God?"

The words hung in the air between us. In slow motion, without a sound, my mother's face deformed into a rictus of despair. She held out as long as she could, fighting for mastery, until with jerky in-breaths and a toss of her hands, she began to cry as she had never cried before, not through the year of Maddy's illness, not during the service, not in the long cold months since, when she was being strong for me. The wordless keening went on and on, as though she had drilled through to a secret source of fuel, while across from her, patting her soft-boned hand where it lay on the table, I watched with alarm and envy this act of nature that I had set in motion and was powerless to stop.

My mother grew quiet. She withdrew her hand and blew her nose.

"Goodness." Her blank eyes looked through me. "Goodness! Where did that come from?"

"Where do you think it came from?"

Now she fixed a hungry gaze on my face. "How," she said, in little above a whisper, "can a person just disappear? It makes no sense."

"Blame God," I said briefly, "not yourself."

"Don't be angry, Eve."

"I'm not." I squeezed her hand. "I'm not." But I was. Underneath my compassion for what my mother had lost and her wrangles with her faith, deep inside my answering grief, I was unreasonably, ungenerously, incurably angry. Mine had just happened. Mine was maternal, the worst kind. I would go under if I had to take on hers too.

"Thank goodness you have Robin!" declared my mother. "Dear, dear Robin."

"Mom," I said, "I'm going to London."

"London?"

"For work."

She looked confused.

"I ran the idea past Claire today. I think she'll go for it."

"Well, good for you, sweetie," she said dully. "That's exciting."

"There's another reason."

"What's that?"

"I want to look up Antonio."

Surprise barely registered on my mother's face. "Walter told me about the letters."

"He did?"

"Don't be mad at him, Eve."

So they had discussed it and arrived at the party line: I was not to be mad at my father. My family spent all their time making sure no one got angry with anyone else. Anger had certainly been in the air when I told them I was going to raise my child without a father. Walter's jaw made of stone, Rose's blurry eyes avoiding mine. They rallied soon enough, and stood behind me, and loved Maddy more than anything, but even so, at the time I had delivered a blow to their life plan.

"You didn't know Maddy and Antonio were in touch?"

"I had no idea. Your father sure can keep a secret."

"So could Maddy."

"Walter said he was kind to her. It was a good

thing she wrote to him. Is that the way you see it? He's not just saying that to justify himself?"

"They wrote back and forth for months. It seemed pretty friendly."

"I just hope Maddy got something from it," said my mother hoarsely.

"Oh, she did!" I leapt on that. "I think it was very important to her."

"Antonio." My mother frowned. "After all this time! Have you thought this through, Eve?"

"I can get his side of the story, at least."

She gazed at me for a moment, her anguish subdued in the lifelong habit of counsel. "Is that really why you want to go, sweetie? To get his side of the story?"

The back door scraped open and the hallway was filled with panting dog.

"Well, why else would I be going!"

"You know best, Evie," said my mother, and I let her pat my arm. My father stood in the doorway, his glasses steamed over from the cold, stamping his shoes, peeling off his gloves, oblivious to what had just taken place.

Maddy

24

So, the place turned out to be awesome. Robin came up with the plan to go, the three of us, on a Friday to avoid the weekend crowds and to fit it in before I went for scans and blood work Monday morning. My mother loved Fallingwater. Robin had never been, and I had gone once when I was eleven. My main memory was of a white-haired lady in the gift shop who let me go behind the counter and punch numbers into the cash register.

The visitor center was in the middle of the forest and made of raw wood. Ramps went up to it on three sides, like it was a waiting spaceship, and there were three pods: a museum in one, a café in one, and the gift shop in the other, where my mother almost bought something for holding letters, with carving on the sides like stained glass windows. She said she didn't get many letters these days. I said that's not the point, Robin said go for it, but then we had to rush to get to the tour and she put it back. My mother can be too reasonable. She denies herself things.

"You'll love this place," I told Robin on the ramp where our group was assembling.

"I do already. Why?"

"All the wood."

"The house isn't made of wood," said my mother. "Remember? It's concrete. The only thing I'm not sure about is the color."

"What color?" asked Robin.

"Pink."

"Pink?" he said. "You didn't tell me that. I would have stayed home."

Frank Lloyd Wright may have been Mr. Harmony-with-Nature, but our tour guide was wearing mascara an inch thick and gold strappy sandals. I guess if it's your job, being natural must get tiring. Her name was Laura. She said her words of welcome, and off we went down some steps that had a birch railing, to a dirt path leading around to the house. To give her credit, Laura glanced once at the scarf on my head, knotted at the side like a pirate's, and after that she treated me like everyone else, except I could see her deliberately slowing down and waiting for the three of us to join the group before she started her next talk. We were always the last ones.

July had been the month of hugs, starting from the moment Dr. Osterley said this new treatment might be doing the trick, and my mother exploded laughing and weeping at the same time. As for me, I searched Dr. O's brown eyes for, I don't know, some kind of sign that meant my body was mine again, but his were the eyes of a man who had seen everything and knew to hold himself back. Sure enough, halfway through August, just when I was daring to think about eleventh grade, the fevers started. The night sweats started. The bruises came. I was as tired as I'd ever been, tired as I would always be.

Robin had a very natural way of helping me. He put his hand on my shoulder as we descended, or around my back when we were on level ground, and he took my arm when Mom was on the other side. He carried the folding stool for when I needed a rest. He set it up, clowning around like I was a queen and he was a servant waiting on me hand and foot. I had no idea if Antonio was the kind of father who put his hand on your shoulder, or whether he would even want to visit a place like Fallingwater, let alone help me down the steps. Antonio would be much taller beside me, and when people saw us together they would know we were father and daughter. But the fact was, I liked Robin and sometimes I even loved him. There was no use wishing things were some other way.

We stopped on the bridge. Robin unfolded the stool, and I divided my attention between the water and the house that leaned dangerously out over it. Okay, imagine a lot of huge concrete shoe boxes clamped together at different heights. Windows in the slits between them. Gray stone chimneys. All balanced like a shelf over a fast-moving stream, and not only a stream but a two-level waterfall that actually goes right under the house so the crashing never stops. The house and the falls were very clear and real to me, now that I was five years older. Five years from now I'm sure I could remember every single detail, not just the gift shop. Which was why I went back and forth from wanting to memorize the place to thinking, What's the point? Just let the water run.

"Something, isn't it?" Mom said when Laura had finished her speech about cantilevered trays, local sandstone, European Modernism, structural daring, and the annex for guests and servants.

"It's not pink," I said. "It's kind of orange."

"It's pinker around the back," said my mother. "Down below where all the pictures are taken, it's totally gray. We'll go to the viewing point after the tour, if we're not too tired."

While we were sitting on some low walls behind the terrace, I asked Laura about the color. She said it was so the building would blend into its surroundings when the leaves changed in the fall. I nodded, but to me it seemed odd to have a house you can't stand the color of for most of the year, just so it looks good in the fall. And anyway, since when are leaves pink? But the fact was, once we were inside the house, it didn't matter about the color and the concrete. This was what we'd come for.

The living room was a huge horizontal space with light coming in everywhere and glass doors that opened onto a balcony above the falls. From the balcony there were steps going down. It was spooky the way the steps ended in this little platform that went nowhere and didn't even have a rail around it. You could drink your coffee there in the morning with your feet in the moving water. That's what the guide said. Back indoors we were shown the bedrooms, which were on different mezzanines. Wherever you went, you could see another part of the house and a part of the outdoors.

I couldn't wait to get back to the main room, and I could see by my mother's face she felt the same. She wandered around in a trance while I rested on my stool, because you're not allowed to sit on any of the furniture. My mother came over and squeezed the knot of my scarf and hovered her hand absentmindedly over my head without touching it. I knew she was thinking about Monday. I knew she was wishing she could forget about Monday and sit on one of the sofas, take a book down from the shelf, and read it leaning on a red cushion by the fireplace built in to the rock, and whenever she felt like it, she could go to the glass doors and presto: her very own waterfall rushing down.

"Could you live here?" said my mother, to no one in particular.

Robin came up from behind and kissed her hair. "*You* could."

"But could you?"

"I don't know," he said. "I've never seen anything like it."

"I've always loved this place," said my mother. "Ever since my parents brought us when we were kids. There's something incredibly peaceful about it."

"Except for the noise," I pointed out. "I'd want to switch it off sometimes. Wouldn't you?"

"I guess so," said my mother. "It might get on your nerves, in the long run. If you know there's no stopping it."

We made our slow way back to the parking lot, having taken leave of Laura and the group. We decided to skip the viewing point. We had seen that view on every single fridge magnet and bookmark in the gift shop. Besides, I was exhausted, and we had the long drive home.

I didn't say this, because my mother doesn't know I do it, but on the way back I was thinking there would be one advantage of living over a noisy waterfall. You wouldn't have to take a shower every time you wanted to have a long, private cry.

Maddy,

These questions you ask me! My boys want to know facts and how things work. I am maybe finding out how different girls are. Part of it is because you are almost an adult and thinking about all the important things, like who are we, what are we made of, what are we like? Am I a loner? My work requires me to be on my own a lot. But I am also part of a team. A family is another kind of team. Though there are times I could do with more time to myself! To be honest I think I might be the odd one out. Erica is very sociable, she loves talking and meeting with people, and the boys have lots of friends. Whereas I like my own company.

As for your other questions, I think that is something for your mother to tell you about. It was a long time ago. I want you to know that I am happy that you got in touch with me, and that I can get to know you a little through these emails. There is of course a lot more to say! Who knows, maybe it will be possible to meet each other one day. It is much easier to talk about complicated things in person.

Antonio

Dear Maddy,

I am impressed by how much you are doing. Music, art, a campaign, not to mention your schoolwork. How do you fit it all in? You must have a lot of energy.

My sons are getting ready to start school again. They complain about the end of the summer but I think secretly they are glad to get back and see their friends. Are you looking forward to school starting? What classes are you taking this year? How is Jack? I would love to hear your news.

Antonio

25

When my cat ventures into an unfamiliar place, she takes a few steps, turns around, and sniffs the doorway to identify her escape route. Then she finds the lowest surface to sit under and stays put. Nothing can get to her while she figures out where she is and what's what. After the visit to Fallingwater, and the day Dr. O told us we were out of options and my mother completely lost it, they dismantled Robin's table and moved my bed down to the dining room, and I took up residence there on millions of pillows. I was right in the middle of the house and whatever was going on. But I felt like I was under a low surface, waiting.

At first, Jack's voice lifted my spirits like nothing else. So did the sight of him in the doorway, taller than before and softer around the eyes. He was more polite with adults than ever. It was as if he had become a concentrated version of himself. He sat by my bed, entertaining Cloud, holding my fingers lightly in his half-closed hand, and playing our favorite YouTube clips, of the lion ecstatically reuniting with the people who had raised him from a cub, and dogs running the wrong way on escalators. Before, when we laughed at the clips, I wanted the lion and the dogs as pets. Now I wanted to be them.

Over the summer, Jack had gone on vacation and we'd barely had a chance to talk about junior year and what it might be like back at school now that we were together. Good thing, really. Without saying too much, we could just slip from the in-between state we'd been in all along, to my new existence in the dining room, a place so wrong for a bed it hardly called to mind the other uses of beds.

One afternoon after we'd looked at everything we could think of online, and said what there was to say about the march to the White House, my animation, which thank goodness was more or less finished, Jack's classes, and the kids we both knew, he sat very still in the chair, his hands on his knees. "Maddy . . ." he began. *"Dearest."*

"Yes, Jack? *Beloved.*" After our visit to the lake, we'd taken to calling each other things like that. "What's on your so-called mind?"

It burst out of him. "Junior year is horrible!"

"SATs?" I said.

"I can't wait for high school to be over."

"You've got college to look forward to . . ."

I watched his eyes fill with tears. "I'm going to hate it, you know."

Sometimes when Jack was with me he looked normal, and sometimes like he'd been hit in the head and was just coming to, but he never cried.

"I know. I know you are." I put on a voice like a mother patting a little kid. I pulled one of his hands close and studied the smooth tanned skin of his knuckles and pressed the pad of each finger. His hands were small for a person of his height, but they were hefty next to mine. Every shadow and crease of his skin looked supersharp in what seemed to be not really daylight, but not any other kind of light either. "Wouldn't it have been great?" I said, fitting his palm to the side of my face and keeping it there. Never let him go.

Jack reclaimed his hand and stood up. He unlaced his running shoes and came over and stretched his long body beside me on the bed, making murmuring noises. The vibration of his voice box tickled my neck, so I laughed and he laughed, and we lay like that for a long time, until his hands started moving over me, sleepily, in the old way. I closed my eyes and took what strength I could from the pressure of Jack's hands and the smell of his T-shirt and his voice. As if all we had to do was get through this and everything would be fine. As if he were still mine.

"My mother's in the house," I whispered.

She appeared in the archway of the kitchen, summoned by my thoughts, and retreated just as abruptly. I pulled away and told Jack my stomach hurt. He scrambled to his feet and stood by the bed, looking lost. My stomach was hurting for real now. That awful punched ache of fear. Ever since we met, I'd done what I could to make myself totally special to Jack. First, best, only. I caught his hand and swung it and kissed it. What good was that for either of us now?

In the evenings, Robin took to leaving the music room door open. If I yelled, or croaked, rather, "What was *that?*" he played the piece again for me, adding his commentary. "Listen to that transition. Stealthy or what? Sneaking up on you . . ." Or: "Everything's sweet until that E natural. That's where the doubt comes in. That E natural will break your heart . . ."

I had avoided the Brahms C-major Trio because Robin was always talking it up, but on one of my good days he made me listen from beginning to end and I went OCD on the scherzo. I played it over and over on my phone. The violins crazily stacking things up, the piano knocking them down . . . and at the end the cello making a point of telling me that no matter what happened or how sad it got, the world was beautiful and I was safe. It was like being chased uphill and running downhill into the arms of your mother. I wasn't too proud to tell Robin that. He might have been the only one I could tell.

Fiona and Vicky came less often and did more of the talking. Vicky had split up with Wade and was going out with Kevin Stockhaus, who was nineteen and doing drama at the conservatory.

"He is so smart. Not to mention drop-dead

gorgeous. We have *so* much in common." She found a picture on her phone and passed it to Fiona, who passed it to me. I raised my head to look and I had to admit *gorgeous* was no exaggeration. Curly hair, rectangular smile, muscular neck. Unlike the ones she usually went for, he looked like a truly nice guy. You can tell by the eyes. Maybe Vicky would get *her* heart broken this time.

I handed the phone back, catching sight of my bony arm as I did so. I was the reason for their visit, but I felt like everyone belonged here except me. I let the pillow take my head. "Are we going to meet him?" I said.

"Definitely. Whenever you want."

"So what's his USP?" asked Fiona.

"His Unique Selling Point," Vicky confided, lowering her voice in case my mother was around, "is his big c . . ."

Fiona was hooting.

". . . car. Family size," whispered Vicky, and the two of them collapsed in their chairs, screaming soundlessly.

When she could speak, Fiona gave a moan. "I'm dying here."

"I'm done." Vicky wiped her lower lids one at a time with the back of her finger. "I am so, so done."

"Are you okay, Maddy?" Fiona's voice floated near. "Did you hear that?"

Her elfin face was above me, ready to do whatever I asked. I longed for both of them to go.

"My hearing's perfect."

"Want some coffee?" asked Vicky behind her. "I can get us some coffee."

"No, thanks. But go in the kitchen and make some. Mom won't mind."

"I love your mother. She's so chill."

"Mine would be a basket case," said Fiona. "I'd be taking care of her."

"What happened to Billy and Carina?" I asked to change the subject.

"She got sick of waiting for him to make a move."

"He's got his eye on Lucy Wall now. I said he could aim a little higher on the food chain, but he won't listen."

"All our experience and good advice," I murmured. "Gone to waste." What was the point in having experience, when I wouldn't be able to use it now?

Fiona was still standing over me. "How's Jack, anyway?"

"Okay."

"Just okay?" I could feel the intensity of her gaze.

"Sometimes I don't want to see him."

"You always want to see us," said Vicky.

"It's not like you have to do anything," said Fiona. "He can just sit and look at you."

"I don't want him to sit and look at me!" I shut my eyes. There was a lot going on in the darkness. Pulsating lines, and tunnels inside other tunnels, and red shooting stars. "I can't take the expression he gets."

"Girls are stronger than boys," Vicky said at last.

"They are?" *Weak* was not the word. I was a balloon all the air had gone out of. Halfway through September, we thought I might get to the first part of the march to the White House, but then I landed back in the hospital, and now I couldn't even get to the bathroom on my own. Sometimes I couldn't lift my arm to hold a glass. I pictured Vicky flinging her shawl of black hair over one shoulder and exchanging looks with Fiona, who had left my side and would be sitting on the desk chair, hugging her knees. "Guess what," I said.

"You're getting married," said Fiona.

I opened my eyes. She was checking a handful of her pale hair for split ends.

"You're getting divorced," said Vicky, scrolling down her phone.

"What, then?" asked Fiona.

"They're showing my animation at the march. Two whole minutes of it."

They looked up together and stared.

"Wow, Maddy!"

"Oh my god. You didn't tell us. Why didn't you tell us?"

"Miss Sedge did it all. Mom signed off on it this morning. We're going to watch it on TV."

"What's the animation about? You never told us."

"You'll see. Promise you'll watch? I'll be a celebrity. For two minutes."

"Longer than that," said Vicky confidently.

"It'll go viral," said Fiona. "Eternal fame."

Maddy,

I have not heard from you in quite a while. Is everything OK in Washington?

Antonio

Hello Maddy,

I wonder if you might have told your mother we were writing, or maybe she found out and that's why you've stopped writing. Just a guess! I know I said I would answer any questions you had and I meant that, but maybe I did not take into account the kinds of questions you have. I'm sorry I could not give you a fuller answer to the story of your mother and me. I will try.

Antonio

A day or a week, or maybe a year later, it was getting hard to tell, Mom said gently, next to my ear, that Fiona and Vicky were there to see me. I shook my head no. Are you sure? I was sure. I tried to explain that I had nothing more to say, and no room inside me to listen. I saw tears standing in my mother's eyes. I think she understood. I had to put Fiona and Vicky in a place where hypothetically I could still laugh with them and argue with them and be best friends forever, but the time had come to turn my attention elsewhere.

Another day, Jack said: "Everything's ready."

His broad face close to mine, shiny bangs he flicked out of his eyes with a scissoring gesture. Crew cuts felt like moss. He used to let me touch his. Maybe deep down we knew what would happen, way back then. "What's ready?"

"For the march. Next week, remember? We've got the portable toilets lined up. We've got the marshals trained. Fences, everything." Jack's smile squinted his eyes, giving him a look of good-humored know-how. I loved that about his face. "Your animation will go on before the speeches. Miss Sedge is totally cool. I can't wait . . ." He was happier than I'd seen him in a long time. "I just wish . . ." he began, bending down to pet Cloud, and instead of finishing his sentence he took off his shoes and came over and climbed onto the bed. I welcomed him in, though

297

my instinct was to shrink away. He was nestling against me, pressing his leg protectively over mine, when without a second's warning even to turn my head, I threw up.

Jack leapt to his feet and was laughing and plucking Kleenex from the box in handfuls when my mother came in. I started crying harder than I cried when Dr. O gave us the news. I didn't care who saw. Enough is enough. He would get used to it and he would get over it. While my mother changed the sheets, Jack went out to take off his stinking shirt, and I never let him back in.

Hospice nurses were like ghosts coming and going, tugging me gently around, putting straws to my lips and pillows between my knees and fiddling with my chest port. One said "upsy-daisy" when she turned me over, one had chapped hands, one spoke like Lisa Simpson, but there was no getting to know them. I had to just let it happen. Breathing was easier if I didn't think about it. Grandma and Grandpa and Robin were nearby, but I guess at a time like this you need one person, and that person was my mother, my amazing, incredible, irreplaceable mother. I couldn't have gotten through one day of this without her, even though I never knew what her face would be like when she came into the room, or what I could and could not afford to say. I couldn't say: Being a kid was the best part. It was worth it for that. I couldn't say: You'll have to tell Antonio. I couldn't say: Wow. Can you believe this is what my whole life was leading up to? Because I think my mother was still holding out for good news. My mother did not know how to stop fighting. Maybe mothers never do.

Grandpa. Mom and Grandma. Robin and Mom. They appeared above me, one by one or two together, against fields of swaying stems or with melting edges, and they departed just as suddenly as the pain returned. Every time, it took me by surprise. Who would want to do this to me? Because my body was no longer divided into parts where pain could be confined, it bullied and burned its way through to where I really lived.

"Has she had her twelve o'clock?"

"Now."

"Turn it on."

The black screen lit up, filling the room with images and noise.

"Where's Jack?" I asked in my new thick voice.

"Out there in the crowd."

"I want to see him. Will I see him?"

"Keep watching. You might."

I could hear my mother was telling me a white lie. It was all white lies now. The people were colored particles, thousands of them, moving like a huge, slow liquid in the space between the buildings. I was hypnotized by the patterns the liquid made flowing forward. Jump to a stage, with faces below, waiting. The screen back of the stage came to life.

"Look," said Grandma. "Is that it?"

My mother was behind me on the bed, holding me up.

"That's it," said Grandpa.

"An animation by Madeleine Wakefield," my mother read off the screen, her arms snug around me, her voice vibrating through my back.

My face appeared, towering over the people on the stage, and then filling up our television screen.

"Who's *that?*" I said. "Who did that?" The gigantic pencil-drawn me was so familiar, every line and smudge of it, but it seemed as though someone older and smarter than me had made it.

My mother swapped a glance with Robin. "That's you, Maddy."

"That's your animation," he said soothingly.

"I know it is."

I'd been half-asleep, drifting and bobbing along with the crowd, but now I was wide awake. There was my head. There were my lips, smiling mysteriously because I knew something no one else knew. There was the earth on top of my skull, with its miniature cities and mountains and trees, and there were my eyes closing in slow motion like I was entering a dream.

Gaps opened up on the surface of the earth.

Only a few patches to begin with, nothing too alarming. But it was like Robin's E natural, that first note of doubt. Gradually the gaps got bigger and ran together, gobbling everything in their way, and at the same time my face below started to crumble. That was the statue coming in. Gouge into the wet paint, let it dry, draw over the ridges. When the whole earth was bare and the beautiful forests and lakes and streets and schools were gone, the sea rose across the earth and blotted everything out.

The clapping went on and on, in our dining room and on the television, and it bubbled into every corner of my heart, swelling it to twice its normal size. They knew. They saw. All because of this thing that I'd made. I was out in plain sight with everyone bearing me up, but at the same time I was disappearing into my unreachable self, the place where no one could ever find me. I knew then that if there was no point in hoping for what I really wanted, I could always hope for something else.

Hi Maddy,

Have I said something to annoy or upset you? I really hope not. But if I have, my sincere apologies. I'm so glad you contacted me. Just say if you don't want me to write anymore. That is absolutely fine. I understand.

All the very best
Antonio

Dear Maddy,

As I have not heard from you in seven weeks—nearly eight—I can only think that you have decided not to write to me for now. Did I put you off when I suggested we might meet one day? Anything like that would be entirely up to you. I won't write again until I hear from you. Please know I will be so happy any time you want to get in touch.

Love from
Antonio

Eve

26

When I put the idea to Alison, she slouched down on the office sofa and tried to talk me out of it.

"People don't just do things. *Why* do you want me to come with you?"

"Most people would give anything for a trip like this."

"I'm not most people."

"I know that."

"Take Melissa. It would be a great opportunity for her."

"I'm not taking Melissa. She doesn't even *like* art."

"How do you know?"

"Has she ever defended it from a lunatic with a gun?"

In the end Alison said yes. It was arranged that we would stay in the home of Philippa, an educator I'd met years ago at a conference. Once the interview contacts had been made and the flights booked, I felt as though some brake had been released and the train I was on was lurching slowly forward. Robin and I started making love again early in the morning when we were only half-awake. It hurt me to see the leap of surprise in his eyes when I reached for him, to hear the softness in his voice when we lay together. Did I give myself away? Could he tell that in the part of me that was not already occupied by Maddy, I was hollowing out a space for someone else?

As November approached, I took the encounters that came my way as signs.

While driving near the high school I spotted Fiona and Vicky on the sidewalk with a girl I didn't know. Fiona was balanced on one leg demonstrating a ballet position, her pale hair curved around her face in a new way. She wobbled and fell theatrically into the arms of the other girl, and Vicky raised her head from her phone at the right moment to laugh.

Fiona had always been my favorite of Maddy's friends, an imp as a child, tart and quirky as she grew. Vicky's more self-sufficient bearing came, I thought, from her large Italian family: she didn't need any more adults in her life. Yet it was Vicky who treated me in the most natural way after Maddy died, not distant at all but warm and solicitous and Catholic in her instinct for ritual and ceremony, weeping openly and speaking of Maddy as though she were in another room. The girls came to see me a number of times after the service, and then their visits dropped off, as their visits had dropped off even before Maddy turned them away.

Her refusal had grieved and bewildered them. I tried to soften it, to explain that she was drawing away from everyone and everything. Two days before she died, Fiona and Vicky showed up with a homemade banner—*We love you, Maddy!!!*—mounted on stakes they insisted on hammering into the lawn under the dining room window. "Do you think she can see it from here?" They conferred, yanked up the sign, rehammered it. I didn't have the heart to tell them. By that time Maddy was barely conscious.

In the seconds it took to slow down and decide not to stop, I saw them clearly: two young women who would always hold pieces of Maddy, but who had accrued a year of extra life and moved on.

A week after the sighting of Fiona and Vicky, Jack and Glenda Sedge came to see me. An unlikely pair, Jack in his sweatshirt, Glenda in her tan coat, they followed me to the living room and settled on the couch. I sat opposite. I had last seen Jack in May, when he returned some drawings of Maddy's. Six months is a long time in the body of an almost-eighteen-year-old. He had bulked out in the chest, cut his hair, lost his pimples, and started to shave. Maddy would never know this composed young man.

"You've grown, Jack."

"I'm taller than my dad now."

"I didn't mean your height."

He flashed me his shy grin. "How are you?" He looked at his hands: a normal question with impossible answers.

"Fine."

He glanced up, relieved.

"We all miss Maddy," said Glenda Sedge in the gravelly voice that the cruel among her pupils no doubt taunted her for. "So much. You've been in my thoughts these months." Her brown eyes sought mine. I blinked away my customary response to uninvited warmth. Maddy too had been buoyed up by that voice and that smile.

"As you know, there was a huge response to Maddy's animation, even from people who didn't know the whole story."

"The clip went viral online," said Jack. "One week it was trending top ten on YouTube. We took it down," he added.

"At least she got to see it projected on the day," I said. "She heard the applause."

Maddy had been sleeping a lot by that time. We nudged her from her dream to watch the march live on television, pointing out the size of the crowds and taking turns to read the signs out loud: *No Oil in Our Soil. May the Facts Be with You. There's No Planet B.* She listened with an inward-looking smile. At one o'clock the speeches were streamed from a stage on Third Street. The last speaker introduced the animation with the words we had agreed on, and the screen at the back of the stage crackled to life. Maddy had been medicated and was resting her weightless self against me, her shoulders made of something flimsier than bone, her eyes in their shadows fastened to the television screen. As the applause went on and on, the joy on her face was something to behold.

"She went downhill so quickly after that," I said to Glenda. "I guess the whole thing went out of our minds."

"The idea of someone with so little time left not only pouring herself into a campaign, but making a film of such power. I don't have the words. The reason we're here," she continued smoothly, as if she had practiced this part, "is to see if we might use Maddy's animation again. It could be just as powerful now—"

"Now that she's gone?"

"If not more so," said Glenda Sedge. "There's the next publicity drive. There's the blog. There are events coming up."

They were both having trouble meeting my eye, whether out of respect for my silence or because I unnerved them. Jack leaned forward, his forearms resting on his parted knees, hands loosely linked between them. There was a new authority in the way he sat, and in the man's watch he wore low on his wrist.

After the vomiting incident, I'd had to tell Jack that Maddy couldn't see him anymore. *Couldn't,* I stressed, not didn't want to. There was no point in being as blunt as she was. It was too awful for them both, she said. What boy in his right mind wanted to be around this? She would send him away before he decided to stop coming. He would thank her one day.

But Jack did not give up easily. The doorbell rang and he faced me on the porch, hands thrust in his pockets, head at an awkward angle, lips set in a grimace to fend off tears.

"Maddy's sleeping a lot," I told him gently. "She's asleep now."

"Can I come back when she wakes up?"

"Next time," I said.

"Tomorrow?"

"Another time."

He turned up again the following day, and again I told him Maddy was asleep. The third time, with a stubborn jut of his chin, he asked if he could come in. I took him to the study. We sat together in our mutual and solitary despair. A few feet away, on the other side of the stairs, Maddy was dozing. I had no right to go against her wishes. His gaze flitted across my shelves and filing cabinets, the alarming stacks of paper on desk and floor that I was unable to put in order or care about. I don't think Jack had ever been in my study. They'd spent their time in Maddy's room or the den.

He was swallowing and blinking rapidly. This boy had loved her body, championed her art, kept her company in illness and relative health. She would haunt him for years to come. The fear on his face was my fear. I longed to seize Jack and hold him to me and be held, even as I fortified myself against him. I stood up, trembling.

"Do you want to see her?"

Dumbly he followed me to the dining room. Maddy was lying on her side, facing away from us. Her body hardly raised the covers. Now that treatments had stopped, her head on the pillow had new growth of soft furry brown, making it look even more tenderly skull-shaped.

"I'll be in the kitchen."

I never knew whether Jack woke Maddy up, or if he just sat watching her sleep. He appeared sometime later in the kitchen, completely dazed, thanked me, gave me a blind wordless hug, and rushed out.

Jack and Glenda Sedge were waiting for me to speak.

"I don't know," I said.

"It's her legacy," said Glenda.

The hands in her lap were as still as her face: the eyes widely spaced, the long upper lip forbidding when she didn't smile. I'd overheard Jack say that her students were her family. At least Maddy still existed for her. But was the film Maddy's legacy? Who was to say what Maddy's legacy was? Jack could be forgiven; he was young. Glenda Sedge was not, and she was a strong personality besides. Activists could be single-minded, obsessive, even. I knew Maddy had liked and respected her very much; but it was possible that, for her own reasons, the woman had persuaded Maddy to do what was needed for the campaign. This had not occurred to me at the time, so relieved had I been that she had companions and activities to throw herself into. I should have kept a closer watch.

Jack ventured: "She worked so hard on that thing. I know she wanted people to see it. She wanted it to be part of the campaign . . . Maddy was a fantastic artist. Everyone said so. She did it all, you know. I just helped on the technical side."

In the long dreamlike months after Maddy died, Jack had come to visit me, I don't know how many times. Through my delirium, I could see that being in our house was a compulsion and an agony for him. His face distorted horribly when he spoke of her. Now, nearly a year later, his gaze was clear, his features smooth and unmarked. Did he have a new girlfriend? Had he written Maddy into an adolescent myth of fate, sex, and death? I would never know and I shouldn't mind. It was what healthy young people did. One day the story would elicit the tenderness of his future wife, and he would seem deeper and more alluring because of it.

"She was very talented," I said. "But you did it together. She needed you, Jack." I saw in his eyes then a flicker of gratitude and concealed misery, a conduit briefly opened to the reservoir of his grief. The knowledge passed silently between us, making me glad, and guilty to feel glad, before he shifted his legs and the moment passed. But I knew without a doubt that Jack was a part of Maddy and one of her keepers, and so, in her own way, was Glenda Sedge.

"It's entirely up to you," said Glenda. "You and what Maddy would have wanted."

Would have: that detested phrase. "I'm not sure. I'll think about it."

After they'd gone, I went straight up to Maddy's room. Her laptop was on the floor of her closet. I plugged it in, powered it up, and entered the only password of hers that I knew. At least when it came to passwords, my daughter was predictable. Her desktop sprang to life with its rows of folders lined up on a cresting wave. Like me, Maddy preferred to have everything out where she could see it. I scanned the titles and opened the one called "Animation." Inside were multiple files. I chose the one called "final final final" and barely paused before clicking on the play arrow.

Maddy's eyes were level and calm, her lips bunched in a half smile. I had not seen this image since the day of the march. I could feel her slight weight against me. Impossible to move or look away or press stop. Applause had given the film a triumphant close. Now it unrolled in eerie silence until the land was shorn of life and the stone face below had crumbled pits for eyes. Watching it had hardly been bearable then, and it was hardly bearable now, seated alone in her empty bedroom. Her knowingness and candor and flair cut straight to the part of me that would never recover.

Before I could summon the energy to press pause, the image began to move. Was there more? There was more. The ruined face slowly smoothed itself into flesh and skin. The knobs of her eyelids opened. Jolt to the heart. Maddy was looking straight at me. Mama! Lips began to quiver. Help me! Eyes flared. Don't mess with me! Brows gathered. All is lost! It took very little for supplication to turn to defiance and defiance to despair. At the eyes and mouth, where most of the changes took place, the pencil gradually tore through the paper until all the features vanished and there was only an empty shape where she had been.

Enough! I should not be watching this. I should turn it off, refuse to look. But I was hungry for more. In front of me the image was changing again and all I wanted was to see what came next.

Marks appeared and began to circle the blankness in search of a worthwhile form. Slowly, sleepily, then faster and with greater purpose, the marks flew to their places, joining into lines and shadows, while the edges bulged to make way for a new kind of head. I caught my breath. I knew by heart those slits of eyes and that particular toothless laugh. "Was that really me?" Maddy would say, holding the old photograph like a holy relic in her hand. "I know it's me, but deep down I can't believe it."

Clearly she had used her own baby pictures for the drawings. But the more I stared, the less it looked like Maddy at any age. I had never seen a face like it. It was a child given over to a kind of laughter no child should know about, triumphant and without hope and indifferent to anything but its own release. While I had been downstairs loading the dishwasher, taking out the trash, assembling trays of crackers and soup that she would thank me for and leave untouched, she had been making this.

When Robin came home, I told him about my visitors and replayed the segment screened during the march. When the earth-head had been wiped clean of habitation, I pressed stop and closed the file.

"Whoa," said Robin hoarsely. "I'd kind of forgotten what it was like."

"Not easy to watch."

"Great that she made it. That she could make something like that."

"Should I let them use it?" I asked him.

"Why wouldn't you?"

"Well, why *would* I?"

I didn't show Robin the new ending. I copied the file to a memory stick and carried it around in my wallet. Whenever I had a private moment at work or at home, I watched the film, pausing the frames, speeding it up or slowing it down, and sometimes, with an image frozen on the screen, I would glance away and whip back to catch it unawares.

The defiant and despairing expressions were painful, the crumbling face filled me with horror, but at least I could understand them. I could not understand the laughing baby's head. And what kept me awake was this: If Maddy had left the ending for me to find, we were in some kind of bizarre and exhilarating contact. If she had made it for herself and herself only, I was trampling on her private life in a way I'd vowed never to do.

27

Thanksgiving came and went unmarked, as it had the previous year. We postponed our family dinner, until the anniversary of Maddy's death. That proved to be a mistake. I had not understood the strange power of calendar dates. The twenty-fifth of November rushed toward me like the edge of a cliff, and that morning the events were upon me as vividly as if they had just taken place.

As in those first terrible weeks, bed was a sanctuary and a trap. If I faced the wall, the frames of misery awaited me. If I faced the door, I could see people entering and leaving, in the weird light that precedes a storm, people who weren't Maddy and never would be Maddy.

"Wouldn't you feel better if you got up?" said Robin, stroking my forehead with one hand and my wrist with the other. "You don't have to do anything. Just come downstairs. Watch TV or something?"

Go over there. By that cloud. I'll swim to you.

"No, thanks."

"Sure? We miss you."

Close the curtains. Is it nighttime?

"Thanks, Robin. I'll be okay."

My father took my hand and held it, saying nothing.

He doesn't know, Mom. I wanted him to love me.

My mother's weight depressed the bed's edge. "You won't always feel this way, Eve. Believe me."

I smiled for her.

Water, please.

My mother stroked my hair. "Beth and her kids stopped by. Everyone's calling. Everyone's thinking about you."

"Tell them thank you. Tell them not today."

She tiptoed out. I turned to the wall.

"Spare me."

Spare me belief of any kind. In the unfathomable will, in appalling luck, in random error, in the life everlasting. Spare me belief that the complex universe can't fit our simple ideas, that bad things happen to good people, that the journey is the destination, the true body awaits, the veil is thrust aside, the person slips into the next room. Spare me belief in the futility of belief.

Spare me the casually alive sons and daughters of my friends. Acquaintances who turn away in banks and aisles with relief in their eyes only I can see, that it happened to her and not me. Spare me the solidification of time. The slackness of the house when I want it to resist me in a way I never asked for and could not foresee. Spare me the tedious sounds I make, and the silence.

Spare me fluorescent glare and aquarial gloom. Plastic tubing, peel-apart packets, fluid-filled sacks, machines that click, hum, suck, or drip; anything pointed, jointed, tapered, or interlocking; anything rubber-soled, rubber-wheeled, padded, or palliative or sterile or collapsible or disposable with extreme caution. Above all, spare me that morning in November, when bearing my tray of dispensables I closed in on the bed, and Maddy rotated her fragile head, and the whites of her eyes said, Spare me.

PART III

Eve

28

During the long wait at Dulles, I asked Alison the standard questions and she answered in a reluctant monotone. She'd grown up in Baltimore, youngest of a family of three, her mother an elementary school teacher like mine. Her father owned a liquor store that went under when she was eleven.

"People in DC all come from somewhere else," I said. "You and I are natives."

"I come from Baltimore."

"Close enough."

She had been something of a prodigy in high school and won a scholarship to Mount Holyoke. Her interest in art came from "just looking at things." When Alison was a junior in college, her father left the family for good, her mother moved to Detroit with another man, and Alison did not do as well as she'd hoped on her exams. Besides, there weren't any jobs out there for art history majors.

"Half the waiters in the country are art history majors," she informed me.

"I thought waiters were all actors."

"Whatever." She bit her nails and avoided my eyes. Maybe she felt exposed for having cut her hair and dressed up for the trip; her black jacket and white top looked brand-new. Maybe it was dawning on her that she was going to be stuck with me for a week in another time zone.

Once we were airborne, I said casually, "Alison, there's another reason I'm going to London."

"What."

"To see Maddy's father."

"Oh?"

"She never met him. He left when I was pregnant." I told her about finding their correspondence. I had been going through the letters again.

"Well, she had a stepfather, didn't she?"

This was not the point, I felt.

Her next question was: "Why do you want to see him?"

"Curiosity?" It was a ridiculous word.

"I mean, if he didn't stick around, he's just some poor guy who plunged when he should have jerked—"

"Alison . . . !"

"Just saying. I have a dad. He doesn't give two hoots about me." She undid her seat belt and peeled a stick of gum, offering me one she knew I'd refuse. "I thought Robin was nice."

"Do you have a boyfriend, Alison?"

"Hundreds."

"Robin *is* nice," I said, pleased for some reason that my partner passed muster.

Alison pulled the flight magazine from the seat

pocket and lowered her head. "What does he think about you going to London?"

"Oh, he's fine with it. Robin is very understanding."

She looked up. "Doesn't he mind you're going to see your ex?"

"No, Alison," I said patiently. "You've got the wrong idea. I'm not going to London to get together with Antonio."

"Well, what are you going for?"

I thought for a moment. "To punish him." Saying it felt daring and a little glamorous.

She gave me a long narrow look. "Wow," she said, flipping her pages rapidly. "You've got yourself one tolerant guy."

I flagged down the flight attendant. Tipping the miniature bottle of wine into the flimsy cup, I had to admit that the sense of purpose I'd been enjoying, landing this study trip and taking Alison with me, was starting to drain away. I put my head back and concentrated on the deep vibration of the plane and the sense that all accountability was, for a short while, suspended. I did not want to land. The further away, the more bearable the world became. Things acquired a pattern from the air that they did not have on the ground. I hardly thought of Antonio. He was in cold suspension somewhere, to be taken out and thawed at the last minute.

When we descended to Heathrow, fires were

blazing just beyond the curvature of the earth. What lay underneath was blurred in places by hanging nets of cloud. Eventually the dotted lines of London pierced the cloud for good. My heart quickened at the thought of arriving. Life, after all, cannot be lived at forty thousand feet. If I could not get off the planet, at least I was moving toward Maddy rather than away from her. Alison was silent, her forehead pressed to the window, absorbed in the sight. The city turned below, as if on a slowly spinning plate, and I saw that the lines of light were more crooked than the ones I had left behind, and uneven shapes of darkness lay between them.

29

I love having a boyfriend, but it's kind of strange. Boys are different from girls that's for sure! Sometimes I'm not sure what he wants or even what I want. Is it that way with everyone, the first time? Jack is always good to me! He is an incredibly nice person and a loyal person. I can't imagine him doing anything unkind. Ever. That is maybe almost a character fault! Just kidding. He thinks about things a lot and then decides what he's going to do. Some people just do what they want in the moment. My friend Vicky is like that, so I know. But she's very popular, everyone wants to be around her. Jack is more of a loner. Well, maybe we both are in a funny way. Maybe that's why we're together. What about you? Are you a loner?

As a meeting place I proposed the PizzaExpress on a quiet corner behind the British Museum. I'd stumbled across it on my first day of interviews. I did not want to be on Antonio's territory when we met. Nor did I want to aim too high in terms of venue. The arched windows and white and green tiles gave it the air of an upmarket restaurant in which decent wine would be served; nevertheless, it was still a pizza place.

I arrived early and found a table in the far corner with a view of the door. Walls were reassuring; corners were better. I shared mine with a metal plaque and a small stained glass window that had no light behind it. Above me hung a cluster of milk bottles made into a lamp. A waiter in a striped shirt and paper hat brought me a glass of wine. I studied the plaque. The building had once been the Dairy Supply Company, bringing high-quality milk from the countryside to London.

At five-thirty on a Thursday, only three tables were occupied. I was thankful that it was not the kind of place frequented by teenage girls. There was a family with a baby and two men in suits, arguing. At the window sat a pair of retired compatriots of mine, judging from their large-framed glasses and sensible shoes, and the self-conscious way they glanced around. I had already observed two kinds of Americans in London. One believed they had a right to be there by virtue of their ability to pay for things; the other knew they didn't belong, which gave them an endearing timidity. This couple and I were in the second category, although I was not merely a tourist. I had business in London; I was staying not in a hotel but in the home of a colleague. The father of my child lived here. The phrase had an antiquated ring to it: the father of my child.

Since Maddy died, I had become more timid in certain ways and more intrepid in others. There were times when I could not enter a room if more than two people were in it. There were times when the idea of answering the phone defeated me. And yet in my former life I would not have dared to make a trip like this, to take with me an eccentric stranger, and to wait by myself in a restaurant for the lover I had not seen in eighteen years.

Was it because nothing on earth mattered now, least of all what people thought of me? That was not strictly true. I had spent a long time at the mirror, preparing for Antonio. I'd arranged our meeting on a day when Alison was visiting her aunt in Norwich.

Against the Art Nouveau swirls painted on the windows, it was hard to spot the entrance of a particular individual while appearing not to be looking. People changed a lot in eighteen years. I had never been the kind of woman to dye my hair. I'd earned my threads of silver. I hoped Antonio had not married someone who went out of her way to hide her age.

The door opened. Two women deep in conversation made their way to a table by the window. My pulse slowly returned to normal. I had thought about this encounter for weeks. Dreamed it, planned it, refused to plan it, formulated sentences and facial expressions, mentally erased them, begun again.

To start: a dignified greeting between adults for whom bygones were bygones. Followed by: quiet appraisal. "I'm curious, Antonio . . . What was it about for you? What were you thinking?" My natural reticence, my skills in withholding and listening, would give him the chance to account for entering into a correspondence with Maddy behind my back, before I had to divulge anything myself. I would listen graciously as he spoke of his wife and children. Then I would tell him. My rehearsals never got past that point. Obviously it was better to inform him in person than any other way. That's what I had decided, and there was no going back on it now.

"Never?" I said. "You never, ever want to have a child?"

He paused long enough to tell me what I needed to know.

"What you mean is, you don't want to have one with me."

My triumph had been raising her on my own. After turning us down in favor of his own plans and interests, or what he took them to be, Antonio had burrowed back into our lives just when we were at our most defenseless. He was lucky I wanted to see him at all.

To keep my eyes from the door, I read the plaque again, concentrating on details I'd missed the first time. The squalid conditions in which urban cattle were kept. The unhealthy character of London milk. The cow with the iron tail—

He was beside me. He had slipped in. There

he stood, blocking the light and taking up all the air, his face a compelling variant of the one I had known so well. His hair was shorter and more barbered, the reddish brown sparked now with gray. His eyes sat more deeply in his head and were ringed with fine tucks and creases. I could not speak. The presence of this living, latter-day Antonio was wondrous and unreal, like seeing photographs of my parents in their youth, only in reverse. The table was between us. I forced myself to stand. As I stood, dread rushed in and I felt like I was in one of those dreams where I had committed an appalling act that could not be undone.

You can't give someone news like this in a pizza place!

Antonio moved toward me, extending his hands to take both of mine, a courtly gesture I remembered well. He lowered his gaze and raised it suddenly, a habit of Maddy's, and smiled at me with her shy, generous smile. The shame of it flooded through me: that Maddy had not made it, that I had brought her into the world and failed to save her, that her father was here and I could not show her to him.

When he saw I was crying in earnest, Antonio waved away the approaching waiter and stopped short of touching my arm, smiling no longer, bewildered at this turn of events and uncertain if he had a right to comfort me when we had not even said hello.

"She's gone." I fumbled in my bag so I would not have to look at him. "Maddy died."

I had never seen Antonio cry before, even in the stifled way he was doing now, clearing his throat and blinking it back, ashamed to let me see. The contortions rendered his face older and more haggard, and at the same time as innocent as a boy's.

"When, Eve?" he asked finally, fastening his eyes to mine. "What happened?"

He listened in silence while I told him about the year of Maddy's illness. I hated to hear myself state the facts so coolly, one event leading to another, fixed irreversibly in place. When his eyes watered, he looked away.

"She never told me. She said you had a friend who had cancer. Why didn't she tell me?"

I shrugged. "Why didn't she tell me she had found you?"

"She stopped writing suddenly."

"Was that in September? Over the summer things looked a little more hopeful. By September it had come back. They did the final scan and sent her home. She was very weak. We set up her bed in the dining room so she could be in the center of things."

"I'm so sorry, Eve. I can't believe it. I really can't believe it."

By the door, the American man was holding his wife's coat with home-on-the-range gallantry. I feared I would never see Antonio again, that this was all we would ever have. "This is strange!" I cried. "Isn't this strange?"

Antonio hailed the waiter, who did not react to our swollen faces. We sat in silence until the bottle appeared along with a bowl of stuffed olives. Antonio poured out the glasses, released his long legs, and sat sideways, one hand on the chair back, the other doing finger exercises on the table.

"You're thinner, Eve."

"You're the same, Antonio. Almost."

"Am I?"

"I shaved my head when Maddy started chemo."

"Your long hair . . ." he began, and did not finish.

"She made me grow mine back."

"Oh, E-vie . . ." He separated the syllables of my name in the old way. That's when I knew that intimacy cannot be undone.

"I wanted to tell you in person."

"Yes."

"I only recently found out you were writing to her."

"I'm sorry," said Antonio. "I'm sorry you didn't know."

"Can you imagine what it was like to find out after she was gone? Never to have the chance to talk to her about it?"

"I wanted her to tell you," he said. "I stopped writing for a while, to give her a chance to tell you."

"But she didn't."

"No."

"And you started again. Maybe you were happy to leave me out of it."

"You've seen the letters," he said. "She was very stubborn."

"She thought it was only fair if you told your family about her."

"I wanted her to tell you," he repeated.

"Well, good for you! And did you tell your wife about Maddy?"

"Not yet."

"Not yet. Were you going to?"

"I wanted to see you first."

"Are you going to now?"

"I am thinking about it."

"You're thinking about it."

"Yes."

"And what exactly are you thinking?"

He pulled a face that once would have made me laugh. He always tried to humor his way out of a tight spot.

"Did you want a private relationship with Maddy? Just the two of you?"

"No, Eve . . ."

"It's easy to impress a young person. With her fantasies of what a father is. When she's never had one."

I remembered well that skeptical retraction of the chin, the indulgent frown. "You're so angry," said Antonio quietly. "Who wouldn't be? The fact is," he went on, spacing his words, "Maddy's the one who wrote to me. She was the one deciding who knew and who didn't know."

I let my voice go soft. "I'm glad for Maddy's sake she got to know you before she died. I truly am. I wouldn't be here otherwise."

"You are?" said Antonio. "Oh, I wish she had told me she was sick!"

"What difference would it have made?"

His eyes watered again. "I don't know. The questions she asked me! Did I think there was life after death! I thought they were just the usual teenage questions. I would have answered in a different way. It seems like such a . . . brave thing to do. Write to me but hide the most important thing."

"The most important thing?"

"Such a thing," he said hastily.

"She was very proud. The last thing she wanted was for people to feel sorry for her. She went ballistic if she thought someone was being nice to her just because she had cancer. She longed for a father. It was a shadow over her, growing up."

"Eve," he said. "You have to remember—"

"Maybe she wanted to make sure you didn't pity her. Or maybe," I said, "it was her way of getting even."

He leaned forward until I could see the amber light in his Maddy-gray eyes.

"I thought there was plenty of time. I thought she stopped writing because she had second thoughts. Or I had offended her somehow. Or she told you, and you didn't like it. I had no idea. I was only guessing." He rubbed the back of his neck. "It got to me, you know. She got to me."

"You have your own children."

"I don't have a daughter."

"You thought you'd borrow mine?"

He held my gaze for a long moment, his lips gathered into an expression I couldn't read. He squinted at the ceiling. "Are those milk bottles?"

"This place used to be a dairy." I pointed to the metal plaque. "I memorized that while I was waiting. Ask me anything."

Eyes on the light fixture, he said: "I've thought about you a lot over the years, you know. If you want the truth, Eve, I thought one day we would all meet. When Maddy was older. Remember, it was a shock for me, the first time she wrote."

"Oh, was it?"

"Erica knew nothing."

The casual way he inserted her name in our conversation stung me. "You know," I said slowly, "there's something I'm not getting here. People find each other these days. Maddy was planning to contact you when she was eighteen. When I could be sure she really wanted to."

He was staring at me.

"What?" I snapped. "You knew you had a child out there. You could have found us first." I understood then that for the whole of Maddy's life I had been waiting for Antonio to find us.

In a voice hoarse with wonder, he said: "But I thought you were getting rid of it!"

"*It?*"

"Her," he said humbly.

"Never! I never wanted an abortion!" The women at the nearest table glanced our way. I lowered my voice to a hiss: "I told you that."

His face was darkening slowly. "Yes, I know, but you changed your mind. That's what you told me," he said. "When you left."

What could I do but shake my head?

"You did, Eve!" His face was distorted, strange. "I kept calling you up, many times."

"Once."

"Lots of times! I can't believe this. I can't believe you're saying this! I left messages on the machine. I went by your apartment looking for you. I left notes."

"I'd gone to stay with my parents. I was sick of talking about it. What was the point? You'd made your position clear."

He studied me for a moment, before casting his eyes down. In a low, reluctant voice, he said: "I think I kind of froze. You know? I was so sure I did not want to become a father. It was not in my"—he smiled unhappily—"life plan. At that time I was obsessed with keeping to my plan. But after you left that day, I was afraid."

"Afraid of what?" An idea was forming in my mind, so hideous that I banished it immediately.

"Afraid I had talked you into it. Or that you would do it to spite me." His face threatened to crumple again. "I really didn't know what I wanted. But I didn't want to get rid of it just like that. I knew I had no right to force anything on you. Either way."

Stubborn as he could be, Antonio was also respectful. That's why he'd backed off when Maddy stopped writing.

"I was thinking all kinds of things," he went on. "If I had been maybe too closed and too certain. But at the end I had to give it up. You did not want to see me. It was very painful." In a low flat voice he added: "I was in love with you, you know." I said nothing and he hurried on. "But I guess the part of me that wanted to get on with my career and not look to the left or to the right—that part was happy to give up."

I sat in stupefied silence. What *had* I said to Antonio?

"What you mean is, you don't want to have a child with me." I waited for him to touch or contradict me.

He might have reached for me. He might have tried to touch me. He might have said other things that were lost to me now. No copy was kept of the past and what had gone on there. It was possible I had said something else, something cold and desperate and calculated to wound. Something I did not mean.

"So why should I want your baby?"

Or: *"What makes you think I'm going to keep your baby?"*

Or even: *"I want a baby, Antonio, but I don't want yours."*

He was playing with the saltshaker, capsizing and righting it in his long, lean fingers. His hands used to cover my face and slide apart so he could kiss me. The dark red privacy, the thrill of exposure. Being so much taller, he had to lean down to do it. I never experienced our difference in height as inequality; rather, it was a gap that had to be crossed, intensifying what passed between us. The tipping of the saltshaker was maddening. I needed stillness. I needed to think. I needed to think and I could not bear to think, because alive in the room with us and coursing like a toxin through me was a monstrous idea: I had deprived Maddy of a father.

That potent and useless construction: *could have.* I could have answered Antonio's phone calls. I could have tolerated his misgivings. Shocked and temporarily cold-hearted, he could have been given time; he could have been persuaded. If Antonio could have been persuaded, then Antonio and I could have stayed together. If Antonio and I had stayed together, then Antonio would have been Maddy's father. I could not look at him or speak. I hated him for the chance I had taken with our lives and, when I finally met his eyes, I hated the knowledge in them that was curdling into pity.

"Eve," said Antonio urgently, touching my wrist where it lay on the table, inert and stunned like me. "Forget it. What happened happened. We have to leave it. Just leave it behind. I blame myself." He smiled the ghost of Maddy's mischievous smile. "You can too if you want."

30

Is a worldview the same as a paradigm? Miss Sedge says we have to start seeing human beings as just one small part of everything living on the surface of the earth. Do you think another scientific revolution could discover the afterlife exists and maybe even God (though as I said, I think there could be an afterlife without God)? You said it's the ridiculous ideas that can lead to discoveries. According to Miss Sedge, if you go the straight route, you get an answer you already know, but if you go the crooked back way, you get something new. She tried it out on Jack and me and we came up with the idea for the animation. I guess that's art, not science. But maybe it works the same way.

I've been so busy. I'm making this animated film. Jack's helping me on the practical side. I started out doing it for the march, but now I'm doing it mainly for myself. You make a drawing and change it hundreds of times, taking pictures as you go with this software that joins them together. I'm also making a secret animation nobody knows about. It's really hard to do, but I love it. I want to be an artist if I could do this all day.

No one was in the hallway or the kitchen. I slipped to my room on the carpeted stairs and curled up on the bedspread, longing for Maddy. I had been in contact with her, but only where she smiled at me through his lips and watched me from his eyes. Jewel-like pictures hung at different levels above Philippa's ivory-painted furniture; a lighter circle on the wallpaper showed where the clock had been. On my first night I had taken it down and stuffed it in a drawer. I never could sleep in a room with a ticking clock.

I rolled on my back, laughed out loud, knew myself to be incurably alone, did not give in to tears. Could the word *misunderstanding* account for what had happened between us? *I blame myself. You can too if you want.* Thanks, Antonio. The carved rose from which the light fixture hung had been painted so many times it had no distinct edges. Slowly it spun out the new alternative worlds. Little Maddy and her brothers skipped around us, tugging on their father's hands . . . Teenage Maddy and her sisters formed a huddle, giggling at us, their parents, the happy outcasts . . .

I found my phone and summoned Robin's voice into my ear.

"Oh, hello, Ducks."

"Sounds like you're around the corner. Where do you get that from, again?" I said.

"What?"

"That name you call me."

"The Rubber Duck Regatta. Cincinnati's big claim to fame. Other than myself, of course."

"Oh, I remember. So, what are you up to?"

"This and that," said Robin gnomically. "This and that."

"Like what?" I heard a piano playing. "What is it, four there?"

"Something like that. Listen. It's the Shostakovich. Second movement."

Even before Maddy grew hungry for music, Robin had opened his world up to me, persuading me of the grace in what seemed ungainly or incomplete. He held his phone near the speaker. The melody sleepwalked into the beat: two against three, four against three . . .

"My favorite part," I said.

"I'm learning to play it. Want to hear?" Scraping, rustling . . . the passage came into my ear again, more distant, from the real piano this time. In Robin's hands it was not yet fluent but just as haunting. It was odd to picture him there, in our cute, functional house, where the ceilings were low, the doorknobs round, and the open-plan kitchen was built with the needs of large appliances in mind. From here, the house seemed like a temporary structure that could easily be dismantled.

"Wow, Robin. Are you learning it for me?"

"You might say that."

"Aren't you working today?"

"No." He sounded buoyant. "I'm going to the lake tonight."

"Again?"

"I'm on a roll with the room."

"It must be freezing up there."

"Not too bad. Anyway, I have the space heater."

I offered details about my interviews, London buses and London weather, my odd companion and my gracious host. Into one of the pauses that developed between us, I said: "I met Antonio today."

I knew from his silence he was taken aback. "Why didn't you say?" The question had an edge to it and he waited before continuing. "Did you tell him about Maddy?"

"He was shocked."

"Do you want to talk about it?"

"He was crying."

The mention of strong emotion silenced Robin again. Then: "Did he get to know Maddy well enough for that? Or was it just the idea of her?"

"Both, I guess. Not the kind of thing you can ask someone right off the bat. It was bizarre seeing him, Robin. Not what I expected at all."

Our words had become points ringed with unspoken thoughts.

"Well, what *did* you expect?"

"I didn't expect him to look so much like Maddy."

I am slim in the way of small-framed women. Maddy had been slim in Antonio's way. When seated, they folded their long legs to one side. Standing, they possessed a natural authority. My fine hair fits my head like a cap. Antonio's hair, like hers, had ripple and spring to it. His gray eyes were hers too, and the way he used them— up for thought, down for evasion, sideways for humor or embarrassment, while his fingers fiddled childishly with whatever came to hand. He spoke at length in a neutral tone, and then all at once he turned his gaze on me as if to say, I'm telling you this, right here, right now, and you have to listen. That was pure Maddy. If Maddy had inherited my lips, they behaved in a wry, twisty Antonio way. Families who grow up together get used to this mirroring; I imagine they hardly notice it. I had found myself unable to take my eyes off Antonio. When I'd known him before, his features had belonged to him. Now he was a variation of Maddy.

"But what was it like seeing him again?" Robin pressed. "For you, I mean."

"It was like she was there and not there at the same time."

"Evie . . ." he murmured, giving up on any real answers. I thought how ordinary my name sounded when he used it. "You're brave to put yourself through this. I hope it helps . . . settle things for you. I really do."

"So do I. Sorry!" I said in a rush. "I have to go. Someone's knocking. Catch you later."

"Do what you have to do, Ducks . . . But don't get too drawn into it."

"Into what? I won't. Have fun at the lake. Robin?" I called, anxious now that he was going. "Be neighborly. I haven't met the husband or kids, but Norma's really nice."

"I know," he said. "I ran into her last week. Reception's crap up there. Text you from the car."

In the doorway stood Philippa, the English equivalent of Claire. Stout and unadorned, with depths of no-nonsense resolve under her warmth.

"Sorry," I said. "I sneaked in."

She peered more closely. "Are you all right? You look as if you've seen a ghost."

"Oh, I have." I smiled. "It's been a long day. I'm exhausted."

"Of course you are," she said comfortably. "How people can fling themselves around the planet and then be expected to *function* . . . I should get an early night if I were you."

Another kind of person would have replied: "No, that's not it. It is not jet lag. Let me tell you what it is," and sat Philippa down on the flowered wing chair, and made use of her intelligence and her easy sympathy. I could not muster the energy to account for myself to anyone. I let her bring me Earl Grey tea on a tray, and gently she latched the door behind her as if I were already asleep.

I raised the sash window. Heat from the radiator clashed with the inrush of cold air. Mist haloed the streetlamps. The houses opposite were closed for the night. In their bay windows, long lines of light leaked between the shutters. I lowered the window and found my phone.

Met A thanks largely to yr encouragement. Bizarre! Interesting. Difficult. Might meet again. Details later.

I undressed, sat up in bed, and wrapped my hands around the warm cup. The life of the senses was all I could rely on. Who was Norma? Someone partial to the color yellow who had a kayak and two sons, one of whom was autistic. Something of Norma's freckled, tactful presence had accompanied me to the restaurant to meet Antonio and was in the room with me now. Had it not been for her, I wouldn't be on this quest halfway around the world, having to live with what I found out. I didn't know whether to thank her or not. How much would I tell Norma? How much would I tell Robin, for that matter?

My phone pinged. *Oh wow. Well done. Getting the bigger picture? Electricity down last week. Workmen cut through cable. In the doghouse with neighbors . . . Sigh.*

I would reply tomorrow. Strange I had never met Tanner. He seemed to leave her to oversee the remodeling. Was everything as it should be there? Where was Tanner when Norma was arguing with workmen and managing the children? The amused affection with which she spoke of him could be a cover-up. If there's one thing women are adept at, it's covering up.

The fact was, I was thankful Norma wasn't here, Robin was at the lake, Alison was with her aunt in Norwich, Philippa had gone downstairs and would not be coming up again. The encounter with Antonio clamored to be shared. But sharing would put it in its place. I did not want to put Antonio in his place. Or rather: What exactly was his place?

When we parted, he had bent and kissed me on both cheeks. Drawn though I was to the center of his face, I dutifully turned my head and received these tokens of decorum. We'd agreed to meet the following week. Our long-ago selves were still intact, caught together in their web of space and time. Or so I believed. But whatever safeguards the past also makes it unreachable.

I switched off the light. After a minute I got up. I could hear the clock ticking. I muffled it with a second sweater and returned it to its drawer. I turned over and back, sat up for water, lay down again. But when I closed my eyes, it was not Antonio I saw but his sons, living their promising, hurtful lives. Maddy would never know them. They made no difference to her now. Through her, they were part of me.

31

We went to this amazing concert. Do you like Chopin? It's so sad! In a good way. I used to play Chopin on the piano. Maybe that's why I still love it. You know what we were saying about being a loner? One place I like to be alone is listening to classical music. Or do I? It's complicated. I want company but at the same time I want to be on my own. More and more. Sometimes I don't even want to see Jack. Or Fiona and Vicky. Don't worry, I am fine! Just saying.

Alison bought toffee peanuts from the stand on the Millennium Bridge and we paused between the single chimney of Tate Modern and the dome of St. Paul's. The cathedral had seemed flat and unreal on our walk from the station, where it was hemmed in by offices and restaurants. From here it inflated magisterially to fill the space behind us.

"This is kind of like the Mall," I said, "halfway between the Washington Monument and Capitol Hill."

"No, it's really not," said Alison.

"No, it's not."

"What I love is the way everything's jammed together. Oh, look, there's Starbucks . . . there's Yo! Sushi . . . there's your four-hundred-year-old cathedral. It's like stumbling on the White House when you go to wash your car."

"We've got more space than they do," I said. On both banks of the river, old and new jostled together without design. "Besides, DC was a planned city. London just happened." Beneath the railing, chrome supports flared out like the wings of a plane. How did it hold us up? No one knew. We trusted our lives to invisible engineering. When Maddy was born, the machinery of her tiny body alarmed me. Shouldn't I understand how she was put together, how she worked? Shouldn't I be in charge of inhaling her air and pumping her blood, keeping everything on track? "Do you know about this bridge?" I asked Alison. "There was some fault. It wobbled when people walked on it. They had to close it the next day."

"Resonance," she said. "Oscillation. I remember from high school physics. There was this bridge that twisted around in the wind and fell into Puget Sound."

"Was there? I'm not up on my bridge disasters."

"No one died. Only a dog called Tubby." She paused. "They used to call me that." But she was smiling, her hair whipped across her eyes by the wind. Her cup gave off the sickly smell of burnt sugar. "It's going so fast! Only four days left."

"Glad we came?"

She would not look at me, nodding instead at the empty decks of a pleasure boat sliding under the bridge. Alison had never been out of the country before, not even to Canada. She had risen to the challenge of this visit as I'd hoped she would. She'd helped me with the interviews at the Whitechapel Gallery and the Serpentine. Her research was thorough and she had a talent for offbeat questions that cut straight to the point. Today, at the Tate Modern, she was going to take the lead.

"Maddy would have loved it here," I said. After a moment: "I hate that phrase! *Would have.*" The grammar whispered that Maddy was no more, I'd had all I was ever going to have of Maddy. Now there was only what I chose to do with the idea of her.

"Is there a better way of saying it?"

"How do I know what she would have loved? She might have detested London. *Would have* has nothing to do with her. It's all about me."

Ahead of us, the chimney of the old power station reared up. Art and tourism filled it now, but the building still spoke of harsher things. Antonio was out there somewhere, south of the river. The idea of him was a bruise, a humiliation, after our meeting, and at the same time it was a warm current buoying me up, prompting me to say things about Maddy out loud. Did Antonio ever go to art museums? When I knew him, he'd been very absorbed by his research; his associates had been other doctoral students, serious young scientists intent on deciphering the codes of life. He'd shown little curiosity about museum studies. He'd thought it was a frivolous subject, or that's the impression I'd had. Maybe in the larger scheme of things it was.

Behind us a man muttered into his cell phone: ". . . it's ridiculous how much comes in and goes out . . ."

I held up a finger. "Did you hear that?" Of course she hadn't heard it. Only one person at a time hears these scraps of passing speech. Since Maddy's death, they had increased in frequency and bizarreness to the point where they seemed like messages.

Turning back to the railing, I said: "I met Antonio yesterday when you were in Norwich."

Alison accepted the change of subject without comment. I knew she would not help me. She would let me flail and drown in my own words.

"It was strange."

"Was he shocked to hear about Maddy?"

"He was upset. We talked about, you know, way back when."

Alison crunched her peanuts.

"We remember it completely differently," I said, "what happened."

"What did happen?"

In a gush of self-pity: "He thought I was going to have an abortion! He says I told him I was."

She thought for a moment. "Did you?"

"I might have." My eyes watered in the wind. "If I did, I didn't mean it."

"Well, he's the one who knocked you up. Women always get the blame."

"He says he kept calling me and coming by, but I refused to see him."

"Why would he keep calling and coming by?"

"He might have changed his mind."

"About . . . ?"

"Yes! We could have been together after all."

She turned her gaze to the far shore, where the low tide lapped at spots of bright plastic among the stones. "Are you sure about that?"

"It was my fault, Alison! I really think it was my fault Maddy didn't grow up with her father. How am I supposed to live with that?"

"That's assuming you stayed together. It could have gone wrong any time along the way."

I had not entertained this possibility. "He has children now," I said. "Boys."

"Of course he does! And a trophy wife, I bet."

"Should I try to meet them?"

She retorted: "How would I know!"

I came to my senses and seized her arm. "I'm sorry, Alison. I'm so sorry. Forgive me. I don't know what I was thinking. Come on. We'll be late." We set off against the flow of oncoming bridge walkers. "Remember, you're in charge of this interview. I'm taking a backseat. Do you have your questions ready?"

"In my head."

"In your *head?* If I were you, I'd take along some notes. Just in case."

"Who did you say was in charge?"

"You are. You are." I halted. "Did you hear that?"

"What?"

"That woman in the blue coat. She said: 'The point at which I'm getting all my organs stolen, I can't afford to . . .' "

Alison laughed. "Do you always eavesdrop on people?"

"What do you suppose she can't afford to do?"

"Ask her. *I'll* ask!"

The woman shook her head at this odd American and her cup of peanuts. I could see Alison did not mind in the least making a fool of herself. She returned in high spirits. "The nerve! She wouldn't tell me."

The curator of public programs rose and touched her fingertips to the table. "I'm afraid I have to go. Sadly. I'll leave you in Ian's capable hands. I hope you've come away with something useful?"

Alison switched off the recorder and together we stood. I did not want to stop. I wanted to weigh up the merits of thematic hangs and nonstatutory learning while Gillian sparred with her Scottish colleague. I'd kept to my word and let Alison run the interview. She had done it masterfully, without notes, her blunt questions conveying not rudeness but genuine curiosity that provoked them both into thinking aloud.

"We'll be putting together a report," I said. "Maybe a journal article."

"Yes, of course," said Gillian. "It's a great shame you can't be here for our opening."

"The Past in the Present," Ian said in his deadpan brogue. "Misrepresentation comes in many forms. Omission. Idealization. Nostalgia . . ." He too was reluctant to bring this to an end. He had a sucked-in, bony face, with cushions for lips and all the color drained upward into his vivid hair. You wouldn't find either of these characters back home, with their offhand wit, their folksy dental work, their refusal of style that was, in its way, stylish. "We want to show the past is something to be tampered with. Defrosted, as it *waire*."

"Shame you can't join us," said Gillian.

"The show's been curated by educators," he went on. "It's the longtime quarrel—"

"Tension," she said. "I've really got to go."

"Tension between curating and educating. Curators came up with the conceptual framework. And then the educators explained it to Mrs. Bloggs."

"Mrs. who?" asked Alison.

"The lowly public. Usually in the basement."

"Why not *Mr.* Bloggs?"

"Oh, Mr. Bloggs too!" Gillian assured her. "And all the little Bloggs." She offered me her cool fingers. "You'll be gone by the fifteenth?"

I glanced at Alison. Her eyes were alive. "Maybe we could stay. We'd love to."

"You'd be welcome," said Ian warmly. "Very welcome indeed."

On the escalator, I murmured, "When did you prepare all that? You're a natural."

"This isn't a vacation, you know."

We would have preferred to go slowly and stop often, but Ian's long stride pulled us through the displays—Structure and Clarity, Poetry and Dream, Transformed Visions—before delivering us to the sloping floor of the Turbine Hall, part warehouse, part mall. We followed him through the arch to a windowless area, where giant slanted buttresses held up the ceiling. The walls were a moonscape of pocked, stained, and riveted concrete.

"The Tanks are through those doors. Where they used to store the oil for the power station. The only gallery space in Europe dedicated to performance and installation."

"Can we go in?" Alison wanted to know.

"Well . . . no. They're open when there's a show

on. And during private views. In 2013 they'll be shut while we convert the Switch House."

"I'd really like to see," said Alison.

Ian toyed with the staff card hung on a lanyard around his neck. He considered us for a moment before ambling over to have a word with the security guard, who led the way to one of the black doors and turned his key in the central dial.

"Thanks ever so much," said Ian. "We'll only be a minute. You won't *tale* on me, will you?"

In his haste to get us through, Ian's hand touched my back, and then the door swung shut and the darkness was complete. There was nothing to breathe, only the stifling, metallic odor. Flare of a light: Ian's phone. He passed the beam over the perimeter of the tank. Cylindrical in shape. Three or four times a person's height. Surface covered with a rusty iron grid. The tank had been emptied and turned to other uses, but it was still hostile to human trespass.

I let Alison ask the questions. But what *kind* of participation . . . ? Who is it for . . . ? Why no light from above . . . ? What about the oil . . . ? That curious and confident voice she'd used for the interview hardly sounded like hers. And Ian's monotone: "Not exactly white cube but not black box either . . . You had to take a lie detector test . . . Tania Bruguera. Surplus Value. William Kentridge. Three sixty, eight channel. Shadow boxing meets the Russian avant-garde . . . North Sea possibly. Africa possibly . . ."

All that oil, enduring year after year in the airless dark.

"Still seeping through the walls . . ." droned Ian. "Art in Action. A space for the short-lived. . . ."

Impossible to breathe deeply.

"Spectacle in place of fossil fuels . . ."

Around me fizzed lights of my own making. I bowed my head. Currents sparked and fused on the sides of the tunnel, rushing to enclose me. A hand gripped my arm, more hands were on me; the door was shoved open, light roared in, and soon I was outdoors seated on a bench under the puffy chrome supports of the bridge and Alison was scrolling down my contacts to find Robin's number.

"I needed some air," I said. "There was no air."

She peered into my face. "Do you have diabetes or something? Should I call an ambulance?"

"Low blood pressure. My mother has it. Maddy had it. We're all prone to fainting."

She pressed the phone to my ear. "Pay attention! It's ringing."

"Went to voicemail," I said, curious to see Alison so agitated. "He must be at the lake. The signal is terrible up there."

I tried to stand. She yanked me back and left her hand there, a reassuring weight on my arm. Somewhere out of sight, a flute was playing.

"Ian disappeared in a hurry. How embarrassing! I don't know what it was about that place."

"It was amazing," she murmured. "I didn't want to leave."

"I'm so sorry," I said. "I'm fine now. Did I scare you?"

"Don't do it again."

The melody threaded through the branches of the caged trees and hung above the river, silvery and medieval and haunting.

"Should we try to stay for the opening?" I asked.

"What, a whole 'nother week? Wouldn't we be pushing our luck? Claire didn't want me to come with you in the first place."

"*I* wanted you to come."

"I don't know why."

"Maybe you'll want to do your master's now."

Her face closed up again. "Who knows? Maybe."

"Wouldn't it be fun to go to the opening?"

She gave me a straight look. "You want to stay to see your ex again, don't you?"

"Antonio?" I scoffed. "I wouldn't stick around for him."

"No," said Alison after a minute. "I think I have to get home."

I extended my ticket for a week, telling Claire, "I owe you big-time . . ." I dropped Antonio an email to let him know my change of plans, and received an equally brief response. Maybe we could meet again before I returned.

"You sound different," said Robin on the phone.

"Claire asked me to stay. Next time you're coming with me."

"Aren't you homesick?"

"It's just another week."

"I miss you . . ." he said hopefully. "Are you seeing Antonio again?"

"Why?"

"Just wondered."

"He's very busy. What's been going on there? I couldn't get through. Are we still having Christmas at the lake?"

"Why wouldn't we?"

"It's going to be as hard as the anniversary."

"I know."

"Have you run into Norma and Tanner?" I said. "From the yellow house?"

"Just a sec . . . thought I had a call coming in. No. Yes," he said. "Norma's been over a couple of times."

"She has? She didn't mention it."

"Why would she mention it?"

"We've been texting."

"What happened was, her workmen cut through a cable. From there to the peninsula no one had power for over a day. She came looking for advice."

"Yes, she told me. Nice, isn't she?"

"Very. Haven't met the husband yet. He seems to leave everything to her."

"Different?" I asked suddenly. "How do I sound different?"

"Hyped up. You're not snorting cocaine, by any chance?"

"Ha! No, being over here is making me feel better. No one knows me."

"Well, do what you need to do, Eve."

"So you don't mind?"

"Of course not!"

"I'll come back now, if you want," I said.

"Don't be silly." He had recovered his good humor. "Are you getting by with your English?"

"They've understood me so far."

"Two countries divided by the same language."

"Who said that? Churchill?"

"Wilde, maybe. Sounds like him. My favorite deathbed quote: " 'Either that wallpaper goes or I do.' "

"Robin . . ."

"Sorry!" he said tenderly. "I'm an idiot. Sorry."

Reluctantly Alison accepted my offer to see her off. On the Piccadilly line to Heathrow, we hardly spoke. She was wearing an old sweatshirt she liked to sleep in, and had spoiled the soft shape of her haircut by pinning the sides. I read my paper. She kept her eyes on the other passengers and retrieved my suitcase when it slid down the aisle of the train.

At a restaurant in the departure lounge, I said: "I'm going to miss you."

A hint of sarcasm: "You are?" She looked up from her bored study of the menu, glasses flashing. "The coast is clear now."

I ignored that. "What's the first thing you're going to do when you get home?" A pointless question, deserving of a shrug. I tried again. "What did you like best about London?"

Alison's face with the hair pulled back was as round and foreign as the moon. "Can't remember, offhand. I'll make a list if you need to justify your expenses."

I let the craving take me over, for Maddy's lovely face, Maddy's curious eyes, Maddy's wit and goodwill. She would be laughing at the toddler at the next table grinding egg into his hair. She would ask what she'd been like at that age. I would repeat the stories she knew by heart. We would link arms on our way out. My yearning for her was monstrous and bodily and doomed. I was in two realities at once: with Maddy, and with this graceless stranger.

"You're so angry, Alison."

She was silent for a moment, unaccustomed to the forthrightness of others. "Angrier than anyone else? Angrier than you?"

"Maybe not," I said. "But I suggest you get on top of it."

"Oh, really?"

"Being outspoken doesn't always serve you well. It could hold you back."

Her voice trembled. "Is that so?"

"Sometimes," I advised, "it's best to keep your opinions to yourself."

Blotches spread like a rash on her pale cheeks. "I'm not your daughter, you know!" She was glaring at me, around me, through me. "Did Maddy have to keep her opinions to herself?"

"That," I said, my voice returning slow and cold, "was a nasty thing to say."

Alison looked bewildered. "My mother kept her opinions to herself. See where it got her?"

"Where did it get her?"

"Stuck with my dad all those years. Miserable. Always will be."

"Does that mean you have to be?"

The waiter appeared with his pad, but not before I had seen the tears standing in her eyes. Not knowing what else to do, we placed an order.

"Besides," said Alison, when he'd gone, "I thought that's what you liked about me."

"What?"

"That I speak my mind."

I was trying to take charge of my face.

"Sometimes I wish I didn't," she murmured. "You can't take things back."

"No," I said huskily. "But it has a way of making things happen." All at once I was exhausted beyond any normal condition of the body. "Know what?" I waited for her to lift her eyes to mine. "I don't know *any*thing. I thought I did."

At passport control, we shuffled forward with the line, standing closer together than we would have a week before. She thanked me twice for taking her along; for Alison, that amounted to gushing. I said I should be thanking her. She didn't ask me why. I wanted to follow her into the departure lounge and board the waiting plane. We reached the front of the line. In a hesitant, unfamiliar voice, she said: "What was Maddy like?"

The officer beckoned us forward with a winding-up gesture.

"Kind," I said. "Funny. Talented. Everyone loved her."

"I could never be like that," said Alison.

"Me neither."

We embraced clumsily and she lifted her carry-on and hurried to the barrier. At the last minute, she turned around and waved with her boarding pass.

I ran up, as close as I could get. "Do you want to come to the lake with us? Before Christmas?"

She gave me the faintest of smiles. "I'll think about it."

32

My philosophy is do everything all at once. And find everything out all at once. Am I impatient? Maybe I am. Mom's friend isn't doing great. But getting back to the question I asked you before, why do you think my mother would be angry with you? Do you think you've had time to think about it? I would be really curious to know. As well as other things. Like where do you go on vacation and what do you play with your boys, and are they any good at art? Cloud's got sharp teeth. She doesn't mean to hurt me. Say hi! She's waving her paw.

The day Alison left, an email arrived from Antonio, wondering if I had time for a drink that evening. We met in a pub on Sicilian Avenue. I asked if he was free by any chance the next day, after my interview at the Hayward Gallery. It turned out he was, and the following day, and the day after that.

We were together by five-thirty and parted by seven. We chose a different place each time, somewhere central. Small talk saw us to our seats, whereupon Antonio raised his finger to summon the waiter. He never struck up a conversation with staff; he did not have Robin's affection for wageworkers, and besides, service had to be prompt. We were short on time.

Once our drinks were ordered, I began talking about Maddy. I favored stories showing her spirit and determination. Fearless at three, poised at ten, learning to multiply and to dive, mothering her many friends. She'd been a favorite of the older girls, big sister to the little ones, and naturally at ease with adults. I had notebooks filled with the witty and touching things she said, of interest to no one but me. I wanted the whole of Maddy to exist in Antonio's mind, and I wanted to give him a glimpse of what he would never have. He let me tell it in my own way, listening in alert silence, his eyes hardly leaving my face. My friends thought they were doing me a favor by not mentioning her. They thought talking about her would remind me of what had happened. Remind me! Antonio let me talk, and as I talked, I felt something that had been displaced was being put back where it belonged.

Eventually we moved on to other subjects: aging parents, gentrification, Olympic stadiums, the chemistry of consciousness. We played the parts of two friends meeting for after-work drinks. I learned again to read his moods, his facial expressions, and his pauses. We started with Maddy and ended with Maddy. We grew increasingly confessional just before it was time to part. I carried my laptop in my bag and the memory stick with her animation on it in my wallet, but the moment never seemed right.

At the Royal Festival Hall bar, I told him about Jack. "Not every boy would have taken that on."

"No," said Antonio.

"Would you have fallen in love with a dying girl?"

He smiled a little. "I see where Maddy gets it from."

"What?"

"These questions."

"Like what?"

"Like: Are you a loner? How does music work in the brain? Are you an atheist? Like what happens—" He stopped to give some change to a man shuffling between the tables.

"What happens . . ." I prompted.

"I said things I would never have said if I'd known."

"So what would you have told her if you'd known?" Maddy's veiled references to her illness and her future had cut me deeply. Why hadn't she been able to ask *me* those questions?

"I'm not sure," he said after a moment.

"When she was around five, Maddy got very worried about death. Mine, mostly. I was putting her to bed one night. 'Mom,' she said, 'you're going to die before me! When *I* die, how will I find you?' "

"And what did you say?"

"I said: 'Don't worry. I'll find you.' "

Antonio's eyes were intense on my face.

"I heard no more about it for a long time."

"My boys don't talk about these things."

"Oh, I'm sure they do, Antonio. Just not to you."

He gave me a long sideways look.

"When Maddy came home after having sex for the first time—"

"How did you know that?"

"I'm her mother! I knew."

"But how?" He was genuinely puzzled.

"She was clingy, and extra-concerned. I had this primitive feeling something had been taken away from me." I paused. "And she wanted to know why you left. She'd never asked me so directly before."

"What did you say?"

"That I didn't know. That you didn't want to have a baby with me."

Antonio was frowning. "That's not exactly—"

"I said it was your loss."

"She didn't know the whole story," he said resentfully.

"Maybe that's why she wrote to you. Anyway, Maddy was lucky. Jack's a genuinely nice boy. She gave him an out, but he stayed with her all the way."

"I'm so glad."

"Not like my first time. My first love left me for my best friend."

"Mine was a complete disaster!" said Antonio. "I could do nothing! She laughed at me."

We had exchanged these stories when we were courting, when everything that came before was recast as a warm-up for our own superior love. I sneaked a look at my watch. Ten minutes to seven.

"Robin," began Antonio. "He is your—fiancé? Boyfriend?"

"Partner."

"Partner," he repeated, as though he didn't think much of the word.

Robin seemed far away and incongruous, but I wanted nonetheless to sun myself in the idea of him. "He's a master carpenter and a musician. Maddy was crazy about him."

"Was she?"

"Robin took her to concerts."

"I'm so glad."

What else could he say? Robin at a Renwick concert, smiling tenderly at me over Maddy's head. I forced the image away. "Maddy's illness didn't make *me* into a better person," I said. "It made me into a tedious, monstrous person."

Antonio leaned across the table and positioned his face very close to mine. Grains of gold swam in his Maddy-gray eyes. He took his time studying all the parts of my face while appearing to be on the brink of a smile.

"What?" I shrank away. "What are you looking at?"

To my relief, he withdrew and hung his hand off the chair back. "I loved the conversations we used to have! Into the night. Remember, Eve? I miss that. Seeing you is like someone put a lost piece of my life back into my hands."

"I remember," I said primly. My head felt weightless, full of light. I kept my eyes on him.

"Time is such a strange thing. The years pass by and you don't even see them go. Family life swallows you up. No one tells you . . ."

"Tells you what?"

His eyes lingered on mine. "Sometimes I think I went to sleep and woke up old."

"Well, I feel a hundred sometimes."

"With good reason. What you've been through!" After a decent pause he smiled. "You don't look a hundred."

In the café overlooking the Great Court of the British Museum, I confessed there were times after Maddy died when I tried to whittle her down.

"Whittle?"

"Diminish her importance. I'd say to myself: Sixteen years ago, I didn't know Maddy. Sixteen years from now it won't matter so much. Isn't that a terrible thing to do?"

"What else are you supposed to do?" he said softly.

Tears sat in my eyes so often during these conversations that I no longer bothered to hide them. "Then I think further ahead, when there's no one left who knew her. Will it matter that she died?"

Antonio frowned and pulled in his chin. Finally he said: "I guess that's why people invent God. A consciousness that remembers us forever."

Didn't he know I had been through every possible angle, from the preposterous to the vaguely scientific to the refuge of the imagination? Each held a grain or two of solace. But none in the end was any use. Across the table my confessor and seducer, the father of my child, waited for me to speak, and I was looking through him to a land so hideously parched and impassable there was no point in putting a single foot down.

"I don't know if I can do it." It dawned on me that, until this moment, I had believed the future was provisional, open to amendment.

"Invent God? Who can? When you know what we know about the human brain—"

"No!"

He frowned. "What, then?"

"Live the rest of my life without her."

He reached over and enclosed my hands in both of his. I tried to pull away, but he wouldn't let me. He held my gaze, or cast his eyes around the room as he spoke. He said she'd made use of the time she had, which is all anyone can do. He said she was gone, but in a way, she never would be. He said she got her spirit and her strength from me. He said these qualities were what had drawn him to me in the first place, and they would see me through. I let him hold my hands and talk. I let the passion behind his speech, his endearing syntax, his certainty that he knew what I was capable of, pour over me as though it were some essential life-giving liquid, and what did not soak in now could be stored up for later.

The last of these evenings took place at the PizzaExpress in Holborn, where we'd first met. Earlier than usual, twenty after six under the milk-bottle chandeliers, I began: "Why do you think Maddy never told you she was sick?"

"Pride?" he said after a moment.

"That's a harsh word."

"I don't always find the best words." Antonio consulted the menu, though we never ate on these occasions, and tapped the table with it. "I don't know. Maybe, as you say, she didn't want me to feel sorry for her."

I had begun to appreciate Maddy's refusal to do Antonio's bidding, her courage in not letting him know she was ill. *Well, are you going to tell your family about me??* It was her bargaining card. I decided her secrecy was a character strength, one that reflected well on how I had raised her.

"At the beginning, she was pretty open about what was happening. But it was so long and so—unrelenting. I guess there came a time when talking didn't help. She used to cry in the shower."

Blinking, he took this in.

"Toward the end she didn't want to see her friends. Or even Jack. She sent them away. But before that, all she really wanted to do was listen to music and make her animation."

"She got comfort from that?"

It was my turn to study Antonio until he shifted in his chair and looked away. Without a word, I unzipped my bag and removed my laptop. I set it on the table, inserted the memory stick, opened "final final final," positioned the screen between us, and pressed play.

Maddy gazed out, in the presence of both of us at last. Our eyes briefly met, and returned to our daughter. Antonio's eyes were fixed to the screen as Maddy's had been during the march. Slowly her eyelids closed and the blanks appeared on her head, joining and spreading to consume all of the earth's riches, and be consumed in turn by the seas, while her face underwent its terrible changes. I pressed stop. Antonio looked up. "Is that the end?"

I nodded, closing the file into its folder. I had left it to providence or instinct or the wisdom of the moment to decide whether to show him the other ending. "It was played after the speeches during the march. Maddy was weak by then, but she got to see it on TV. The response was amazing. The applause. You should have seen her face. You should see *your* face."

His voice was muffled. "I'm knocked over. I'm so impressed. I wish—"

"Don't wish."

"She was courageous," he said simply.

"They want to use it again, you know, for the campaign. They're asking me to release it. I might not. I might want to keep it private."

"Would Maddy want you to?"

"How do I know!" After a minute, I said: "It's complicated. Maybe the fact is, if she can't be here, I want it all to happen."

"What?"

"Catastrophe. Cities underwater. Everything destroyed." He was silent. "I don't really mean that."

"Don't you?"

"Only a little. Sometimes."

Antonio kept me in his gaze for a long moment, weighing something. "Do you know how it felt when you told me Maddy was dead?"

We were free to touch each other within certain limits, arm or shoulder, for a second or two. Now I touched his wrist on the tabletop and left my hand there. My fingernails were blank. I had not painted them in months. "How?"

"Like she had been brought to life again, and then killed in front of my eyes."

I withdrew my hand. Antonio sat back.

"First I had the shock of Maddy writing to me. Then I grew a little bit fond of her. Then she stopped. Okay. She had second thoughts. Or maybe I said something wrong. But I was thinking no matter what, we would meet one day. And there you were"—he gazed around like a sleepwalker at the stainless steel ovens, the waiters striped like cartoon convicts—"in this place, actually, and I thought, Okay, Eve and I will find a way to know each other again. We have Maddy between us. And then—" He sliced the air.

I bent my head. "I'm so sorry, Antonio. Really I am."

"Did you do it on purpose, Eve?"

"I should have told you before."

"Yes. You should have." The way he shifted in his chair felt like a giant shrug, but his voice was soft. "We both have things to be sorry about."

"I guess that's one thing that can't happen to a woman. You can't have a child out there you know nothing about. Even if you give your baby away, you know you've had one."

He was playing with the bud vase on the table. "I felt guilty about it for years. I used to be a good Catholic boy, you know. When you are raised the way I was raised, it is in your blood." He paused.

"That's why I was angry with myself. For being stubborn. Driving you to . . . Or thinking I did."

"Is Erica a good Catholic?" I said, trying out an Alison-like version of myself.

Antonio looked shocked. "Why are you asking that?"

"I want to know about your family."

He crossed and recrossed his legs. "She is not a Catholic. She is not anything. She puts down Church of England on forms."

"Why?"

"That's what they do here." He continued with reluctance. "She's a wonderful mother. Like you, I am sure. We've been twelve years together."

"What does she do?"

"Before the boys, she worked for a publisher. She went back for a year after Oscar, but when Daniel was born, it was too much. She was too divided. She wanted to be home with them."

I turned sideways, resting my elbow on the chair back. "What's it like, where you live? Stoke Newington, where I'm staying, feels like a village. "

"London's made out of villages. Blackheath is an old village too. "

"This city's so big," I said.

He smiled. "It's home for me."

In Washington, Antonio had been the outsider and I the native. This had magnified me, no doubt, in his eyes. "Do you feel English now?"

"Oh no. Of course not! Not if I was here for forty years. Erica and our friends, they are talking about their childhood, their teachers. I know about the dinner ladies. I know all about the eleven-plus." I raised my brows. "This exam they used to give to kids to decide their future. The point is, I have nothing to say. I did not grow up here. I'm not going back to Spain," he added. "That is for sure."

"Why not?"

"I am a happy transplant."

"Completely happy, Antonio?"

He looked up. "Yes, of course. Why do you ask that?" He spaced his syllables evenly. "Wherever you raise your children is home." He paused and repeated: "Why do you ask?"

"Tell me about your sons."

"Eve, really . . ."

"They are Maddy's half brothers. I have a right to know." I kept my voice light. "Oscar must be eight now and Daniel's six?"

"How did you know?"

"The letters, remember?"

"They are a handful. They argue sometimes. I guess that's normal. But the older one looks out for his brother."

"Are you going to have any more?"

He smiled at the intrusive question. "We have not decided for more. But you never know. You cannot always plan these things."

"Really?" I said, mocking. "Can I see a picture of them?"

Again he looked shocked.

"Please. I'd like to."

He found one on his phone and handed it to me without a word.

The boys sat on a low wall, gripping it with both hands. Their mother leaned down from behind to fit in the frame, an arm around each boy in the green-gold of summer. Hold still. Smile for Daddy . . . The instant the picture was taken was nothing to them now, a forgotten speck of time. I did not trust my voice. Enlarging the image with my fingers, I studied each face in turn. Of course he would have an interesting wife. Alison was right. Of course she would be much younger than he was. The older boy had Antonio's springy reddish brown hair, the same confident backward tilt to his head. The small one was fair like his mother, with her wide-apart eyes and pointed chin.

"Do they like school?"

"They don't like sitting still all day! It is hard on boys to sit still."

"They're at the same school?"

"Year two and year four. All Saints is very good. One of the best in Lewisham. The Church of England can't hold on to its members, but it still runs good schools."

His phone had gone dark and I handed it back.

"They are both great readers," he was saying. "We try to keep the screen time down."

"Good for you."

"Erica would have been heartbroken if they did not like reading."

"Shame she had to give up her job."

"She might go back to it."

"It's not easy to work your way up, later on."

Antonio shrugged. "I don't know. I think you can."

"Would you want her to go back to work?"

"She loves being there for the boys." Abruptly he got to his feet. The wall clock said twenty after seven. He had a home to return to, excuses to make.

I stood too. "I'm leaving Monday."

He hid what looked like alarm under his courtly smile. "So soon?"

"I did tell you." I gathered my things and stepped to one side so the table was no longer between us. "There's an opening at the Tate Modern on Saturday night. Would you like to come?"

He took my hands and kissed me on each cheek. "Thank you. I'd like that."

"Can you get away?"

"Yes, I think so."

"You think so? Or you can?"

"I can, as a matter of fact. Erica's taking the boys to her mother."

Late as it was, we parted on New Oxford Street. I watched Antonio's long coat dwindle rapidly toward Kingsway. When the road bent to the left, he disappeared along with a turning fleet of black cabs, one of which I knew he would hail as soon as he was out of sight.

33

Do you think there is any hope for us? The human species, I mean. Jack thinks we are probably doomed. Not right away but eventually. In the very long run there are asteroids. And entropy. Or we will fall into the sun. He says people are the worst thing that ever happened to the earth. Do you agree?

I missed my train at London Bridge and made a wrong turn out of Blackheath station; it was three-thirty by the time I found the road leading down to All Saints School. Through the drizzle, I could see the bright coats of the parents clustered like balloons at the gate. The redbrick schoolhouse fit snugly across the cul-de-sac. It looked smaller and friendlier than the photograph on its home page. Families were already coming up the hill as I hurried down, agitated and out of breath and half hoping I was too late. A pair of mothers and daughters passed in matching coats; a father flicked the rain cover into place on a stroller; older students cut their own giggling paths. A woman in a purple jacket came forward, with a boy on either side.

"Mum, I've still got one in my bag—" said the taller one.

"Give it to Daniel. Go on, be fair—"

"But I've only got *one*, Mum—"

"Really, Oscar!" Abreast of me now, she flashed me a smile I was too bewildered to return. It was the face I'd seen on Antonio's phone, leaning down to fit between her sons. The suddenness of the encounter, the ease with which I had found them, and her amused, conspiratorial smile paralyzed me. I'd imagined no further than wanting to be in their company. She opened an umbrella; the older boy tugged her arm, still arguing; the younger one skipped alongside. I watched them climb the hill toward where the spire of a church pierced the sky at an odd angle. At the top they tilted over the edge and disappeared.

Friday morning, I completed my final interview at the Royal Academy and in the afternoon I set off again for Blackheath. There would be no other chance. The Tate opening was the following day, and Monday I was to fly home. I arrived early this time and settled on a low wall near the school gate.

When Maddy was small, an even greater pleasure than taking her in the mornings had been picking her up after school. I'd shared that task with my parents. Tuesdays and Fridays had been my days. I could see that in good weather, English parents stood around as I had once done, knowing their children had been kept safe for another day and would be returned to them soon.

The last two houses on the street had been converted into classrooms, their windows now covered with paper snowflakes and letters of the alphabet. Staff with clipboards crossed the courtyard to open the gates, and the children spilled out. Erica was easy to spot in her purple jacket. I watched the boys run to her. Oscar soon veered away to wrestle with another boy, but Daniel stood looking up into his mother's face, playing with the toggle of her zipper. She was talking to someone, resting her hand unthinkingly on her son's head.

I stood. Antonio would be furious to see me there. He would rush his family away and never speak to me again. I could feel the child's skull under my hand. If I left now, no one need ever know. I forced myself down, gripped the edge of the wall, and fixed my gaze on the pointed dormers of the school, until the unruly group of Erica, the boys, and their friends moved together up the sidewalk. They passed close enough to reach out and touch me.

Once they crossed the road bordering the heath, they kept to the low ground while I made my way to a bench partway up the slope. Crisscrossed by footpaths, the yellow grass stretched down to a gray-stone church that looked defeated and out of place on the bare heath.

Erica was easy to keep an eye on, milling below with the other mothers while their boys romped. She pulled off her hat and her hair fell in a loose braid down her back, rendering her younger still. This woman ran Antonio's life. She slept in his bed. She loved his children. She was like a fictional character I had conjured up so successfully that she roamed around paying me no attention and doing exactly what she felt like doing. It could have been me standing on a patch of grass in the flattening light of a winter's afternoon while our boys played. I was the fiction. My own life did not exist.

Oscar was marching the others around lampposts and over the dead grass. He would grow up to be someone of importance. I saw it in the way he held his head, the way he shouted at his friends and laughed raucously before they had a chance to reply. He took up all the air, as ambitious people do. One had to cut off parts of oneself to be with them. Space and sound were oddly elastic between where I sat, the cluster of women, and the running children. I could barely hear their cries, but I could see them with dreamlike clarity, these boys who were free to play and grow up, never knowing they had a sister who had died. They would greet the news with puzzlement, then indifference: a fairy tale that had nothing to do with them.

Daniel had been trailing halfheartedly after the

group. He broke away to follow his own path of widening circles, talking or singing to himself. Would he come to me? Nearer . . . Nearer . . . I caught my breath, not daring to move. He strayed so close I could make out the Velcro straps of his shoes, his slender wrists protruding from his cuffs, the soft spikes of his hair, finer and paler than Maddy's. He stopped a few feet away and studied me, wiping his nose with the back of his hand. I smiled. He smiled back, uncertainly, and turned to squint under the visor of his hand to where his mother was calling him. But he didn't go to her. Instead he offered me his face again, appraising me with Maddy's intelligent eyes, Maddy's stillness. The seconds stretched and trembled. I held him in my gaze, refusing to let go until he did. In that moment, I held her too.

The boy turned and zigzagged down the slope without a backward look. At the bottom he joined his family and they moved off, growing smaller and less distinct until the ground dipped and they disappeared. No doubt by the time he got home he had already forgotten the lady on the bench.

34

Sorry about not being in touch. I haven't had a lot of time to write. It's sad that summer's almost over. Well, I'm feeling sad in general these days. I used to love going back to school. So every baby that's born is a miracle, no matter what, right?

I suggested meeting on Hungerford Footbridge. I made a point of crossing the Thames whenever I could, even if it meant a longer, more roundabout route. The human scale of the bridges drew me, and the way two or three of them could be seen in either direction, like straps fastening down the shoreline while the river moved freely underneath.

He was resting his forearms on the railing, the sides of his long gray coat hanging down. Behind him the cranes formed red constellations above the glitter of the night city. He turned and watched me approach, kissed me on both cheeks, and briefly gripped my hands. He'd cut his hair even shorter. It made his lips prominent, made him look more Spanish. This grown-up Antonio scared me a little, reminding me of the small part I had played in his life.

"Is your family gone?" I asked, to keep everything out in the open. Let there be no nonsense between the progenitors of Maddy.

"They left this afternoon."

"Thanks for coming with me. It's no fun going to these things alone."

"At your service," he said with mock gravity. He took my arm and we set off. During our year together in Washington, we had done a lot of walking along the Potomac, under the foaming cherry trees or their skeletons, and around the basin to the outlying monuments. We strolled through Georgetown and down the length of the Mall, cutting our earnest talk with laughter, stopping to embrace, my heart expanding to house the future that I believed was ours. It was a giddy sensation now, being in London with Antonio, without Maddy. All the traveling I'd never done, the adventures I had deferred to the mythical future! I would not tell him I had stalked his family. For one evening I would not think about the past, or what our lives were made of now.

"Can we stop a minute?" I let go and went to the railing. I had inherited the childlike delight my mother took in looking down at bodies of water. In the wide view, the river appeared almost motionless, but nearby, around the pilings, the muddy water coursed dangerously fast.

We set off again. Antonio's hands were jammed deep in his coat pockets, his shoulders so square and straight he seemed to be leaning back into the arms of a following wind. My eyes fixed on the glossy black tips of his shoes. Poor Antonio! While I'd been applying waterproof mascara and cream blush, carefully so as to suggest the high color of health, not the tragic masquerade of an ex-lover, he had been polishing his shoes for me.

"You are so quiet," he said, shooting me a glance. "Is everything okay?"

"Okay as it ever is."

A violinist wearing fingerless gloves was performing at the end of the bridge. Antonio tossed some coins onto the man's tartan rug and we descended to the South Bank.

Once Maddy fell ill, I had been treated not only to routine makeovers but to pedicures, exfoliators, mud masks, Dead Sea salt scrubs. I'd gone along with anything she wanted. Why not in all the years before? It had been our game. She badgered me; I laughingly refused. Given long enough, Maddy might have turned out to be an ascetic like me. Or maybe our clash of pleasures had in itself been pleasurable. There was no pleasure in it now. I longed to feel her hands steadying my temples, her earnest patting and tugging ministrations. Why had I not let her fuss over me when she was seven, ten, twelve, when she wanted to help me be a glamorous mother? Instead I tried to teach her that a woman's worth did not rest in her appearance.

We joined the crowds beside the river. I made Antonio stop to read the paving stones commemorating the Queen's Jubilee. I took a picture of him looking urbane by a serpent-twined lamppost. He took my arm again, and the place where he touched me felt warm, even through my coat. By sheer effort of will I could open myself up to the here and now. The boats churning past, the toy buses sliding over the toy bridges, the flow of strangers on the pavement who seemed to be generated from a hidden source, some of them no doubt with disasters in their lives worse than mine. By the time we reached the caged birches in front of the Tate, I no longer felt disloyal for taking pleasure in the evening, for walking freely by the Thames with Antonio. I was not turning my back on Maddy. I had her with me.

Gillian and Ian were chatting in a small group. While we waited for them to notice us, I faked interest in the view of the Millennium Bridge that Antonio was admiring, hands behind his back. He had only been here once, years ago. I felt the place belonged to me now.

Ian came forward, an iPad in his hands, slashes of pink on his cheeks. "Come in. Into the belly of the beast." Gillian in her bat-wing blouse introduced me to the others, and I presented Antonio as an old friend, causing Ian's gaze to alight on our faces briefly in turn. I plucked two glasses of wine from a passing tray.

"Yes, I believe Mr. Bryce *was* an early postmodernist . . ."

"The permanent as well as the temporary . . ."

"I expect you're a victim of your own success? *We* are . . ."

Returning to work after Maddy's death, I had been painfully alert to every averted gaze, every brave question, every conversation that dried up as I approached. Here no one was afraid of me. Antonio was a highly presentable escort and his presence protected me from the wounding I had come to expect on social occasions. I did not mind sharing him with these women, the one with fiery hair braying, "We've got to ring the changes! If we don't ring the changes . . ." and the other one coaxing him away with her painted eyebrows. "If you do nothing else, go down and see the Tanks. Oh, you *must* . . ."

I nudged Antonio in the back. "Stop . . ." he whispered, and his lips did what Maddy's did when she was trying not to laugh.

On my other side, Ian was holding forth. ". . . isn't there a danger these hybrid practices th*rr*ive in a liberal environment, but in a con*sair*vative one the picture looks different. V*err*y different indeed . . ."

"Change the subject, do," Gillian murmured

in my ear. "He's about to tell you he's an old warrior of the left."

"Do you have any children?" I interrupted, regretting it at once.

"Girl and a boy," said Ian. "For my sins. Twenty and twenty-two."

"I've got one twelve, one fourteen . . ."

"Mine are four and eight . . ."

Antonio was silent.

"Sixteen," I said. I was still a mother.

"My daughter's in Egypt."

"My son's been swimming with dolphins."

"Mine got hepatitis B."

"They survive."

I pointed to Ian's iPad. "Will you take our picture?" He obliged and passed it to me. I remembered that Antonio did not smile for the camera. He raised his brows, which made him appear dignified and enigmatic. I was reluctant to give back the picture and its curious distancing and doubling effect. Antonio and I lived in two places, in ourselves and in the image of us.

"Can you send it to my cell?"

"Are you in prison?"

"Mobile." I laughed. "Send it to my mobile."

"Your *mo*-bull?" said Ian.

Antonio touched my waist. "Shall we go look at some art?"

We made our way through the rooms. Older works from the collection had been paired with the contemporary—Monet's lilies and Long's stones, a Sickert interior with a Kienholz tableau—and upcoming artists had rooms to themselves. Antonio pressed on to the farthest display, in which houses sewn from colored fabric had been torn, stretched out of shape, and glued to slabs of handmade paper. He moved rapidly along the frames, reading the labels out loud. "Home One . . . Home Two . . ."

"The past exists in the present," I said, "but it can't be lived in. I think that's the idea." Desolation was always there, biding its time. No reprieve could last. No escape was far enough. I could reason out a curatorial concept, but that's not what I saw in this art of the flattened and torn. Would I ever be able to look at the world and not perceive bodily damage or the possibility of damage?

"Let me guess . . . Home Three?"—leaning in—"No! Travels in Inner Space. Oh, E-vie, help!"—chortling—"Is this art? This can't be art."

I did not reply. My alliance with Antonio did not go so far as to make me want to join him in cheap shots at contemporary art. Plenty of men like him came to my gallery talks, dragged in by wives eager to talk about meaning. Of course art could be pretentious and fake, ridiculous, even. But the impulse to art was not ridiculous. It was not ridiculous to try to make something out of nothing, to think with materials. Art allowed you to look at what you were afraid of. There was humility in it, and courage.

People had emptied from the galleries back to the reception. The speeches were about to start. It dawned on me then that Antonio had maneuvered me away from the others so we could be alone. I started to laugh. I slipped my arm out of his.

"Want to see something?"

35

We took the stairwell instead of the elevator to ground level. The gift shop was dark and so was the cloakroom. Too late I remembered our coats on the racks upstairs. Side lights marked out the sloping floor of the Turbine Hall under five stories of empty space.

"Did you ever sneak around your house at night when everyone was asleep?"

"I don't remember," said Antonio.

"I was scared, but I liked having the place to myself."

We reached the arch in the foyer to the Tanks. A single security guard sat at the outer desk, punching the keys of his phone.

"Where are we?" Antonio's voice was slightly blurred from three glasses of wine. I had stopped at one.

I sent the light of my phone running across the naked ceiling pipes and down the walls where the mouths of torn-out ducts gaped in the stained cement. Antonio aimed his own light above the arch. A row of sunken squares with bolts for eyes.

"They look like Iberian masks."

"I think they are the ends of T-beams."

"The South Tank is through there. It's where the oil was stored in the old power station. It's the only museum space in Europe made for installation and performance." We stood in silence. The Tanks had been opened for viewing, but everyone was upstairs now. We were out of sight of the guard. "Want to go in?"

I switched off my phone and made Antonio do the same. The foyer lights penetrated a short distance into the gloom. I released the prop at the bottom of the door, and as it swung shut I waited for sirens, running footsteps, the ignominy of being found out. Nothing happened. The door sealed with a clunk and darkness came at me like a cloth pressed to my face. No space, no distance; only the sharp mineral smell of liquids oozing in to reclaim their rightful place.

Nearby Antonio chuckled.

"Shhh . . ." I whispered, though with the thickness of the walls and the seal of the door, I knew we could have shouted in there and not been heard.

"Let's find our way to the other side. Want to? No lights."

"Is this . . . performance art, Eve?" His hand glanced off my shoulder and moved down, groping for my hand.

I snatched it away. "No hands."

I led the way with a halting gait, arms extended, waiting for something or someone to stop me. No point in opening my eyes. No way to tell if I was walking a straight line or not. The floor was hard and sticky underfoot. Twice my shoe caught and I saved myself from falling at the last minute. Each time I stopped to let my heart rate return to normal. After a while the dark became a friendly soft material that parted to let me pass and closed behind me.

"Antonio?"

"I am here." His voice was off to my right, not where I thought he was at all. The tank did strange things to sound, swallowed it up or moved it from one place to another. "This is crazy."

"Just keep going. We're almost there."

After a moment he said tersely: "I don't like this. I'm turning on the light."

"No! Don't! Please, Antonio."

Cats had whiskers, bats had sonic radar; I had whatever skills had been forced on me in the last two years to navigate darkness. I no longer knew where Antonio was. I could hear only my breathing and the sound of my shoes, which left tracks on the air, like smudges of charcoal that vanished as soon as they appeared. How far had we come? Impossible to keep track of time in an empty oil tank. Impossible to know how long it was before my arms went out again of their own accord: a coolness, a thickening of the odor; my hand struck the wall.

"I'm here! Found it!"

From the angle, I knew I had veered to the left

rather than traveling the full diameter of the tank. I was exploring the ledges that covered the sides, gauges for the depth of oil, I guessed, or for extracting machines to latch on to, when Antonio lost patience and switched on his light. Without warning, my pale hands were before me, groping the rusty wall. Everything was smaller, dirtier, and more ugly than it felt in the dark.

"This is really crazy." He made his way to me, bringing his jagged shadows with him. "You could have hurt yourself."

I turned and fitted my back to the wall. "Maddy had this thing," I said, "when she was three or so and we were at the lake, she used to float around in one of those inflatable rings. She wanted me exactly the right distance away. 'Go back, Mom, back. There! By that cloud! Now close your eyes.' Then she'd paddle over and pounce. When she was six, she'd turn off the lights in the basement and make me stand by the door. Then she'd spin around to make herself dizzy and find me in total darkness."

"I see," said Antonio. The light made strange shapes on his neck and face.

"What do you think that was about?"

"I don't know. Did she learn that from you?"

"She didn't get it from you."

"Eve?" He sounded out of breath. He slipped his phone in his pocket, and the dark closed around us again.

I spoke rapidly, whatever came into my head. "Have I told you that when Maddy was born I thought I already knew her?"

"E-vie . . ." said Antonio softly, separating the syllables.

Words were all I had to put between us, to keep him from coming any closer. "How far can newborns see, maybe a foot, foot and a half? I think it's the distance to the face of a person who's holding them. So this nurse put her in my arms." The wall pressed into my back. "I swear Maddy gave me this look: It's me. Mama, it's me."

"Eve." His voice was low and warm and very near. "What's going on?"

His arms and long body drew me to him. I tipped back my head. We were the only things in here made of flesh. We began to kiss the way we used to. Blood in my ears; taste of desire in my mouth. I felt him swelling, strangely high against me, and pressed myself there, courting ruin. I sensed rather than saw the forms against the dark: the heaving shoulders of my mother, my father's backhanded salute, Robin lying wounded under the water-grained slab. Antonio's mouth was taut and leathery, tasting of wine and peanut skins. No one knew we were here. Smiling Erica didn't know, and neither did her boys, flinging themselves across the grass. I had hunted him down, I had brought him here. I had the power to make things happen, to fling and smash, to inflict damage.

His hands cupped my jaw and neck. He came up for air to murmur, "It's still—" or maybe "You're still—" and in a panic I shoved him to pry us apart. But Antonio would not hear of it. He was gathering me up, finding my lips again, pressing on with the drama we had both started, as he'd always done and I'd always let him, as though it was unstoppable. He inched his hand down the front of my body, whispering. I was weak. We had done it standing up before, in the shower or the kitchen, laying ourselves down to finish. The channels were already cut. We would remember what worked, what pushed us over the edge.

Antonio began kissing me again, his fingers locked behind my neck, both of us straining to get to what we needed in this underground place where everything echoed and nothing rang true. His hand slid into my blouse and found the naked point of my breast. I jumped as though stung, and shrank away. Desire swerved and stalled. No! Not there. Not for you. He moved his hand to the small of my back.

The darkness enclosed us, a barrier nothing could pass through. All I wanted was her shy, shining face, in pencil so hard to look at and impossible to reach. Beseeching eyes, stubborn lips, smooth young features in the skull of babyhood and death. We wanted things from each other we could only partially and poorly give. She was with me. She was watching me. She was waiting for me to speak. Longing shuddered up my spine, numbing my arms, blocking my throat, trying to escape from my feeding mouth. She was spoken for. She was gone.

I forced him away, violently this time. "Sorry," I whispered. "I can't."

Antonio let me go. He was breathing hard.

"Oh, Evie," he said at last, arms at his sides, knowing better than to touch me. "We are only human."

His accent had always given clichés the patina of wisdom. I set off along the perimeter, groping in my pocket for the light. "Speak for yourself."

Antonio followed me back across the tank. Our lights found the chrome bar of the door at the same time. We propped it back open. When we passed the desk, the guard gave us a sharp look but didn't stop us. As we climbed the stairs to the third floor, I tripped and had to lunge for the railing. Antonio put his hand out but did not touch me. He'd done the same thing when I broke down that first night and told him about Maddy. On that occasion he had stopped short of touching me out of confusion and respect. Now he was letting me know that his body was no longer available to me. From the gallery came the hum of voices. I fumbled with my coat. The sleeve seemed to have been sewn shut. I pushed at it with my fist, panicked that someone would come out and find us there. Antonio righted the sleeve and held it for me from behind. I wanted to sink back into him and be indulged and forgiven, but he had already moved away.

"I'll walk you to St. Paul's."

"You're going in the other direction. I'll be fine. Really."

"No," he said. "I will."

We crossed the bridge and the two intervening streets, and circled the empty steps of the cathedral. The dome above was dark and remote and looked to be carved from solid stone. It was the station entrance around the corner that was alive, lit up and noisy, sucking passengers in from every direction. We stood at the top of the stairs. In Antonio's eyes I read puzzlement, pride, and something more sorrowful. In all likelihood I would never see him again.

"I'm sorry, Antonio."

"No, I'm sorry."

"Well." I tried a smile. "We can both be sorry." The uselessness of words! I cast my eyes over a darkened coffee shop and a lit-up pub, refuges barred to us now, and waited for him to speak. Antonio had removed himself from our drama already and was waiting for the moment when he could take his leave without giving anything away.

After a minute, I said: "I saw them, you know."

"Saw who?"

"Your boys. I went to their school."

He shot me a look of warning.

"Don't worry. They didn't know who I was. Neither did your wife." People in dreadlocks, torn jeans, suits, and stilettos detoured around us and down the stairs, scowling at the obstruction we made. I risked a glance up into his angry face.

"You wait 'til now to tell me?"

I said nothing.

"You got me to say the name of their school. Didn't you?"

I shrugged. "Maddy would have loved a brother or two."

"Was that a good thing to do, Eve?"

"Don't I get some credit for discretion?"

Coldly: "You had no right. And you know it."

I stared at him. "*I* had no right? What about you? Would your wife be interested to know what just went on over there?"

Antonio's face was rigid. "You play games with me, Eve." He started to speak again and stopped himself, scanning the pavement up and down Cheapside. "Should we be talking about this now? Here?"

"When else will we talk about it?" I tried to sound challenging. "Do you think it was easy? I thought I would feel connected to your boys through Maddy. I did in a way. But they're your kids. They don't have anything to do with her. Not really."

"No," said Antonio.

"At first I thought—There's a piece of Maddy! She's not completely gone! She's still walking around, just in a different form."

His eyes were glistening under the station lights.

"But she's not," I said.

"No," he said. "She's not."

"The older one takes after you. The younger one is more like Maddy, in temperament, I mean. You need to watch out for him. Don't assume he's okay just because he doesn't give you any trouble."

"I told Maddy about the boys," he said tersely. "She asked me about them."

"And you wrote to her behind my back. And you did meet me. Not just once." For your own complicated reasons, I thought, you did offer yourself to me. I could only hope his reasons were complicated. "Of *course* she would have asked about your boys. She would have been desperately interested in them."

"I guess so."

"But you know what would have been the main thing, for Maddy?"

"What?"

"She knew you loved them more than you loved her."

There was nothing to say to that, and Antonio said nothing. The passengers parted and flowed around us. Robin stepped into my mind, as if he could see us standing at the top of the station stairs, not knowing how to end this.

Antonio's hands were back in his pockets. My tone had reassured him I was not going to tear his family apart. He looked cold and forlorn. I felt sorry for him. I no longer wanted to know why he was with me, or what mix of vanity, curiosity, marital stasis, lost youth, true love, or the glamour of tragedy had been behind his passion in the Tanks. I had no urge to explain what he meant to me. Let him tell himself what he wanted about our encounter. I would keep to myself what I knew, or refused to know, or barely knew about it. We had met, and we had done nothing irreversible.

What is it about tall men that always makes me think they can help? I reached for Antonio, and was surprised by how long and how tightly he held me, pressing my face sideways into the rough wool of his coat. When he let me go I rushed down the steps as if released by a spring, waving one hand behind my back in case he was still watching.

36

The airplane's shadow rushed sideways over grass and runway apparatus, growing smaller and more uncertain, an earthbound version of itself that the plane was shedding as it rose up. In London the winter sun never parted from the horizon for long, and set at four in the afternoon. But up here the sun was high and unblinking, and it hunted down every line and curve of water and silvered it fleetingly.

I had spoken to Robin the night before. He couldn't wait to see me, he said. With many air miles already between me and Antonio, everything I had been tamping down erupted to the surface. The unnatural darkness and inhuman smell; backing up to the laddered wall . . . The images were powerful enough, it seemed likely that Robin, wherever he was, would be able to see them.

Maddy put a high value on loyalty. She once told me that cheating on someone was the meanest thing she could think of anyone doing. Would she be appalled, or would she exempt me because I was her mother or because she longed for a parental reunion, something children of divided families supposedly do?

When I closed my eyes, Robin was there,

gaining volume and definition as the plane hurtled toward him. I hoped time spent at the lake had put him in a philosophical frame of mind. Robin would understand. He would have to. Maybe Norma, who had planted the idea in the first place, could explain the nuances better than I could. They had met. The subject must have come up. I would impress on him how essential it had been to see Antonio, how the echoes of Maddy had unhinged me a little but it was all behind me now, as far as London was behind me and the Atlantic was below, shifting its miniature waves. How much would I say? A conversation with Robin was not something to rehearse for.

Clouds were moving in like a slowly gathering herd, packing together to hide the earth from view. Don't look. Don't be fooled by the magical sight of what we were about to destroy. Sip cheap wine, feed from a tray, spin tales until the real tragedy swallows up our little personal ones. Don't think about pulling up to the silent house and going inside. I began my special pleading to Maddy, wherever she was, in whatever form. Forgive the missing father, the faulty genes, the late diagnosis. Forgive me for being stubborn, divided, bitter, alive. And a new one: Forgive me my trespasses.

In the pickup zone outside Dulles airport, I was lifted off the ground and given a midair kiss that had more pressure behind it than passion. When Robin was nervous, he went in for theatrical gestures. We stood apart, breathing white shapes into the cold air. He clapped his gloved hands together. So surprising was it to be on the ground in the presence of Robin, large as life and all in one piece, that it took me a moment to notice the beard, an elfish goatee grayer than his hair.

"Very cute," I said.

"Cute? I was aiming a bit higher than cute."

"Dashing, then. Mysterious."

Robin loaded my bags and slammed the trunk and we got in. "Turns out," he said, starting the engine, "the line between stylish and homeless is a thin one. I see people staring at me: Is this urban chic, or is it that living in your car makes it hard to shave?"

I laughed in the old way. "Do I have a say in it?"

"I thought you'd like a change."

"No, I like it. I do."

"The thing about facial hair," said Robin, "it's zero commitment. It can go at any time." Easily he laid his hand on my knee. "Feels like just yesterday I was seeing you off."

"I know."

"And it feels like it's been years."

"I know."

He took his hand back to change lanes. The freeway signs wheeled past, Bethesda, Baltimore, white letters on green, the places we had to circle around to get home. His eyes never stopped moving, making their private, minute-to-minute decisions. Inside the ring of beard, his lips were fuller and more self-possessed. Why had a beard never occurred to me before? He looked like a very good likeness of Robin. No matter how close you get to someone, the deep strangeness of the other person is always there, waiting to rush in.

We were off the freeway, heading south toward Silver Spring. The lights of a winter evening wheeled past: streetlights, porch lights, flashing lights, green and pink neon lights: big, human versions of what I'd seen from the air.

"It hasn't snowed yet," I said.

"It's been cold enough. Freezing or below freezing for a week."

"If it rained, it would snow."

"That's one way of putting it, Ducks."

I allowed ten seconds of silence. "Robin, would you mind not calling me that?"

"Why not?"

"I've never liked it much. Sorry. Nothing against Cincinnati. It's bizarre," I said, eyes on the road, "changing worlds like this. Air travel has a lot to answer for."

He shot me a sympathetic glance; he was not one to take offense. "Did you ever stop to think that before the steam train, no one had traveled faster than on the back of a horse?"

"Do horses go faster than clipper ships? Anyway, I don't like it. It's too sudden. I don't know who I am."

He slowed and stopped at a crosswalk. "Tell me the best part of the trip. What you were saddest to leave." Robin liked to ask for details in the form of lists. Three things I liked about my job. The worst vacation I'd ever had. My five favorite movies. He didn't really rank experience like that; it was his way of opening up a conversation.

"Just London," I said, not playing along. "Everything about it."

"We'll get you home and straight to bed." As if sleep was the answer to changing worlds, to speaking in generalities, to whatever ailed us now.

The car lurched to a stop. Robin's arm shot out, though my seat belt had already stopped me. He raised an apologetic hand to the honkers behind. A large woman in slippers had stepped onto the crosswalk just as we were rolling forward. First testing it with her foot, she advanced like someone crossing a rope bridge over a ravine.

"There should be a minimum speed on these crosswalks," said Robin.

"For the pedestrians, you mean?"

"Drivers could hold up signs to say how long they're willing to stop. Over Ninety Seconds, Can't Make Any Promises!"

"The Risk Is Yours." I leaned over, laughing,

and kissed Robin on the border between beard and cheek. I hadn't realized just how much space Antonio took up, with his long coat and his top-flight career and his obliviousness to the asymmetry between us: my part in his life, his part in mine.

At home I poured us both a sedative glass of wine and kept Cloud on my lap while Robin told me about his commissions, a lucrative built-in closet and a coffee table in the shape of California. I filled him in on the last interviews, my dizzy spell in the Tanks, and the opening, while the cat pushed her skull under my hand and the empty house bore down on me. I had left the country, I had come back, and still Maddy wasn't here.

I gave Antonio no special weight alongside the other stories. I drafted in a corporate vocabulary. Seeing Antonio had been "challenging" and "valuable"; we'd spoken several times; I had not met his new family, nor did I want to. Nothing I said was, strictly speaking, untrue. Cloud left me to see if there was anything in her bowl she didn't know about, and I ran my hand along the crack at the straight-cut end of the table. The butterfly joint that bridged it was as smooth as a scar.

Where had Robin gone? He was behind my chair, reaching his arms down the front of my body, casual as a parent preparing to pick up a child, careful not to touch anything personal. I knew his tactics. Drawing the space around an object renders the object more acutely. I turned to meet his lips, bare and warm in their furry surround, and upstairs I allowed myself to be undressed, caressed, and cajoled into hunger of the kind that makes its own decisions, that kicks things off and kicks things away. We had not been together long enough for boredom to set in—tragedy had set in—and now it was Robin I wanted, our particular history and our private games; but what was happening was impossible to separate from Antonio. The force of that encounter had been trapped in me for days. It had to go somewhere.

We lay together, Robin's rib cage moving against mine. In an old film we would both be smoking. I kissed his hand and carefully replaced it on his chest. Pleasure held dangers, new ones all the time.

"What are you thinking?"

He gave me a postcoital smile. "I'm thinking how much I've missed you." He eased his arm free and sat on the bed's edge, looking down at me, his face in shadow. "I don't mean when you were in London."

Watching his sinewy back and pale flanks recede to the bathroom, I glimpsed the tail end of an idea just before it slid out of sight.

37

You'd think a homecoming like that would have cheered me up. The next day Robin sought me out with tender high spirits, backing off when he saw what a terrible mood I was in. I unpacked, did three loads of laundry, made a pointless trip to the drugstore to get out of the house, and, when questioned, blamed it on jet lag. An hour and a half was taken up by a visit from my parents. No one asked me about Antonio. In our family, delicate subjects were only broached one-on-one. After they left, Robin and I drove to get a take-out pizza and ate it at the dining room table from the box.

"Feeling any better?" asked Robin hopefully. "Have you landed?"

"Now I have to turn around and pack for the lake. Do you think we could invite Alison up?"

He folded the box in half. "Unless you want it to be just us?"

"I felt bad she had to go back before me. She doesn't have much of a family life. Mom and Dad won't mind."

"Is it part of the transition?" he said, studying me across the table. "Settling back?"

I shrugged. "Maddy loved Christmas."

"I know."

"I don't even remember Christmas last year. It's completely wiped. It might help to have other people around. You've been up at the lake a lot," I said. "Weren't you lonely without me?"

"Desperately. Did I tell you about the power outage?"

"Norma did."

"Bad luck," he said. "Being a newcomer, especially. Did not endear her to anyone."

"It endeared her to you."

He narrowed his eyes as if trying to bring me into focus.

"You always go for the underdog," I said.

"Norma's not an underdog."

"No," I admitted. "She's not. Did she stop by the house?"

"She dropped in on all the south shore lots to explain. Grovel, actually. Everyone without lights got a bottle of wine."

"Boys at the grandparents?"

"She had them with her. You can't get mad at someone who has a cute kid on each hand."

"Did you get to see their house inside?"

"Once."

"What's it like? I never went in."

"Oh, it's nice enough, but run-of-the-mill, wood-wise. Hollow doors. Click flooring. Very Home Depot for a high-end architect."

"Maybe her husband's not really an architect."

"Oh well." Robin grinned. "I say it's great to see the rain forest being put to good use."

"Did she come over to ours?"

"Once or twice."

"Was it once or was it twice?"

"A few times. I don't remember."

"Why?" I persisted, feeling on my shoulder the symbolic restraining hand of my mother.

"Why don't I remember?"

"Why did she come over?"

He shrugged. "Being friendly, I guess."

To buy time, I ran my eyes over the hutch, an ugly fifties item of lacquered maple I had picked up at a garage sale. Robin regularly offered to replace it with something magnificent of his own making, but I took the view that not every piece of furniture in the house had to be tasteful. Besides, the top drawer of the hutch was where I always kept Maddy's school photographs. On its uppermost shelf circulars, coupons, and mail accumulated in messy piles. Now these papers stood on end in a carved wood letter holder.

I lifted it down, tipped out the papers, and turned it on its side to examine the design of overlapping ovals that Frank Lloyd Wright used for his chair backs and room screens. I had last admired this object with Maddy in the gift shop at Fallingwater.

"I went while you were away," said Robin. "I'd never seen it in winter before."

I felt as though I had strayed close to the edge of a great height. "And you brought this back for me."

"Yes."

"That was so sweet." I returned the holder to its shelf and sat down. "And what was it like in winter?"

"Magic. The falls were running but everything else was iced over. The stream had to force its way through the ice."

"I always said I wanted to see it in winter."

"We'll go," said Robin quickly. "You'll love it. In winter the house looks even more a part of the mountain."

"Is it a mountain? I didn't think it was a mountain."

"Hill," said Robin.

I smiled encouragingly. "Did you go by yourself?"

He checked my eyes and made a rapid decision. "Norma went with me."

Blood surged to my head, blotting out Robin, the table, the room, all sense and decency. Images rushed at me as though they'd been waiting to be released. On bridges, over falls, in underground caverns he pulled her close, bent over her, and did the things he did to me with a passion born of craving and denial. Clever of her to send me away! But she'd only met him that day on the dock. Even so! Ways were always found where betrayal was concerned. The two of them writhed together, finding what they needed. Her eyes shut, her white throat exposed. All welcome snatched away. All help gone. No one for me, ever again. No place for me, ever again. Once more I felt the invisible hand on my shoulder, sensed rather than heard the voice that, when I was a young person, had enraged me so: Step carefully until you're sure; things aren't what they seem; impulsiveness does not always serve you well.

"All these mysterious trips to the lake?" I sneered, turning my mother away and silencing her. "The mythical husband? The blackout!" The biggest insult of all was starting to sink in. "Fallingwater. Really, Robin? *Really?* Go ahead and fuck her. But don't take her to Fallingwater. That's mine. Mine and Maddy's."

"Stop it, Eve. Stop for a minute! Listen—"

Neither his astonishment nor his hurt seemed faked, but who could tell? His hand went out; his table was between us. I was standing by this time, my knuckles on the beautiful wood, ready to bolt from the room, the house, the planet, to be anywhere but here, and anyone but myself.

"I bet you lay there afterward and talked about me."

His mouth was an ugly shape. "Seriously, Eve?"

"Why not? She's a basket case. She's off the rails. Her life is over anyway." I did not recognize my voice; at the same time it seemed more profoundly my own. "What a drag! You think I don't know what a drag I am? What a colossal bore I am? What a great chance this was—"

"*Ser*iously?" he cut in, measured and cold.

But there was no stopping me.

"Say something! Tell me I'm wrong!" My voice sank. "Look at you. Sitting there lining up your excuses."

Robin's arms were clamped to his chest. He was scanning my face as if he'd never seen it before. Is this how the end comes? Misdeeds on every side, a souvenir in the wrong place, fury in search of a worthwhile cause? Calamity breeds calamity. Another one could happen just like that, and no one would be much surprised, least of all me.

"Go to London," he jeered. "Go back to the lake. Go see your ex. Do what you have to do. I'll be here. I'll take whatever you dish out—" His scornful tone was so unlike him, and so closely matched my own, that I had to cover my mouth to keep from laughing. He swatted the air with the back of his hand. "I don't know what you did over there. I can guess."

I found the table's edge and held on to it to get the spinning room under control. I felt like someone coming out of a fever dream. "Nothing," I said meekly.

"Nothing!" He bit off the word. "*I'm* the one who did nothing! Not that I wasn't tempted."

"I promise you—"

A warning palm. Come no closer. "You know what the problem is, Eve? The problem is you."

Barely above a whisper, I said: "So am I wrong?"

"You think you're the only one who lost someone?" His arms locked again over his chest. "You think you're the only one who misses her? It's all about you. You're incapable of seeing anyone else. You don't care about anyone else. The problem is *you*."

I asked it again, as though an answer to this one question would fix everything: "So I'm wrong?"

He gave me a look of such derision that it was hard to imagine he had ever loved me. I knew then without a doubt that whatever the truth was, whatever had happened or not happened in my absence, I was the one who was wrong, profoundly, grotesquely, irreversibly wrong. Loyalty to Robin had not stopped me from seducing Antonio. I had stopped because of Maddy. I had been prepared all along to sacrifice Robin, though in my arrogance I never believed it would be necessary. He was right. I was wrong. Wrong to the core, wrong at the cellular level, the kind of wrong that brought about disaster and ushered in ruin even as I protested my innocence. Maddy's death had stripped off the veneer and exposed what was really there: cheap, second-rate, nasty.

"Find a handyman," said Robin. "Get yourself a babysitter. It's not going to be me." Sucking the air like someone about to weep, he quit the room without looking back and I did not dare try to stop him.

At three in the morning I awoke, aching and shivering. The sheet beside me was empty. He'd slept in the music room. When I went to the bathroom to vomit, flakes of snow were floating down the window, silver on one side, dark on the other. By their speed and size I could tell it was the kind of snowfall that sticks.

For two days I could do nothing but lie flat and be sick. Reading was out of the question; so was watching television or listening to music. My body was not my own; it did what it had to do, and I took a grim pleasure in kneeling to hug the cold toilet bowl, in the stink and the release. No one ever talks about the pleasures of throwing up. Rose and Walter stayed away, not wanting to catch anything before the holidays. Cloud stood by me. Robin spoke of foreign germs and recirculated cabin air and brought me what I needed with the remoteness of a private nurse.

"What's going to happen?" I asked on the third day, sitting up to drink tomato soup from a mug.

"I don't know."

"Are we still going to the lake? Everyone's counting on it."

The suspension of time and the absence of a follow-up conversation gave our fight a dreamlike quality. Whenever I saw Robin's face I knew I hadn't dreamt it. I went downstairs in my bathrobe; the letter holder was still on the top shelf of the hutch. The storm had stopped, but the Eastern Seaboard remained in the grip of a freeze, and the plow drifts along the roads were intact though increasingly filthy.

"We have to," he said at last, with great reluctance. "I've got something to show you."

"What is it?"

"Mind your own business."

I rushed to ingratiate myself: "I still like the beard . . ." But he was halfway to the door and either had not heard or chose not to turn around.

38

Packed snow could be as slick as ice, the difference being that on snow the tires had a chance of digging in and finding purchase. We turned left at the country store and started the climb up through the National Park.

"Not too slippery, is it?"

Robin tapped the brakes. "Fine for the moment."

I turned to smile at Alison, roly-poly in her gray ski jacket in the back seat. Black, gray, and white were the only colors she ever wore. She was scowling out the window. Robin and I were putting on a good show, but surely she sensed the tension, and anyway, the ease that had developed between Alison and me in London would take time to re-create.

"I'm glad you could come." Just having her in the car was a small victory. Robin would indulge her; Rose and Walter would cheer her up.

Alison always ignored pleasantries. "Will the lake be frozen solid?"

I hid my smile. "It never freezes solid, that depth of water. Just the surface."

Irritably she asked: "Well, can you walk on it?"

"We've got something called an auger to drill down and check how thick the ice is. We say six inches, minimum. Some people say four. If it's blue ice."

"Blue ice is frozen shit," said Alison, "that leaks out of airplanes."

"Blue ice," said Robin, "is when the ice is compressed without a lot of air bubbles trapped in it. It's stronger than white ice."

"Have you ever been to a lake in winter before?" I asked.

She shook her head. "I want to walk on it."

"Robin goes out on the ice no matter what."

"A lot of people say three is safe," he said.

"It depends on the conditions," I told Alison.

"I know that!" Robin said sharply. "I'm the country boy, remember?"

Since our confrontation, he'd maintained the air of a wounded animal whose patience was not to be tested. He did not respond to my overtures and offered none of his own. My illness had left me scoured out and meek; I did not want to clarify what had gone on between us.

"Sometimes the ice cracks under your foot," I said.

"There are thicker and thinner areas," said Robin. "You can always jump to a stronger part of the ice."

"What he means is, he's gotten away with it so far. He loves to scare us."

Long loaves of snow sat on the caretaker's porch railings and a round one on each gate pillar. "We never used to come at Christmas," I told Alison as we drove through. "When my father built the place, it wasn't even winterized. The caretaker plows the shore road. We pay him to keep our driveway clear." The roadside gullies were filled to the brim with snow, stippled by the stalks of dead ferns. Two big banks marked the turn into our lot. "This is it. We're here!"

A kink in the drive kept the house hidden until the last minute, and as it curved into view, I had a flash of astonishment that the place was still there, the two-step back porch, the chalet roof with its burden of white, the sunken stillness of the frozen lake beyond, that all this had not vanished too.

My father met us at the door, his neck thrust forward from a lifelong effort to peer closely at things. He hugged me and gave Alison a dignified squeeze around the shoulders; they had met once before. Strangers, bashful people, strays, and underdogs always received his special attention; he was like Robin in that respect. I thought I saw Alison nestle into him for an instant before pulling away. From what little she said, her father had been abusive or neglectful or both. She kept her family apart from whatever went on between us; or maybe the truth was I had not shown a great deal of interest.

In the living room, I was assailed by the sharp sweet smell of pine. Gloves and mittens had been spread to dry on the raised hearth. Maddy's straw angels, each one playing a different instrument, were arranged as always on a silver tray. The tree in the corner was strung with unlit lights and tinsel, but as of yet no ornaments. It was our tradition to decorate the tree together, lifting the ornaments one by one from the segmented boxes. Remember the gingerbread man, Mom? Remember the reindeer I made in second grade? I love the glass bell. Don't you love the glass bell?

I had resolved not to prepare myself for the reality of Christmas, and now I pushed away the voices. I forced myself to see through the eyes of Alison, who had never been here and could not miss Maddy: the front window filled with lake; my mother smiling her way from the kitchen, wiping her wrists on a hand towel sewn to her apron, a gracious, old-fashioned mother who could move with the times; Barney prancing around, on everybody's side.

I had warned my mother things were rocky between Robin and me. After welcoming Alison, she kissed the two of us and scanned our faces, intensifying the wattage of her smile. I felt she was taking my little hand and putting it in Robin's little hand and urging us to make up before lunchtime.

My father went down to the dock to check the depth of the ice, taking Rose, Alison, and Barney with him. Robin stayed behind. He lowered himself into an armchair; he got up and scurried to the utility room, deciding finally to shovel the deck while I withdrew to the kitchen. I was putting peanut butter and spaghetti on the shelves when a knock came on the back door, so soft that I mistook it at first for a tapping branch.

Norma stood on the mat. In her white parka and gloves she looked like something carved out of a snowbank. Her cheeks were scarlet from the cold. When she pushed back her hood I saw that her reddish gold hair was cut short and sprayed out from her face without bands or clips. For one paralyzing moment I thought she had come for a tryst with Robin. But no: she was smiling freely and hugging me as if meeting me for the first time after some kind of close call.

I shouted for Robin. I watched carefully as they greeted one another with workmanlike smiles, and then I led the way through the hall so they couldn't see my face.

Behind me, Norma whispered: "Has she seen it?"

I stopped. "Seen what?"

"I was waiting for you," said Robin. He went over and pulled the trapdoor down by its strap. He unfolded the hinged steps and secured their rubber feet on the floor.

"You've finished the attic?" There was a time when I'd loved surprises.

His face held little expression. "You go first."

At the top, the step now fitted onto a landing from which the whole room was visible. Mutely I stood and waited for Robin and Norma to join me.

Deep reds and purples, spiced yellows, burnt-orange-colored rugs and hangings glowed like hearths against the white walls. Long low sofas. In-built bookshelves. Floor cushions at a low table. Dark floorboards with the eddying sheen of stone. Fallingwater was built on rock over a stream. This room was built from wood up in the trees. No concrete encased it. No waterfall roared underneath. Yet the same kind of horizontal grace had been achieved, the same rich colors, the same invitation to curl up and take cover in a place that was everywhere exposed to the outside world. Light came in from all angles, seemingly not from windows at all, though there were windows in every direction, a long slot of them along the eaves, slanted ones in the roof space, and an arched window at the end that I had last seen propped against the wall, wrapped in plastic. Snowy branches filled it now.

Why didn't Robin say something, even if I couldn't? We had not discussed the details. I'd had no idea it would turn out like this. Because the new room had not been finished in time for Maddy, I had taken little interest in it once she got sick, and none after she died.

"We tried to get the spirit of it." Robin's voice was subdued, wary.

"We?"

"I made all the cushions and things," said Norma shyly. I had almost forgotten about her. "I found the rugs and hangings. I'm ashamed to say I'd never been to Fallingwater before. Living so near!"

"You helped Robin finish the room?"

"Oh no." She smiled. "I just came in at the end and dressed it up a little. I like interiors. I'm not artistic. Not at all. But I'm good at sewing." I knew if I tried to speak again I would cry. "They didn't let you take photographs indoors. I took notes, and there were some pictures online. We got the colors pretty close. Didn't we, Robin?" They exchanged a glance of the kind nurses exchange over a patient's head.

"The staircase still needs to be built. I thought I would just go ahead and get everything else done while you were away." He was talking rapidly. "Instead of, you know, waiting."

"You mean I'm no good at making decisions these days?"

"Obviously change it around!" Norma rushed to say. "If you don't like anything. It's yours."

Shame kept me from meeting her eye. My cagey performance on the dock and on her picnic bench, my mission to conceal and disclose my anguish. Why had she bothered? Why make soft

429

furnishings for a dream room for someone you barely know? People did irrational things; people did all kinds of extraordinary things. Walter and Rose were in on it too. Built by my father as a cabin-in-the-woods, the house had been enlarged, redesigned, and improved on for forty years. The attic would be the last refinement.

"I like it," I said. "I love it." The uselessness of words!

Joy would have been on Maddy's face had she stood where we were standing. Maybe the others were furtively noticing and tactfully ignoring whatever was on my face now. The room had the melancholy of fires and aquariums and libraries and late afternoons; that could not be helped, but there were riches too, beyond the melancholy, or hidden deep inside it.

It was too intimate, the three of us standing together in this space they had made for me. I went over and picked up a cushion in a geometric design of blue, red, and black, studied the fine overstitching along the border; put it down; stroked the heathery weave of a throw; touched the deep red cushions and the wall hangings, edged like vestments with gold.

The bookcase held a few paperbacks. Propped on one of the shelves was a small frame. I picked it up: a black-and-white photograph of Maddy, aged seven. At the time her hair had been a close-fitting cap like mine was now. Her hands were tucked in the pockets of her denim jacket. She gazed out of the frame at we who were assembled in the room that would never be hers, with an expression that was tolerant and childish and quizzical and humorous, made from all the tones of photographic gray. *I live here now.*

Downstairs the others crashed in, stamping and barking, in high spirits from the cold.

Four and a half inches the auger had measured and the decision was made not to walk on the ice. Everyone trooped up to the attic to admire the room. At the table for sandwiches, Norma tried to engage Alison in conversation. I could see they would tolerate each other but never get along. Alison turned instead to Robin. He explained to her in a low voice how to start a fire with a lemon, while at the end of the table, Rose and Walter assured each other once again that fracking would never come to Tawasentha Lake.

I sat in a daze. My arm was taken; Norma's clear concerned eyes searched mine. "So how did it go over there? Not a complete disaster, I hope?"

"Long story," I whispered. "Life-changing. Tell you later."

Robin had started quizzing Alison about London, her job, her ambitions. "Fine arts?" he scoffed. "Applied arts? What does that mean? No, we need something much more objective.

What about how you clean it? You'd have the dustable arts, see? The sprayable arts. The dry-cleanable arts . . . ?" If anyone could open her up, it was Robin. It was the kind of nonsense he used to spin with Maddy.

I turned back to Norma, who wanted to know about London and my job and our holiday plans. I let her do the work, while trying to listen and return the questions, but I was having trouble seeing her from the correct distance. It was not just the haircut and the winter pallor and the blue of her eyes, deeper than I remembered. Too much had been said, whether in her presence or not. When I looked at Norma, time dilated and shrank. In white shorts she shoved off the dock and raised her paddle to wave. I flew away and returned. She made her cushions. I made my accusations. We sat at the table drinking chocolate in thick sweaters. Maddy was nowhere to be found.

At the door I thanked her again, so insistently that she drew away and exited with an embarrassed, indulgent smile, and I spent the afternoon by the window watching the snow float down. By dusk it had stopped. My mother cooked lasagna, I won a game of Shanghai I had no interest in winning, and my parents and Alison turned in early.

We kept finding things to do instead of going to bed. Robin cleaned the kitchen; I tried to read.

When he headed to the basement to tinker with the boiler, I pulled down the trapdoor steps and slipped up to the new room. I had not yet had a chance to sit on the couch, which turned out to be a padded shelf that floated off the wall with no visible means of support. I'd brought the portable house phone with me. I tapped in the number before I could think better of it.

Glenda's thick, peculiar voice added to the distortion on the line. "That's very good news. We are so grateful. We'll use it wisely."

Who said "wisely" anymore? "I want to be consulted at every stage, you know. To retain control."

"Yes, of course." We both knew it was an illusion. Who can control anything nowadays, let alone the use of images?

"My thinking is," I said, "Maddy made it for the campaign, and she gave it over to the campaign. She must have been happy for it to be used."

"I think she was."

"She must have wanted people to see it."

"The fact is," said Glenda Sedge, "it's out there already."

I hung up and kept my body very still on the floating shelf, beside the black-and-white photo of Maddy, hands in the pockets of her child-size jacket. Careful! she said. Careful! I said. You've been at Jack's? It's not deep. It's nothing. Had I opened my hands and allowed another precious thing to be taken away? Her shadowed eyes, her penciled face, changing continually on the screen inside a screen. When her ruin was complete, the applause began. In private she could laugh. Joy undid her. She was out there already. A free, shining thing.

Branches blocked the window with their burden of snow. Clods of it fell silently to the roof below. If I didn't clutch and grasp and I didn't turn away, maybe the rich colors and horizontal grace and the warmth of the side lamps could be assimilated piecemeal and one day the room would be mine.

When I came down, Robin was in the hallway. He watched me retract and latch the steps. "I wondered where you went."

"It's beautiful," I said. "Better than I ever imagined." I wouldn't blame him if he left me now, room or no room. Maybe a part of me would welcome it.

"It wouldn't be half as good without Norma."

"I don't know why she bothered. She hardly knows us."

He shrugged. "She's that kind of person. She wanted to do something." Exhausted as we both were, sleep was out of the question.

"Want to go down to the lake?"

39

A winter lake is alive with sound. Ringed with snow and under a lid of ice, it would seem to be the last place to make any noise. But static comes out of it, and strange gulping sounds, and sometimes the crack of a whip. Most unforgettable is the groaning, as if a colossal thing is rolling, dragging, and breaking apart. It seems to issue from the sky or from inside your own body. That's the lake's trick. It's impossible to tell exactly where the sound comes from, and there's no telling when it will start or end. You can only listen for as long as it lasts and not ask for any more.

We stood on the shore where the dock would have been. Late as it was, the moon had been high for hours, a cold half circle piercing the blue-black sky. In winter the dock was dismantled in sections and stored under a tarpaulin by the woodpile. One section we propped up sideways on the ground to put the chairs on. They sparkled now with frost. When we sat down, the chill burned without delay through my coat. Robin held himself stiffly.

"We got it out just in time this year."

"It's always a gamble," I said. In the old days my father used to pull the dock up on Labor Day, but in these warmer times, we often pushed it back to October.

"I think your dad likes the gamble. Has the dock ever gotten stuck in the ice?"

"Once, I think. It had to be hacked out." The time was past when my father could do any heavy work alone. The time would come when he couldn't do it at all. "Thanks for helping him, Robin. When you came along, he could see a future for this place."

Snow had a gleam of its own, duller than water. In winter there was no reflection and hence no doubling of worlds.

"I called Glenda Sedge."

"You did?"

"I told her she could use Maddy's animation."

From the way Robin smiled with his lips together, I knew he'd thought all along that's what I should do. "Feel okay? Now that you've done it?"

"I guess so."

"That's a good sign."

"I could always say no later on."

He studied me, ice crystals glittering in his beard. "I don't think you will."

"Maddy's the one who put it out there in the first place," I said. "For the campaign. It was her way of . . . facing things. But still it's scary."

"Because you don't know exactly what they'll do with it?"

"You never can be sure what the world's intentions are toward your child. Do you feel that about Vince?"

"All the time," he said. "That's another story. But as a parent you don't have a lot of choice. They have to go out there in the end."

I was grateful to hear myself described as a parent. I would be, until the day I died.

Robin's mustache hid his upper lip and made him look secretive and holy. I wanted to rip it off and expose his true expression. What had really happened between him and his ex-wife? After three years I thought I had the measure of Robin, but how much could we really know about each other and what we were capable of? Antonio's long body, Antonio's eyes and lips, existed in another dimension, outside the logic of what was happening to me now.

My eyes lingered on Robin's profile. The lines radiating from the corners of his eyes were dignified and warm. Which expressions were true? "I'm the one who did nothing! Not that I wasn't tempted." That's what he had said. In anger, possibly. Righteous anger, or something more complicated. Which expressions were true? Maddy's serenely shut eyes, her quivering lips, her defiance, her naked despair? Or the laughing baby's face, that invited me in and shut me out? Most of us would never reach the depths Maddy had gone to, facing what she faced, knowing what she knew. I resolved to keep "final final final" for myself, and not to speak again until Robin did.

I heard myself say: "Have you forgiven me?"

He didn't turn his head. "I don't know."

"Can you see why I might have thought . . . ?"

"Kind of," he said. "I can kind of see it." He paused a beat. "But it's an awful way to treat someone."

"I know. I'm so sorry, Robin. I went off the rails. I was imagining things."

He turned his head to look at me, shapes from his breath dissolving in the night air and forming again. Beyond him the shoreline trees made a chain around the lake. With their cladding of white, they seemed closer together and blacker at their centers than in summer. Robin's silence and the smug lines at the corners of his eyes suddenly galled me.

"So *were* you tempted?" I said, with Alison-like bluntness.

"Was I what?"

"Tempted."

He studied me. "Not really."

"Not really? What does that mean?"

"Were *you?*"

On a cliffside, looking down. "A little." The words hovered in the air between us and then I was pleading with him, sick with fear for what could not be recovered and for what else could go. "Nothing happened! I told you, it was extra-ordinary circumstances. It'll never be like that again."

Hands in his pockets, shoulders rigid, he turned his head toward the lake. After what seemed a very long time, he said: "Do you know why everything is blue at night?"

"No, why?" I'd heard it before, but I needed him to tell me something, anything at all.

"Night vision is sensitive to the blue-violet end of the spectrum. It's why in twilight everything takes on a blue tinge. Your rods are taking over from your cones."

"But that's not why moonlight is blue."

"I guess that comes from the moon itself. I'm not sure."

"There's not a lot to say about the moon, is there?"

His eye creases deepened. He looked at me. "Not really."

"Too much has been said about it."

"All of it true," said Robin. He got to his feet and clapped his gloves together. "Want to walk on the lake?" Without waiting for an answer, he stepped down through the drifts to the ice.

"Are you sure four inches is safe?" I called.

"Up to you!" He looked like a friar, with his black ski jacket cinched at the waist and the hood up. "I'm going out on it."

I plunged through the snow after him, testing

the ice first with my foot like the woman in the crosswalk. Solid enough, although the hollow grinding sound my boots made was unmistakable: we were walking over water.

"Your dad plays it safe," said Robin. "Especially when there's a guest he feels responsible for."

"Don't you feel responsible for people?"

"I'm not worried about four inches. I've been on four inches many a time."

Behind us the side bedrooms were in darkness and so was the attic room, hidden up in the branches, but the front window was ablaze with light, and the four terrace lamps shone in their cages.

"How long do you think those lamps will last?"

"They're supposed to be outdoor-proof," said Robin.

"Didn't you put them in that first year you came up? They've held out for two winters."

"We'll have to wait and see."

I turned my back on the lit-up house. Around the shore, the other cottages were mostly in darkness. Norma's gave off a reassuring glow. I felt a pang to think of her asleep over there with her all-night porch lamp on. "Their house is even more visible in winter."

"Yes," said Robin.

"It doesn't really matter, does it?"

"No," said Robin.

"Or the color. I kind of like it now. Sometimes I get all worked up about nothing."

He was backlit, his whole face in shadow.

"The ice is thinner than it used to be," I said. "We had seven or eight inches when I was growing up."

"Even thicker up north. We used to drive onto the ice and fish from the seat of a pickup. I wouldn't do it now."

"Have you seen that program about walrus mothers fighting for space for their pups? They're crammed together on these little chunks of ice. They push each other off."

"No, but I've seen icebergs calving. It's happening so fast."

The snow stretched out before us in long smooth scallops, ridged like bone.

"If you'd never seen water in solid form, would you guess it would be like that?"

"No," said Robin. "Ice kind of makes sense. But snow is more like sand."

"Look at the colors!" Not only the blues, but the violets, grays, purples, and pinks read as variations of white against the dark fringe of the shore. "Doesn't it seem impossible that all this could go?"

"Once it goes, it goes."

I kicked at the snow. "Don't think about it."

I could not see Robin's face, but I could feel his eyes on me. Some things were too big to talk about. Eventually he said: "Shall we sneak Alison out here? Not tell your father?"

"Tomorrow night," I replied, happy to be conspirators again. "She'd love it. I don't think she's spent much time outdoors."

"You two got close in London?"

"I don't know about close."

"She admires you."

"How do you know?"

"Male instinct. Though anyone prepared to be that awkward, I find a little scary."

"Anyway, I'm glad you like her." I turned around and Robin turned with me. A line of boot-shaped holes led away, connecting us to the shore. "Maddy never saw the room," I said.

"The moon?"

"The *room*."

"I should have finished it a long time ago!"

After a moment I said: "It's finished now," and I lunged across the ice, plowing up giant petals of snow. He did the same, in another direction. We stood looking at each other. I made my way to him over the churned-up surface.

"When was she last at the lake?" he asked.

"In June. She drove up with Jack."

"Did she know it would be the last time?"

"I hope not."

A giant whip cracked under our feet and lashed toward the far shore. I froze in place. I had never been on the ice when it happened. Robin reached for my hand, and, glove in glove, not daring to speak, we made our way toward the shallows, where the ice was thicker, instinctively forcing our boots flat along the surface instead of lifting them. Moving on ice was something you did either with great elegance or with great clumsiness.

We came to a stop on the blank place where in summer the dock juts out from the shore. Now that we were safe, I was reluctant to leave the lake. The house seemed far away, half ablaze and half in darkness.

"It wasn't a real crack," said Robin. "Just the lake making random noises."

"I want to hear it again." All at once the need was urgent. "I want to hear it! *Any*thing!" I pulled off my hood and let go of him to listen. What currents were moving in the midnight air seemed to converge where we stood, waiting for the lake to declare itself. Speak! Give a sign! No sign came. No second crack, no murmuring, groaning, or clapping, no promise or hint or response of any kind. Only the two of us, breathing into the frozen silence.

Coda

40

"Can you tell me when my mom's coming back?" Yank the stranger by the chin like mothers do to drive their point home to a kid, though mine never had to. I always tried to be good and so did she.

Her fingers gripped my chin with surprising strength. Defiant *means: Don't mess with me.* What does beseeching *mean, again? Please help me. I could not move or look away or press stop.*

"I'm here, Maddy! Right beside you."

Here was the last place I wanted to be, but I could not be anywhere else. That was the trick that had been played on us.

Leave it to my mother to take the stranger's place just in time. Swollen eyelids and mouth the wrong shape, but definitely hers, and her warming voice. Not the words but the music of her voice I've been hearing forever and ever.

"Water, please."

The head was positioned. The mouth made a circle to suck.

"As much as you want, Maddy. Just say."

Thirst was huge and without end. Water alone would not quench it. But for now I could ride the cool column down, past clouds colliding with their reflections, and lopsided trees where what

447

was stunted on one side grew lavishly on the other, down to the stage where, dressed in black, they were adjusting their valves and barrels, getting ready.

"Mama . . . ?"

"What is it, Maddy?"

"Go over there."

"I'm right here. Can you feel my hand?"

"No, over there, Mom! By that cloud. I'll swim to you."

"Feel her fur, Maddy? She's looking at you. Does it hurt?"

No pain. That's all they could give us. A talented one could draw blood painlessly, regardless of the number of times or the condition of the veins. Most of them were talented in every way. Powerless, as we were, but never heartbroken by it. We were on our own now. Gently lift the cat with both hands, so soft and light, knowing nothing, and set her on the rug.

Pressure on the shoulder, pressure on the ribs. Could have been the shoulder and ribs of anyone. Ragdoll kittens go like this. The limp thing she was fastened to came up into the air with her—let me go, Mom, I'm cold!—before being curled down again and covered. Once the wings came off they were done for, but if I carefully removed the spiderwebs the dragonflies flew away, shimmering and forgetting me instantly. I'd forgotten something. What had I forgotten?

Thoughts were being thought and body parts were being moved, but where this was happening and to whom it was hard to say.

"Take that end, Eve. I'll tuck in this side." Wobblier voice than my mother's, but strong underneath because of the backup she had.

"Better, Maddy?"

"Warm enough?"

Warm eyes. The closer you went, the further away they got. Bravo! He was proud of me. Always had been. Wherever he was, he made me strong. Bass clefs and quarter notes perched on the wires, and the light tried to force its way in. Easy to scare them off. Any movement and up they would lift to the sky, a giant flap of marks, black on one side, silver on the other when they turned.

"Close the curtains. Is it nighttime?"

"No, it's morning now. The sun's out."

"He doesn't know, Mom."

"Water, Maddy? Just a sip?"

"He doesn't know, Mom. I wanted him to love me."

"What's she saying?" said Grandma with great interest. "Who?"

The new head was way too young to laugh, but she was laughing anyway. Not *Him*, Rose!

"You did it," whispered Grandpa. His voice was smiling. I was going to give him a high five and a handshake, but I had descended so far and the pressure per square inch was so immense I was unable to move, let alone speak or open my eyes.

"She won't drink," said Robin. "Yesterday she couldn't get enough."

"She will when she needs to."

"What if she doesn't?"

"Rub my neck," said my mother, greatly weary.

"There?" said Robin.

"No, there."

"Shall I sing to her?" Grandma started at the descant, my favorite part, in her silvery voice. " 'Soft the drowsy hours are creeping . . .' "

"Can she hear us?" said Robin.

"They can always hear."

The applause went on and on and on. The joy on her face was something to behold. Pain at the center of me flared out in savage waves. The time had come. Say something. I can't hear you!

" 'Hill and dale in slumber sleeping . . .' "

"Where did that lullaby come from?"

"Her mother used to sing it to her."

Grandma's mouth half opened, Grandpa's quivered shut; Robin left the room; my mother stared through rips in the paper. The faces were changing, one into the other, each into itself. But not Jack; he had come and gone already. The little brick house had its carriage lamps lit, and the ironwork on the door was like long rounded knives. That's where I was going to live,

Mama. Forever and ever! I loved that purple door. Mounted on the wall, the green man shook his head. Such a long, long, long day. Carried through all the corridors. Prodded and punctured at every turn. I am impressed by how much you're doing. How do you fit it all in? Don't roll me. Let me get up and walk. I want to walk! So much to remember. So much to do—

"It's okay, Maddy. Shhhh. Just lay down. Lay back."

She was turning the key at the port on my chest. Coolness spread through my arm and up my neck into the tiniest branches and the stars trapped in them. Expertly she prodded the strings, pressed my forehead, and brought her hand to rest on the slope of the wood. Breath whistled in and through, in and through. Listen and forget. Listen and forget. Who I might be hurting, who I was leaving out or leaving behind. Would she know where to look when the time came? Tuck your chin or you'll hurt your neck. Relax and roll, relax and roll down the hill into the arms of the cello, shedding all my bright drops.

My mother was murmuring and holding my head. For her I made the effort to take back my lips, haul my voice up from the deep, and force the syllables out one by one.

"Remember, Mom . . ."

I can move stones. Cry and the milk comes.

"What is it, my darling?"

In my hands the curve of her grown-up head, its openings closed long ago, its pelt starting to grow back. Why come into my life if you're going to leave? Go! Go if you have to. I'm not going to end this life inside me. I refuse! Stroke the surface one way and then the other. Short and soft. Soft and short.

"Squeeze her hand, Evie, so she knows we're here."

"She *knows.*"

" 'I my loved ones watch am keeping . . .' " sang Grandma, pausing for suspense. " 'All . . . through . . . the night.' "

It was my turn. Had I told them before or only Jack? Only Jack. This was the funny part. It would make her cry. She was crying already, my head tight between her hands, my mouth stretched wide around the bulging words.

"Anything good happens to you? It's me!"

Crack of laughter. The ice groaning.

It's me, Mama. It's me.

Acknowledgments

My deepest gratitude goes to Lynne Neufer Dale, who has shared her experience with me in such an openhearted and generous way. I am grateful to all of Summer's family; Al Dale and Jordan Dale; Marna Neufer; Paul Neufer; Dave Neufer; Nancy Neufer; Holly Batchelor; George, Paul, Will, and Emily Batchelor; Cynthia Gentry and Charles Williams for their support of this book.

I am indebted to my fabulous and formidable agent, Clare Alexander, and to everyone at Aitken Alexander in London, especially Lesley Thorne, Lisa Baker, and Anna Watkins. I am very grateful to Kathy Robbins in New York.

Enormous thanks are due to my editor, Valerie Steiker, for her tireless and insightful editing and sharp attention to detail, and to Nan Graham for essential editorial guidance and support. I am indebted to the entire Scribner team: Roz Lippel, Colin Harrison, Kara Watson, Ashley Gilliam, Kelsey Manning, Sally Howe, Jaya Miceli, Abigail Novak, Laura Wise, and Susan Brown. I am grateful to Lisa Highton at Two Roads, and to my other publishers and translators.

I am grateful to the Goldsmiths Creative Writing MA, my tutors, Francis Spufford, Blake Morrison, and Maura Dooley, and fellow writers

(2014–16) who nurtured the book in its early stages.

Thanks go to United Agents for awarding the novel the 2017 Pat Kavanagh Prize when it was still a work in progress, and to Ventspils House in Latvia for the writer's residency in January 2018. Thanks also to Selma Ancira for walks by the frozen Baltic Sea and her stunning photographs of water, and to Ribbons and Taylor Café in Stoke Newington, where a great deal of rewriting took place.

So many people have, directly and indirectly, had a part in shaping this book. I am extremely grateful to: Miriam Robinson for constant close reading and invaluable discussions; Francis Spufford for creative and practical advice throughout; Lindsay Clarke for long-standing counsel and comments on a late draft; Teresa Thornhill and Sue Goss for decades of conversation and writing camaraderie; Mandy Hetherton and Oliver Shamlou for generous and perceptive reading; Kelly Morter and her friends for being teen consultants; Nick Manning for comic inspiration and insight into Dupont Circle, Fallingwater, and life in general; Ron and Christopher Hopson for their knowledge of Washington and environs; Mimi Babe Harris for the history of her table; Dr. Bradley George of Atlanta, Georgia, for medical advice; and to the numerous friends, colleagues, students, and my London book group, who provided encouragement and dialogue along the way.

I am grateful to the Neufer and Raney families for a lifetime of summers at the lake, a place that has worked its way into my imagination more deeply than I knew.

Finally, special thanks to my husband, Greg Morter, for his original views and unending support, and to my daughter, Kelly, without whom this book would never have been written.

About the Author

Karen Raney recently gained an MA in creative writing from Goldsmiths, University of London, with a distinction and was awarded the 2017 Pat Kavanagh Prize for *All the Water in the World* when the novel was still a work in progress. Born in Schenectady, New York, Raney attended Oberlin College, graduated from Duke University, and worked as a nurse before moving to London to study art. She lives in London and teaches at the University of East London.

Center Point Large Print
600 Brooks Road / PO Box 1
Thorndike, ME 04986-0001 USA

(207) 568-3717

**US & Canada:
1 800 929-9108**
www.centerpointlargeprint.com